GOOD KARMA

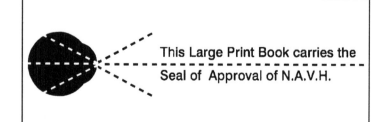

This Large Print Book carries the
Seal of Approval of N.A.V.H.

Good Karma

Christina Kelly

KENNEBEC LARGE PRINT
A part of Gale, Cengage Learning

GALE
CENGAGE Learning®

Farmington Hills, Mich • San Francisco • New York • Waterville, Maine
Meriden, Conn • Mason, Ohio • Chicago

LP

GALE
CENGAGE Learning®

LIBRARY OF CONGRESS CATALOGING-IN-PUBLICATION DATA

Names: Kelly, Christina, 1962– author.
Title: Good karma / by Christina Kelly.
Description: Large print edition. | Waterville, Maine : Kennebec Large Print, a part of Gale, Cengage Learning, 2017. | Series: Kennebec Large Print superior collection
Identifiers: LCCN 2017017083| ISBN 9781410499318 (softcover) | ISBN 1410499316 (softcover)
Subjects: LCSH: Man-woman relationships—Fiction. | Savannah (Ga.)—Social life and customs—Fiction. | Domestic fiction. | Large type books. | BISAC: FICTION / Family Life. | FICTION / Contemporary Women.
Classification: LCC PS3611.E44585 G66 2017b | DDC 813/.6—dc23
LC record available at https://lccn.loc.gov/2017017083

Published in 2017 by arrangement with Harper Paperback, an imprint of HarperCollins Publishers

Printed in Mexico
1 2 3 4 5 6 7 21 20 19 18 17

To Bill, my dreamboat.

Those who don't believe in magic will never find it.

— ROALD DAHL

You never know.

— NORA EPHRON

CHAPTER 1

Behind her, Karma was getting restless. Catherine could hear him stretch, stand, and shake, his ID tag hitting the hard edge of the doggie seat.

"Don't look at him," Ralph warned, his hands clutching the steering wheel. "He's fine."

"But maybe he needs to stop again."

Ralph adjusted the rearview mirror. "Don't project."

"Project?" Catherine asked. "What do you know about projecting?" She'd had it with his amateur psychology.

"A bar of soap has more sense than that stupid dog."

Catherine turned her attention back to the Savannah map, to try to get a sense of the city, to somehow pinpoint where they were. They'd been on the road so long, it was hard to tell. She turned the map ninety degrees and refolded it. It reminded her of a math problem. If a car were traveling at sixty miles an hour heading due east, and a Boston terrier was in distress in the backseat, how long would it take for his bladder to explode? At what velocity would the poor dog erupt into a mushroom cloud and take her husband and his golf clubs with him?

"Look." Ralph pointed to a small sign that directed them to the island. "Only five miles."

They were approaching the end of the parkway, that much was clear. Three lanes merged into two, and orange detour barrels dotted the shoulder. She placed the map back into the glove compartment and grabbed the Seven Oaks brochure. As Ralph focused on a lane change, she pulled down the sun flap and watched Karma in the mirror. He seemed to be comfortable, but she could never be sure. He always breathed as if he were wearing scuba equipment, his little pushed-in nose struggling with the simplest tasks.

The brochure to Seven Oaks, at least, felt solid. Some companies had sent only a glossy three-fold leaflet and a website address. But after spending a week with real estate agents looking at places to retire, she knew not to trust websites or fancy brochures, even though she and Ralph had done their research. They'd collected all the magazines they could find with headlines like "Top Ten Places to Retire" and "The Next Chapter," but not all developments had met their expectations. They'd visited Asheville and Charlottesville and Hilton Head. They'd toured housing communities with names like the Sanctuary and the Farms and Sunset Estates. They even visited a subdivision called Trilogy, whose three parts were touted as "Golf. Tennis. Fun."

They wanted warmth, but not Florida; several friends who'd relocated there had died within the first two years. Catherine's divorced sister, Martha, had moved to the Villages, a gated community north of Orlando with the motto "Florida's friendliest hometown." Martha loved it, but got a venereal disease within the first month. "What can I say?" her sister told Catherine. "It's just a lifestyle decision."

They'd just spent two nights in Charleston, at the base of a cabled bridge on the Cooper River. But their room had smelled of unfamiliar fur, and Catherine had found cat kibble under the bed. Only Karma had seemed to be in a good mood there. They'd squandered two afternoons walking through Low Country cottages with eat-in kitchens and screened porches with an agent who looked as if he were on spring break. He was young enough to be their grandchild, if they'd had one. What did he know about retirement or 401(k) plans? Or why a master bedroom on the main floor was actually a practical solution for their knees, not just a theoretical idea, good for "resale"?

She'd wanted to fall in love with Charleston, with its history and Southern charm, but the city had felt overpriced and sprawling. They could just stay in New Jersey if they wanted that. The historic district, with new shutters and fresh paint on old buildings, like an aging woman with too much eye shadow, just made her sad.

"It says they have a dog park," Catherine said, flipping through the Seven Oaks brochure. " 'A picket-fenced six-acre playground of meadow and woods will keep your pooch and his people happy.' "

Karma shook in the backseat.

"Yes, baby. You'll get your own dog park. With t-r-e-a-t-s." Catherine spelled out the word, careful to enunciate each letter.

"Don't encourage him."

"Treats. Treats. Treats."

Karma barked.

"And I'll tell you again, once and for all," Ralph added, "he doesn't understand English. He's a d-o-g."

"Oh, really?" She might have said more but resisted. He had done most of the driving, after all, and had been touchy since he'd retired four months earlier. Since he'd arrived home one Friday night with an engraved plaque from his going-away luncheon and a single cardboard box of personal effects from his forty years at the bank.

"Or do calculus. Or appreciate fusion or the power of compounding or . . ."

Catherine unclipped her seat belt and swiveled around to the backseat. *"A dog park!"* Catherine shouted, too loudly for the small car. She was sorry at once. "It's just he's sensitive and you never, ever appreciate him," she said quietly.

He laughed a bit and shook his head.

"And you never have."

Fewer cars were passing them now as they headed east, toward the island. The road narrowed and Karma settled again into his car seat.

It was time to make a decision. They were all going a little crazy. The last Charleston listing had been a roomy three-bedroom on a cul-de-sac in Mount Pleasant. They were standing in the vaulted entryway when the young agent mentioned a local Thai restaurant and Ralph had erupted, "I don't care about noodles, for god's sake! I just want to play golf!"

All the properties they'd seen had been adequate for their needs, but none of them had a sense of community or security. Living in a gated community wasn't on her bucket list, but the glossy print about the twenty-four-hour manned gatehouse and twelve-foot perimeter fence did sound comforting. Catherine wasn't as trusting as she used to be. That's why they'd gotten the dog in the first place. Even if she sometimes treated the dog like a baby, dressing him in colorful hats, Karma would certainly alert them to an intruder. At least that was the plan. But, bless his heart, the dog either didn't care or didn't know about security. When a serviceman knocked, he'd lift his head from the dog bed, then go back to sleep, annoyed.

Ahead, the cirrus clouds melted into the horizon. A streak of orange appeared by the larger, distant bridge, the one that would transport them to the island. The gray-green marsh grass carpeted the shore. Catherine looked down and recognized that they were at the exact spot where the inside cover photo had been taken. There didn't appear to have been any airbrushing of telephone lines or sleight of hand with a computer; the marsh was actually lovely in the fading light of afternoon. A motorboat idled in the Intracoastal and she could see the outline of large houses on the far shore. Maybe this could really work.

Karma snorted again.

"Just give us five minutes," Ralph whispered to their dog.

Catherine continued reading aloud, certain her voice would soothe Karma and maybe her husband. " 'Seven Oaks offers a community of all ages with gated security and patrols. You'll find tranquillity in the seclusion and safety of our island, which is conveniently located only twenty minutes from Savannah's historic district.' "

She looked up as they reached the next bridge, a sleek structure that felt like a springboard into another country. It wasn't that they were exclusionary, she thought, but they deserved to feel protected. They'd earned it.

A sign at a single traffic light indicated the entrance to an assisted-living facility and small shopping complex that included a café, grocer, bank, and golf cart retailer. On the sidewalk, an elderly couple strolled, the woman's arm looped around the man's elbow.

"Arrrr." Karma stood again and restlessly scratched the seat.

The light turned green and Ralph accelerated, too fast. Ahead they could see the shiny steel gates of an impressive gatehouse. The road split into two lanes, one marked RESIDENTS ONLY and the other GUESTS. Both had thick mechanical arms blocking the enclave. To the right was an elaborate bronze sculpture of a tree, its muscled branches embracing a sign: WELCOME TO SEVEN OAKS.

Suddenly Karma yelped uncharacteristically, a high-pitched squeal of discomfort.

"Shit!" Ralph muttered.

Just before the entrance, Ralph careened to a stop on the shoulder. In one motion, Catherine undid her seat belt, flung open the door, jumped out of the car, and unhooked her dog's harness. As she pulled him out with one hand, she struggled to attach his leash with the other. Before she could, Karma escaped from her grasp, leaped to the ground, and rushed to the wood chips beneath the sculpture.

Lifting his back leg as high as he could, he sprayed the thick trunk as his parents watched helplessly.

Karma was home.

CHAPTER 2

The next afternoon, Catherine sat in the back of Audrey Cunningham's Mercedes sedan while Ralph took the front passenger seat. Audrey, a member of the platinum sales club at Seven Oaks, had picked them up at their three-night Discovery Package rental. She'd already shown them five listings, but they had yet to see a house they'd be happy in. Catherine wondered, really, what it would take.

She'd been studying the back of Audrey's head and trying to decide what color her hair was. Marigold? Canary? Saffron? It was supposed to be blond, of course, but the actual color was yellow and swung from her head in a waggish bob that had been secured in a sparkly headband, a look appropriate for a teenager, but not a fortysomething Realtor. At one time Catherine might have done something fanciful with her own hair. Perhaps she could have colored it a natural auburn when the silvery hairs started sprouting, but the change had seemed so sudden, like Ralph's retirement, and now it felt too late. One day she had it high and tight in a bouncy ponytail, the next loose and parted to one side, hoping to cover her thinning patches.

"Honey." Ralph swiveled from his place as copilot. Catherine thought he should be wearing a fancy headset, the way he was pretending to help navigate. "Audrey asked you about your tennis."

Catherine came to as if waking from an appendectomy, feeling as if there were something missing inside. "Sorry, I'm just taken by the landscape."

They were in the southern half of the kidney-shaped island. That much she knew. The magnolias towered over them, creating a comforting canopy, with shafts of sunlight breaking through the branches at irregular intervals. When she and Ralph got married forty years earlier, they were going to have the ceremony under similar trees in her aunt's backyard. But it had rained on their wedding day, so they exchanged vows under a blue plastic tent that whistled whenever the wind blew.

Audrey chirped in: "What are your *expectations* for tennis here?"

Audrey had used that term nearly a half-dozen times. *Expectations.* She specialized in four-syllable words. *Amenity. Community. Immaculate.*

"Well, I'm on a 4.0 team back in New Jersey." It didn't sound very impressive, so Catherine added: "One year we actually made it to regionals." She hoped this conjured something more impressive than what it had been — a long weekend spent on hard courts outside a Holiday Inn in Hoboken.

"And where do *you* play in the lineup?" Audrey asked.

This was sort of like asking her weight or bra size. Did it matter? And how could she explain that now she was just the floater, the one on the team who adapted easily to various styles of play? The younger sister. The Virgo. The one who never rocks the boat. The one who could return from either the deuce or ad side.

"It really depends," Catherine answered vaguely. She would start a new tennis life here. She could do or be whatever she wanted.

"They call her the *floater,*" Ralph added. "Because she can play with anyone." He grinned stupidly at Audrey. "She's a good sidekick."

19

Yes, that's right, Ralphie, you tell her, Catherine thought, but said, "I'm looking for a solid partner now. That is my ex-pec-ta-tion."

Ralph pressed his lips together.

"Well, you'll find our teams spectacular." Audrey made eye contact with Catherine in the rearview mirror. "Beyond our regular team play, we've got a nice junior program, tournaments, and even a husband-wife mixer." She turned to Ralph. "You do like to mix it up, don't you?"

Ralph laughed, a deep baritone noise that came from his abdomen. He was acting like a teenager. "Sure, I like to mix it up sometimes."

Then suddenly the thought came to Catherine: *Take him, Audrey. Just take him. And take his laundry and his grassy golf stains and the clearing of his throat. Take his stinky egg salad sandwiches and his toe fungus and opera CDs and his hypochondria.* But another part of her, the part she hadn't accessed in months, maybe years, told her: *But he's mine.*

Although they'd fallen out of active love, the breathless feelings all young couples believe will never fade, a shared history held them together. A loyalty of working through the years. Finally, at their new home and with the freedom of Ralph's retirement, maybe they could reconnect and find the magic that had once brought them together. That was her ex-pec-ta-tion. Her hope. For if she didn't have Ralph, what did she have?

Catherine shrugged, stretching the tight muscles in her shoulders, rocking her neck back and forth. She looked at her watch. "We should head back soon. Karma will need to go out."

The car was quiet. Quieter than it had been all morning. "I said, Karma will need —"

"Stop it! Stop it with the dog! He is fine!" Ralph's voice erupted like a summer squall, coming from nowhere, low over the horizon, in a single thundering clap. After a moment he added, as if he had to apologize to Audrey and not his wife, "We've been looking for too long. We really need to find a new home sometime soon."

Apparently, Audrey had seen this all before. She was part salesperson, part psychiatrist. "Don't worry." She patted Ralph's knee, then reached into her tote, pulled out a listing sheet, and handed it to him. "We've got just one more today. It's been on the market for a year. The owners spend most of their time up North. It's got an incredible layout with a remarkable view of the marsh — twenty-five hundred square feet, new appliances, close to golf, view of a small lagoon, and a patio for al dente entertaining." She puckered her lips together and made a popping sound with her mouth.

"Al dente?" Catherine asked. "Is that so?"

"And a large backyard for her dog."

For her *dog.*

It was getting hot in the car. Catherine had read that on a sunny day, the inside of a parked car could reach a hundred and fifty degrees in ten minutes. She imagined Ralph running to the hardware store and leaving Karma in the backseat. That was something Ralph would do. He would return with a new hammer and wonder where the dog went, why all that was left was just white bones and fur.

They pulled up in front of a traditional two-story Georgian home. As Catherine got out of the car she could smell salt from the marsh. She brought a hand up to shield her face from the sun, while Ralph moved around to open Audrey's door. Catherine noticed that Ralph's thick gray hair had started to grow over his collar. He'd stopped getting regular cuts, so she made a mental note to remind him.

The three of them walked together toward

the brick path that led to the front door. Audrey pointed out plantings to Ralph, who had shown a sudden interest in azaleas and boxwoods. He seemed fascinated that the camellias would bloom wine-colored in the fall. Meanwhile, Catherine was eager to see the inside. To see the gas stove and marsh view. If there was enough room outside for Karma to roam comfortably without wandering into the high grass.

Audrey went to the lockbox, punched in a code, retrieved the key, plugged it into the lock, and flung open the door. "Ta-da!" she shouted.

In front of them, the room opened into a large living area with cathedral ceilings and a piano in the corner. Catherine liked the sudden freedom she felt.

"You'll see the space is sensational for entertaining," Audrey said, swinging her arms out as if she were a hostess on a game show. "And here, before we go any farther, let me show you this exterior space."

Ralph followed Audrey through the living room, and she unlocked and opened the sliding glass doors.

"I'll be right there," Catherine said, "I'm just going to the bathroom."

Catherine moved back and inhaled sharply. It felt like she hadn't breathed in months. She watched Ralph and Audrey talking on the deck. He was animated, stupidly bobbing his head, agreeing with whatever the younger woman was saying.

At one time I loved him crazily, Catherine thought.

When they first got married, Catherine was out of her mind with the thought of him. While he spent long days at the bank, she worked mornings as a librarian. In the afternoons, she'd spruce up their one-bedroom rental, her heart swollen with happiness, and spend hours preparing *moules marinières* or moussaka, complicated recipes her mother had sent her. She folded napkins in the shape of cranes. When he walked through the door at the end of the day she would wrap her arms around his neck and breathe him in, taking in the gingery smells of the city, and know that she was complete. But in the last few years they'd taken to eating grilled cheese sandwiches with trays in their laps while watching the news.

Maybe I can change that, she thought.

To her left, on a built-in bookshelf, Catherine spotted a row of small glass jars. Perhaps they'd once held exotic spices like fiery curry powder or savory saffron. Taking a closer look, she realized that each contained sand of a different color and texture, from fine pink alabaster powder to peppery flakes. Each was labeled: *Barbuda; Virgin Gorda; Cozumel; Mykonos.* Catherine inhaled again. She and Ralph had always talked about retirement as a time they'd learn new skills or travel. She could take up beekeeping or the bagpipes and wander beaches she'd never seen.

She walked into the master bedroom, just off the living room, and was entranced by its view of the marsh. Through the wide windows she could see Ralph and Audrey wandering across the lawn toward the reeds. They weren't close to each other, but Ralph was standing straighter than he had in years. Posing, Catherine thought. Then they started talking excitedly, like old friends, tilting their heads this way and that, moving their hands recklessly.

She stood and studied the furniture, the elegant window treatments, the recessed lighting. She liked the feel of the house, though knew it had been tidied for potential customers. Staged, Catherine thought, like a crime scene in a murder mystery. A king-size bed took up most of the far wall. Across the room was a wide shelf that held just a few books and a pencil drawing of a Labrador holding a sign: TO ERR IS HUMAN, TO FORGIVE CANINE.

Catherine felt a sudden romantic giddiness about the idea of living on an island, like Robinson Crusoe or Mrs. Thurston Howell III. Especially with a strong steel bridge connecting the security of Seven Oaks to the excitement of downtown Savannah. She liked the idea of being both isolated and insulated.

In the distance, Ralph and Audrey reached the edge of the property. Bands of long yellow-green grass rustled behind them. They turned toward each other briefly and Ralph raised his hand to point to something in the reedy distance. Audrey moved in to follow his arm. When they both leaned back again, Ralph placed his hand on their agent's shoulder.

You a-toll a-hole, Catherine thought suddenly, still thinking of islands but hating that Ralph was acting so chummy. It was the type of pun she might have liked to share with him at one time, but no longer. So her thoughts moved from living on an island to living with someone who took her for granted. Someone who'd gone from being her lover to someone who reminded her to take her statins.

Walking toward the center of the bedroom, she spied the hallway that led, no doubt, to the master bathroom. On the right was the laundry room, the washer and dryer stacked by the doorway and a large utility sink in which she could wash Karma; to the left, a closet door. She opened it to a wide walk-in closet with colorful summer dresses and organized shoes and —

Catherine yelped, a noise so feral for a moment she didn't know it was her own.

Before her crouched a young woman in a tan sweat suit, legs drawn up beneath her like a puppy, index finger drawn to her mouth to indicate quiet.

"Please," the woman whispered. "I need your help."

CHAPTER 3

Catherine stood at the closet doorway and tried to settle her breath as she stared at the female figure before her.

"I'm sorry," the woman whispered, "but I *do* need your help." She sat on the ground, her legs curled under her. Her brown hair was pulled back in a long ponytail and she held a dog leash and a baseball cap in her hand.

"No, no. *I'm* sorry. *We* are sorry. Our agent should have called for an appointment." The woman blinked at Catherine again and again, but didn't move. She reminded Catherine of a trapped animal. "Wait. Pardon me, but is this *your* house?"

The woman breathed heavily, leaned forward to push herself up, then whispered, "I'd like to say yes, but it is not."

"Then what are you *doing*?"

Raising a toned arm, the woman pulled out her ponytail's rubber band and nervously shook her head, her thick hair cascading forward. Catherine remembered having hair like that when she was in her thirties — hair that meant something — before everything on her body wilted.

"I'm lost."

"Lost?"

"I think I'm . . ." the woman hesitated, searching for the right word. "Will you help me?" She started to stand but stopped as her head caught on golf culottes above her. She forced an uneasy laugh. "You know, will you help me get out without them seeing?"

Catherine had several questions. What was the woman doing here, and why was she in the closet? Was she a neighbor? A house sitter? A burglar? She didn't look like a burglar. Burglars wore masks and gloves. They carried sacks or had tattooed dragons on their forearms. This woman looked like she could have been a professional cheerleader. "I'm confused," Catherine said, not sure why she was whispering, too. "What are you *doing* here?"

The woman nervously curled the rim of the baseball cap, something a pitcher would do before a big out. "I just sort of wander through houses. It's not *bad.*"

"You break in?"

"I don't break anything."

"But —"

"I like to live other people's lives. I don't know how else to explain it."

Catherine had friends back in New Jersey whose grandchildren played video games in which they wandered through virtual houses seeking virtual treasures. She'd even played such a game once, wearing a broad headset similar to the wraparound sunglasses she'd had after cataract surgery. But this was real.

"What's your name?"

"Amity. My name is Amity."

Catherine felt a tingling in her hands, as if a part of her body that had long been dormant was just awakening. She knew all about fantasizing. She'd been doing it for years. And she knew what it was to be trapped. Suddenly she understood.

Sensing this, the woman smiled. "So will you help me? Please?"

"Wait here."

Catherine stepped back, away from the closet, and strode across the bedroom to the sliding door. Audrey was heading up the deck stairs with Ralph close behind her, a puppy at her heels. She could hear them speaking indistinctly. When she turned around, the woman was standing right beside her, even taller and thinner than Catherine had first thought, and Catherine noticed the fanny pack hooked around her waist.

Catherine now had a plan and a motive. She strode out to the living room, to the pocket door of the kitchen. She could block the view to the entryway or perhaps even create a dramatic diversion to distract her husband and Audrey. She had the vision of letting a fawn free after it had been entangled in a net.

But it didn't matter. Ralph and Audrey remained on the deck, focused on each other, and by the time she turned, Amity had slipped out the front door and was halfway down the walk, her dog leash coiled tightly in her hand.

CHAPTER 4

"Bowser's got stage five cancer. That's why they haven't been around."

"Stage five?" Fred asked.

"Yeah. Of the intestines or rib cage or something. It's eaten through his gut."

Fred turned from watching their dogs and looked over at Ernie. He was a nice guy all right, but he wasn't going to be elected to the local chapter of Mensa.

"Five is the kind they don't even talk about. Nobody mentions it because once you get it, even a bruiser like Bowser" — Ernie drew his finger across his butterball neck in a slicing motion — "you can just say sayonara."

The two men occupied the metal benches at the eastern edge of the dog park. These seats were best midafternoon, since they remained shaded from direct light as the sun hung above the leafy canopy of trees. The morning crowd took the western benches, closer to the front gate, parking lot, and puppy park. Across the newly mown field they could see Seven Oaks Way, the route that led in from the main gate, and the landscaped central circle where the road split into branches to the community's three subdivisions.

Fred's dog, a giant harlequin Great Dane, ambled toward them. Sequoia was drooling, as usual, the saliva sliding in rivulets from her lower lip. She carried a half-chewed rope toy coated with slobber, and deposited it on the bench between the men before wandering off again.

"Good girl," Fred said quietly. He picked up the frayed rope, wrapped it in a plastic bag, and placed it in his jacket pocket. Another dog could easily choke on the toy remnants that got chewed up by the tractor during the park's weekly mowings. Fred had never taught Sequoia this retrieval habit; it was, remarkably, just part of her thoughtful nature.

Fred didn't want to talk to Ernie about Bowser, their friend's basset hound, or anything really. He was at the dog park to exercise his dog. He was there to get out of his house. He was there because his grief counselor had suggested it. After six months of being a widower, he still needed a schedule to adhere to, to simulate an ordinary world.

Not one to embrace silence, Ernie started again, "First Bowser couldn't eat, then he couldn't sleep. I heard he had a tumor the size of a grapefruit. And do you notice that anytime they find cancer, whether it's in a dog or a person, it's always the size of fruit?" He grabbed his Chucker, a long plastic ball launcher, and brought it up to his mouth as if it were a microphone and spoke with a newscaster's serious tone. "Which reminds me, why did the eggplant grow so large? Because it had good aubergenes!"

Ernie's dog, Lulu, a terrier mutt with a shock of white hair framing her face, just like her bearded master, stormed over to the bench when she saw the Chucker. She sat in the dirt in front of the men, waiting expectantly.

"I don't know," Fred added. "Maybe we should avoid all fruit, just to be safe."

He'd said it as a joke, but Ernie nodded in agreement.

Fred preferred to come to the dog park in the quiet afternoon, when a breeze often blew in from the marsh and there weren't packs of marauding mutts. Sequoia could do without the yippy smaller dogs at her feet. She'd squat in play position, then simply swat them away, gently annoyed. He also wanted to avoid the stay-at-home moms, who often arrived at the park mid-morning. Seeing his large animal, they would remark on her size. "Why, she's big enough to ride," he'd been told time and time again.

Lulu whined and pursed her mouth expectantly. Her short body shuddered with anticipation as she tilted her head to one side.

"Okay. Okay." Ernie took a dull pink rubber ball out of his jacket pocket and, while firmly holding the long handle of the Chucker, placed it in its teeth. Fred remembered that the ball had been fluorescent red when new and Ernie could throw it clear across the park. If the light hit it just right, it became a neon meteor swooping across the sky. At one time it had been bright enough to spot in the grass from a distance, but after years of use it had faded, its shiny material now soft with gray age spots.

Ernie used the metal armrest for leverage and pushed his large frame to a standing position. Lulu bent down, chest to the ground, ready to follow the ball to the end of the earth. Her tongue fell out in suspense. Ernie took the Chucker back, elbow bent, wrist flexed, and released it into the air. It lurched hardly twenty feet. Lulu, unimpressed, caught it after one bounce. She looked at Ernie with what seemed to be disdain, dropped the ball, and continued on to find Sequoia.

"Ungrateful bitch," Ernie muttered as he slowly lowered himself back to the metal seat.

Across the field, Fred saw one of Seven Oaks' security cars pull into the lot. The three energy-efficient hybrids that patrolled the island could barely catch a greyhound or whippet but could certainly overtake a golf cart if they had to. Three was hardly a fleet, but really, how many did Seven Oaks actually need? The last crime Fred remembered had occurred two years earlier, when someone reported a stolen golf cart. Chatham County Police had even been called in to investigate before they discovered that the man had gotten a late-night ride home from the nineteenth hole and had forgotten he'd left the cart behind. And the closest thing the development had to a gang was the three standard poodles who always seemed to arrive at the dog park with the ten o'clock crowd.

The bright yellow security car stopped and a tall redheaded officer in a dark-green uniform emerged. He paused to wave to the men.

"He's new," Fred said, nodding to the guard. "Someone told me they call him Rusty."

"Well, these guys do a damn good job keeping us safe before we get to the pearly entrance of our *next* gated community." Ernie laughed as he pulled out an extralong strand of white hair, either from his ear or beard.

Fred continued to watch the security officer, who punched a code into the electric tower by the front gate then moved off to review regulations that lined the bulletin board. NO FOOD OR TREATS. NO GLASS CONTAINERS. NO STROLLERS. "Nothing is safe," Fred declared. "No matter what you think. No matter how hard you try to protect someone . . ." His voice trailed off.

"You know, counselor, what you need is a girlfriend," Ernie said as Lulu scampered over and jumped up to sit between them on the bench. "I bet the casserole brigade is beating a path to your door."

"Oh yes. The endless ravenous women." Fred knew Ernie wanted to live vicariously through the fantasy of widowhood, but he was tired of explaining it was just the stuff of legend. Of course, several women had invited him to play bridge and a few had suggested a movie, but lonely women did not bring pallets of casseroles to grieving widowers. It was sort of like the myth that falling cats always landed on their feet.

"Somehow all those aging kittens skirt right past an eligible divorcé like me," Ernie said. "You'd think they'd be on me like ducks on june bugs."

Fred remained quiet, focused on the security officer, who was now checking the trash container. He tried to imagine a life, even a day, with anyone else. Lissa's sickness had been heartbreaking. She'd lost part of her hair during treatment, but it didn't fall out in great clumps the way they were told it would. Rather, they'd be out walking Sequoia and fine strands of her hair would gently float away in front of them, as if they were dried white seeds from a dandelion.

Fred focused on the words his therapist had suggested when he felt waves of incoming grief: *Breathe. Deeply. Breathe. Deeply.*

Fred checked his watch, then stood and whistled. Sequoia looked up from sniffing a rough dirt patch by the side picket fence and started for the gate. "Don't you worry about me," Fred said. He leaned down to scratch Lulu behind her ears. Suddenly, Fred was tempted to pet Ernie's head, too.

To gently stroke him and tell him that he was a good boy. That he knew Ernie meant well in encouraging him to get out and find a new friend, but there were some things that were out of their control. "Until tomorrow," was all he said.

At the front gate Fred hooked the leash to Sequoia's collar. It was embroidered with trees, a green-gray yarny copse of majestic oaks. A final gift from his wife, as if he needed more reminders of her. She'd sat in chemotherapy for days on end, carefully stitching the pattern with a hypodermic needle hooked into the port by her collarbone. When she moved to the bathroom, she'd wheel the pole that held her IV bag and infusion pump, as if she were taking her cancer for a stroll.

Sequoia walked ahead of Fred, down the rough gravel path to the parking lot. The dog herself had lost a step since his wife had gotten sick. When the X-rays with the mass came back, Sequoia didn't eat for three days. Sometimes even now, in the middle of the night, Fred would hear his dog rise from her oversize bed in the corner. She would stand, stretch her legs, and shake her enormous head. Then she'd ramble over to the sliding glass doors, where she'd remain transfixed for hours. A dark, hulking shadow looking out to the moonlit trees, as if eager to welcome Lissa home from a long trip abroad.

CHAPTER 5

Fred hadn't been prepared for Lissa's death even though, of course, he'd *known* it was coming. She'd been sick with cancer for five years, the bad cells in her body slowly overtaking the good. A truck barreling down on them while they waited like old dogs in a crosswalk. But still her death had felt instantaneous. Once it hit and she was gone, he was dumbfounded. *Where had that come from?* he'd thought.

Some days he became overwhelmed with the sadness, the devastation, the finality. That was the word that kept popping into his head: *finality.* His exuberant wife hadn't been afraid of anything and was known to take risks, and she'd always emerged unscathed. She never hesitated to dive into a conga line or a cold lake. She liked to close her eyes on roller coasters and keep them open during Alfred Hitchcock movies. She even went skydiving once on a dare. *It wasn't a dare,* he could hear her say, laughing. *It was a scare!* And toward the end, when she was being transferred from the ICU to hospice, when they rode in the back of the goddamned ambulette as if it were a limousine, he thought there'd be more. That she'd somehow saved part of her enthusiasm for an encore — an escape hatch in the van that would transport them back home.

They'd lived at Seven Oaks for more than thirty years, so they had plenty of friends. Or at least at one time they had, until most of them relocated closer to grown children, moved to assisted living, or had sudden chest pains on the golf course. It seemed all the same: when people exited the gates and crossed the bridge to the mainland, in a moving truck or an ambulance, they were gone forever.

Fred climbed the stairs one at a time to the second-floor landing. At seventy-five, his knees felt brittle and his hips achy, and he cursed gravity, which, of course, was only doing its job.

"Tomorrow and tomorrow and tomorrow," Fred said to Sequoia, who had followed him to the base of the steps.

The eight-year-old Great Dane dragged her back right leg slightly, looked at him with plaintive eyes, then let out a little moan, a gentle directive that said, *Be careful.*

He opened the door and the heat hit him. Even though it was November and only seventy degrees outside, the temperature in the attic was at least eighty.

Hot enough for a chicken to lay a fried egg! Though Lissa had faded over the months, she still came in loud and clear whenever she felt like it.

He stepped into the cavernous attic that he and Lissa had never gotten around to weatherproofing or organizing. There they'd stored all the things they were going to review one day when they had time — report cards, old letters, his law school textbooks, photos of long-dead relatives. He hadn't been inside the attic in months, maybe years. Lissa's sickness had overwhelmed their lives, as if her cancer had been a handicapped child that took their total focus and energy.

Fred started in the center of the room, opening boxes, trying to prioritize. The first box held Lissa's travel diaries. She'd vowed to reread them someday, to give them the attention they deserved. Inside another was a shoe box filled with dusty memorabilia from their early years in Savannah. Maybe his daughter, Danielle, would want a photo of them crouching by a gassy bulldog named Uga or at a crowded book signing with John Berendt. He liked to think Danielle would do a scrapbook one day, but she had priorities of her own. For the funeral, she had flown in from Maine on a bereavement fare, leaving her nine-year-old son, Tommy, in Maine with a case of tonsillitis and a babysitter.

Just like Lissa, Danielle had meant to start clearing the attic, had threatened to several times during her trip, but they'd been busy with other things. Exactly what, he couldn't remember. It had been a blur of phone calls, shopping, meals, bill paying, and housekeeping. He'd sat through what seemed like an eternity of watching video clips of his grandson running across a playing field. "That's Tommy," Danielle would say, pointing to a red-shirted blur on her computer screen. "Isn't he amazing?"

Fred, coming from a proud clan of agnostics, was never good at death. His family didn't hold wakes or have large, formal funerals. They didn't celebrate the lives of the deceased with extravagant religious ceremonies, complicated send-offs, or an endless assortment of finger sandwiches on extended buffet tables. "When I'm gone, just flush me down the crapper," his father

44

had told him for years.

And so he had expected Lissa's memorial to be small — a few old friends, his daughter, and some hospice personnel. But waves of women, young and old, arrived to offer condolences. She'd made friends while shelving books at the village library, collecting worn housewares for charity tag sales, and holding court at lively canasta tables. Though it didn't necessarily surprise him, he had no idea how many lives she'd touched.

The contingent from the dog park paid respects as well. Even Ernie had shown up, with a wrinkled tie and his beard combed ceremoniously. Thoughtfully, Ernie'd remembered to leave Lulu at home. Fred couldn't recall whether Lissa had met Ernie, unless it was in passing at the grocery store.

Maybe between the Kal Kan and the calzone, he heard his wife say.

Fred pulled a cardboard box from the pile. It wasn't large, but was heavy and old enough that it sagged at the base. The equivalent of a box having bad knees, he thought. He held the bottom with both hands and carried it down to the living room, carefully taking the stairs one at a time. Sequoia clattered behind him and lay at his feet.

He pulled out a packet of letters neatly tied with a plaid ribbon. On the front, he could see Lissa's smooth penmanship, her elongated words and looping letters. He picked up the first one and brought it to his nose, hoping he'd be able to smell his wife, or the essence of her, on the paper. He'd done that for weeks after she'd died — entered their walk-in closet and pushed his face into her sundresses and scarves and button-down shirts. But the truth of the matter was that though there were many ways to remember Lissa, smell wasn't one. She didn't douse herself in perfume like some women, and her shampoo was plain, usually whatever was on sale.

He opened an envelope and took out a pair of reading glasses from his front pocket:

Dear Dani: We are so glad to hear you are enjoying Camp Kehonka. Daddy and I are very proud of you for making the swim team. We have lots of fun adventures planned for when you get back home. Be a good girl. Love, Mommy

Fred had a vague memory of Danielle partaking in music lessons and field hockey, but didn't recall her swimming competitively. Come to think of it, it was only the *bills* for the overpriced violin and hockey stick that he remembered — not even a concert or a game. The fact that he had to write checks for objects that he knew wouldn't get used had stuck in his craw.

Your craw? He heard Lissa. *Where is that — somewhere between your cranium and your jaw?*

Maybe Lissa had dragged him to some swim meets years ago, but he just couldn't pull the image into focus. It was the type of thing he'd like to ask his wife, if only to fill in the blanks of his life.

He placed Lissa's letter back into the thin envelope and saw an old brochure for Seven Oaks. The cover featured the community's original logo, before a new marketing team chopped off the roots of the tree silhouette and colored its leaves bright green.

They'd first visited Seven Oaks as a lark. They'd been in Savannah on vacation from their home in Mount Kisco, a leafy suburb north of New York City, and had done Bonaventure Cemetery, Fort Pulaski, and Tybee Island. They'd ridden a horse-drawn carriage, eaten beneath the low rafters of the Pirates' House, and bought Danielle a rag doll on Broughton. And then they saw an ad in the *Savannah Morning News* to tour a new development. "What the heck. It'll be an *adventure,*" Lissa had said. That was the phrase she always used, whether they were going to the dentist or the drive-in.

Once they'd followed the signs out of the city and over the rickety drawbridge, it seemed that they'd been dropped onto another planet. Phase One of Seven Oaks was just being completed. There were no sidewalks, no tennis courts, no clubhouse, no marinas. A slick trailer housed the real estate center, and the salesman who showed them orange-flagged lots drove a four-wheel-drive Jeep and wore a revolver, in case of errant foxes or wild boars.

The only finished project was the gate-house, a two-story shingled building with spotlights and security cameras. Even then, safety was the development's priority. Not that downtown Savannah was so dangerous, but the marketing department knew Northern folks thought the South was populated with rattlesnakes, white supremacists, and warring clans like the Hatfields and Mc-Coys.

The real estate trailer, covered in wall-to-wall carpeting, overlooked a narrow lawn and embankment that bordered a large kidney-shaped lagoon with a center island. At one time there'd been talk of setting up a paddleboat concierge there, but then several alligators had been spotted in the muck and those plans had been scrapped. In the trailer's front room, an architectural model rested, consisting of green foam marsh, tiny plastic palms, and a mock-up of the golf course with green felt representing lush fairways to come. Miniature golf carts and mailboxes, the size of toothpicks, dotted the roads.

The decision to move south had been easy. They'd had enough of northeastern winters, and Fred was readily hired as in-house counsel at Gulfstream, headquartered near Savannah's small airport. Even Danielle, only in grade school, adjusted without a hitch.

Fred and Lissa didn't know it then, but that was the time of their lives. They weren't that young, but they still *felt* young. They could walk eighteen holes in the morning and play three sets in the afternoon. They hadn't started to take Lipitor or calcium supplements. With their lives seeming like a game of golf in which they could control their own rate of play, they made a pact to grow old gradually and together. They'd expected they'd live well into their nineties, since both sets of parents had.

So decades later, when Lissa's pain came, it took them both by surprise. Lissa thought she had a kidney stone. She'd had one once before and knew the feeling — an intermittent blaring sharpness in her side — and had been forced to wait three uncomfortable nights in the hospital for it to pass. She said she'd rather be home this time, so she sat on the living room couch for days, as if expecting a pizza delivery. By the time Fred made arrangements to see their family doctor, and then got an appointment to see a specialist, it was too late. "Don't beat yourself up," the oncology nurse had told Fred, trying to make him feel better. "It probably had been growing inside her for years."

On the other side of the sliding glass doors, a squirrel skittered across the deck. Sequoia lifted her head, but didn't move.

Fred flipped through other papers in the box and pulled out a playbill, torn in one corner. On the front was a headline — *The Magic Show* — and a line drawing of a giant eye. It had starred Doug Henning. Fred couldn't remember going to his daughter's swim meets or what he had for breakfast, but knew the name of the magician who had starred in a show he'd seen decades before. Oh, how his mind played tricks with him.

He had taken Lissa for a big birthday, maybe her thirtieth or thirty-fifth. He'd wanted to surprise her, and he had. He couldn't remember the details of the evening, only the specifics of her retelling their friends: *He hired a limousine and had chilled champagne!* It was just a town car and sparkling wine, but he never thought to correct her.

It had rained that night, because he remembered the Saw Mill Parkway had been closed and they had to reroute along the Bronx River. The storm had descended on them Hollywood-style, as if they'd been cast in a revival of *Singin' in the Rain.* He as Gene Kelly; she as Ginger Rogers.

Debbie Reynolds. Not Ginger Rogers!

They'd gone to Sardi's after the show; it was *the* place to see and be seen. The walls were lined with caricatures of famous actors, people who had accomplished something. It was the seventies, when celebrities didn't make a living out of being famous. When empires weren't built on just showing up and snapping photos of each other and posting them to an iCloud over Shanghai.

Really, Fred? Shanghai?

They'd shared a corner table, sat knee to knee, and a famous actor came in. Fred could picture him — rugged star of stage and screen — and he'd sat alone (*He's alone!*) and at the bar.

Even now, Fred couldn't come up with his name. Karl? John? Jim?

Let's talk to him. It'll be an adventure!

Jack Klugman. That was it.

Fred hadn't discouraged her from going over alone to say hello, because she was so excited. Fred wasn't much interested and, really, didn't want a fist in his nose. He'd read somewhere that Klugman could be a prickly drunk. And so Lissa had approached him. In a few minutes she was sitting with him and clinking glasses, laughing comfortably like they had gone to their high school prom together.

An hour later, as Fred and Lissa were leaving the restaurant and Klugman was on his third martini, the actor grabbed Fred's arm and pulled him close. "Don't ever let this woman go," he slurred. For years afterward, Lissa would joke: *But Jack would take me on that cruise* or *But Jack wouldn't be such a party pooper.*

Now, decades later, Fred opened the playbill: *Lissa: Happy Birthday! Your (new) friend, Jack Klugman.* And that was it. A faded autograph. A glossy brochure. A distant memory.

But then as Fred put the playbill away, he thought he heard a whisper: *But Jack would've gotten me to a doctor sooner.*

CHAPTER 6

The day after finding Amity in the closet, Catherine and Ralph were in real estate mode again. This time, they were seated at a conference table across from Audrey.

"So while we are on the topic of different neighborhoods, let's talk decision making. Let's talk narrowing choices. Let's talk taking the next step." Audrey spread out five listing sheets before them.

"You're right." Ralph nodded enthusiastically. "We need a future here."

Catherine was finding it hard to focus on anything other than Audrey's low-cut blouse and the whisper of a lacy bra. A push-up kind with built-in continental shelf, Catherine assumed, from the way their agent's breasts jiggled when she spoke. Catherine had tried that sort of bra once, but by the end of the night a raised rash spread across her torso as if she'd been stung by jellyfish.

"Okay. So it seems to me, and I can't sway

you one way or another due to my fiduciary duty, but the property on Laughing Heron Lane is out." Audrey picked up one of the sheets, scrunched it into a ball, and tossed it into the trash basket.

"Wait," Catherine said, "which one was that?" She'd gotten the houses confused again, couldn't keep the crown moldings, screened-in porches, and Sub-Zero appliances straight.

Ralph and Audrey both blinked, as if annoyed she couldn't keep up with them.

"You know," Ralph said gently, "the one near the community center."

Audrey added, "With the white columns out front. Looked like a funeral parlor." She turned abruptly to make sure the door to the welcome center was closed and looked relieved. "Okay, moving along." She held up a photo of a stucco house with a front porch swing. Catherine could have sworn the chair swing belonged to the colonial, but Audrey threw her a life ring. "You might recall the two thousand square feet. Square dining room. Square bonus room."

"Where we could have square dancing across the square lawn," Ralph chimed in.

Catherine remembered the yard. "With square roots on the trees?" she added, but their comedy routine had ended.

"You didn't like the electric cooktop," Audrey advised. "Kitchen needs a makeover."

"A gas stove *is* pretty important. Do you cook?" Catherine imagined a burner's flame searing Audrey's lacy bra.

"Cook? No, I work too hard. I've got a career." She smiled. "But I'm sure over the years *you've* become the hostess with the mostess."

There it was again. Yesterday, when Ralph had wandered off to pretend he knew something about a circuit breaker and left her and Audrey alone, Audrey had made an offhand remark about stay-at-home wives. But what did she know? Catherine hadn't had the *need* to have a job. She had found fulfillment in taking care of Ralph and their house. She'd been in charge of the social calendar, the general household repair, and the travel plans. She was responsible for remembering birthdays, anniversaries, and holidays. She did the shopping, cleaning, and cooking — the thousand working parts of a marriage that came together to put ironed shirts in his closet and a nice roast on the dinner table.

Audrey turned back to the listings. There were three left. "You remember One Happy Rabbit Lane, don't you?" she asked Catherine, her tone implying that Catherine was a familiar but fading great aunt who came for Sunday dinners, someone to draw into conversation every now and again just so she didn't drown in her soup. "Remember? Ralph and I wandered outside while you found a bathroom."

Catherine didn't recall much of the house, only the woman in the closet. Amity. Of course she remembered every detail of that moment. Her long brown hair and ponytail. Her athletic body. Her fanny pack and dog leash. Her delicate laugh. Her saying, "I like to live other people's lives." Catherine decided that Amity must have entered the house after walking her dog. "Yes, of course. I liked the feel of that property."

"Great." Audrey nodded and then spoke to Ralph: "And you told me the marsh view reminded you of the windswept views on that course in Oregon. Abandoned Dunes."

"Bandon Dunes," Ralph said. "You really don't miss a beat, do you?"

"But alligators," Catherine chimed in. "What about the lagoon? What about the marsh? I'm worried about Karma."

"After they reach six feet they are *relocated,*" Audrey replied, as if they were discussing misplaced refugees. "And smaller gators are around, but it's not like they are great white *sharks* or anything. Do you think some guy would retrieve his ball from a lagoon if he thought he could lose a hand?"

Audrey did have a point. Ralph had shown Catherine highlights on the Golf Channel of professional golfers chipping muddy balls from lagoon edges while their caddies stood by, protecting them with sand trap rakes.

"In fact, as proof, just look at old Mr. Peabody."

"Mr. Peabody?" Catherine and Ralph asked simultaneously.

"We like to think of him as our office mascot," Audrey said, standing and moving to the wide picture window where Catherine and Ralph joined her. She pointed a manicured finger past the grassy lawn and steep bank of the lagoon. On an island an Olympic-size-pool-length away, Catherine saw an elongated gray shape. He was halfway in the water, sunning himself on the bank. She might have mistaken him for a burled log if she hadn't been told otherwise.

"Completely harmless. He's been there going on twenty years I'm told."

Ralph's attention, predictably, focused on the fairway behind the lagoon. "And which hole is that?"

"Eighteenth of Greenleaf Park. Long par four. There's a dogleg right with a big trap just before the turn."

Ralph licked his lips stupidly, as if they'd been discussing steak on the menu. "If you hit it more than two-ten off the blue tees you'll be fine," Audrey continued. "What do you shoot, Ralph? Two-thirty? Two-forty?"

"With a little wind, maybe."

"You'll be fine." Audrey pat his arm.

At the very least, Catherine was impressed with Audrey's multitasking — selling them a house, dismissing the wildlife, flirting with her husband. It reminded her of the topless central African women in *National Geographic* who weave baskets, collect honey, and raise children while their breasts sway in the heat.

"But what are those guys *doing*?" Ralph asked. They watched a foursome drive their two carts to the edge of the fairway and into the rough, near the lagoon. One of the men got out, golf club in hand, and hurled it into the water.

"Oh, that." Audrey shook her head. "Little local tradition with the boys. If you've totally mucked up your score — you know, twenty above your handicap — you throw a club into the lagoon as sort of an offering to the golf gods. Must be a hundred rusting six irons in there. DEP hates it — really gets their hackles up — but there's not much they can do." Then she turned to Catherine. "It's funny. You just never know what a man will do when he's in a rut."

CHAPTER 7

Fred felt a particular sadness for the artificial tree in the corner of his grief counselor's office. Its glossy leaves had been spray painted tractor green, and its trunk listed toward the window as if it were trying to get out. Chances were, the tree had been part of someone's estate. Fred knew that some clients bequeathed everything to hospice, from spatulas and hair scarves to well-worn convertibles.

Hunter had just asked him a question, but Fred had no idea what it had been. The man was half-smiling, waiting him out. In a game show there would have been a giant stopwatch ticking somewhere offstage. Hunter was a more expressive, younger version of himself. A version that had his hair cropped short, close to his head, and wore round glasses. A version that kept a plastic tree in the corner of his office where a live one might have worked a little better, considering the circumstances.

"Pardon?" Fred asked.

"I said, what does feeling stuck *mean* to you?"

Feeling stuck. That's what Fred had been stewing about. His life was not moving forward, or moving backward. Stalled on the shoulder of an expressway. Lissa was gone and he was all by himself. His few out-of-town friends had stopped calling regularly, and he was getting tired of taking every meal alone.

He'd been surprised by the random things that people sent him after Lissa's death — a box of tropical fruit, a sympathy basket of chocolate, several bottles of French wine. Even his dog park friends had chipped in together to purchase a wreath of red and white roses. When it arrived Fred mistook it momentarily for a lifeguard ring, as if he could strap his arms through it and be saved. It now lay in a grayish clump in the wooded area behind his house.

"I don't know. I feel . . ." He tried to come up with a synonym for *stuck,* but his mind didn't work that way anymore. Years ago he could have tap-danced his way across any conversation — rattled off names of Supreme Court justices or debated the ethics of human cloning — but now he couldn't come up with a synonym for *stuck.* "A fly to flypaper. All eight legs in glue."

Six legs. A fly has six legs, Lissa told him. "I mean six legs."

Hunter nodded, encouraging him. He had that look, his raised eyebrows saying, *And?*

Under different circumstances, Fred might have invited Hunter to play golf at Seven Oaks, to try out the fast greens of Greenleaf Park or challenging bunkers at Palmetto Pines. They might have spent a pleasant afternoon discussing the advancement in putters or the direction of interest rates. But when Fred had first come in for counseling, he'd commented on the watercolor above Hunter's desk, a large canvas of a wide fairway with a half-dollar green. A small red smudge indicated a distant flagstick. "Oh, I don't play," Hunter had replied when asked. "That picture's just a metaphor for life."

The silence felt uncomfortable, so Fred tried again. "Unable to move on. Paralyzed, I guess."

Hunter nodded as if to say, *Now we're getting somewhere.* "So tell me, were you able to get back on the course this week?"

Fred laughed suddenly. A real laugh. A sound that came straight from his gut. The first laugh he hadn't manufactured and pushed out of his abdomen in months.

63

"Yes. I even shot a forty-eight." He'd dragged himself out of the house before dusk two evenings ago and played the front nine alone. "It's not worthy of an invitation to the Masters, but a personal achievement nonetheless."

Hunter nodded, encouraging him.

"So I guess I'm not stuck in golf."

"Certainly not."

"Maybe someday I'll get back to my tennis, too."

"I think that'd be great for you." Hunter hesitated. "And Danielle? Have you heard from her?"

"She calls. Mostly to tell me about Tommy. Mostly to berate me for not checking my email. And she wants me to visit them at some point."

"And what do *you* want?"

What did he want? To be more helpful in the only way he knew how. To sue his ex-son-in-law, the bastard who left his daughter. To fight for child support. "I want to help her, but she won't let me."

"I see."

But how could Hunter see? No amount of Freudian training could prepare a man for understanding the complexities of fatherhood.

"And Lissa's dresses and jackets?" Hunter asked.

"Coming along." Hunter hadn't taken any notes, but apparently he'd been listening. Fred wondered if his grief counselor raced to his computer to type up notes after their sessions. How had Hunter remembered Lissa's clothes? Fred barely remembered them. "A box a week." So what if he exaggerated a bit? What was the harm?

"Really?"

"I was able to get rid of some stuff."

Fred was going to say *junk. I was able to get rid of some junk.* Yet it wasn't junk but souvenirs of clothes worn, meals eaten, a life well spent. Mementos from their wedding and their marriage and their past. Proof that they'd had a full journey. Stamped passports from European vacations, fancy stiff menus, and engraved party invitations.

It's trash, Lissa whispered. *Just get it out of there.*

"Remember, being stuck can be temporary. Feelings aren't facts," Hunter said.

Fred had been suspicious about the benefits of talk therapy. He felt it plausible that it could help, if only to spend time with someone else, but it wasn't that different from what he did at the dog park. Sit there

65

and talk to Ernie. Granted, they didn't discuss Lissa, but still. *Your dog is pooping. Stop digging. Did Lulu get groomed?* It got him out of the house, at least. "So, what you're saying is that maybe I'm not as stuck as I think."

Eureka! Lissa almost shouted. *Give the man a door prize!*

With the tiniest speck of hope and Lissa pushing him, Fred got into his car. He must have taken his usual route home — left out of the parking lot and onto Eisenhower Drive, right on Waters, straight over the Intracoastal — but he had no particular memory of it. He usually considered stray litter on the causeway or the clumpy remains of roadkill, but he didn't have a conscious thought until he reached the gates of Seven Oaks. *That was quick,* he thought as he drove under the raised security bar. In tennis it was called muscle memory, hitting a ball so cleanly off the strings without thinking or trying, action in perfect harmony with the universe.

Sequoia must have heard the garage door opening, because when he entered she was there to greet him, her tail wagging. He leaned down and took her muzzle in his hand and kissed her on the forehead. He felt her breath on his face but didn't linger.

Before he could get stuck again, before any amount of second-guessing got in his way, he went to his office and clicked on the mouse so that his computer screen lit up.

His daughter had set up an account for him a few weeks ago. She had sent him a letter with his password (Tommyturns9) and complete instructions for logging on to Facebook. Perhaps he could reconnect with college friends and stay in closer contact with Danielle and Tommy.

He picked up the envelope from his desk, and out fell a small, square photo of Tommy. This time his grandson was in a coat and tie and looked like a miniature man. Tom Thumb posing in front of a piano. He was an attractive, amiable child, but how many pictures could his daughter take of one person? Danielle had recorded her son's progress as if he were an endangered flower in a time-lapse photography experiment.

Her note read:

Dad: I'm sending you this the old-fashioned way so you can't pretend you didn't get it or didn't know your password. Come join the 21st century . . . You don't have to be alone. We miss you, xo D.

Danielle worked part-time as a life coach,

whatever that was. *You know what it is. I've explained it to you a hundred times.*

I know what it is, but I don't get it.

You mean, why can't people just coach themselves? Why can't they just make decisions and lead unexamined lives? Why can't they get through and done with their grief without going to a counselor? Why can't they push on despite the loss of a loved one?

Look at me. I'm going. It's what you wanted. But you're not listening.

But he *was* listening, and to him it felt like Danielle never let Tommy out of her sight now that she was divorced and Tommy's father had moved to Chicago. They took vacations together and ate dinners together, and watched movies together. She even played video games with him — badminton and table tennis and drag racing — swinging an invisible racket and pressing a pretend gas pedal. When Fred was employed and supporting his family, negotiations were in person, face-to-face, in corporate boardrooms across Middle America. Sometimes, even, he went overseas when a turbaned sheikh wanted to look him in the eye to discuss contract specifications for a G200. There was no such thing as a virtual meeting. You got to know someone by whether he ordered steak Diane or chicken Kiev at a business dinner, whether he drank martinis or Tom Collinses. It was a time when people actually talked to one another, not texted what was for dinner.

Fred was getting used to the modern world, but didn't trust technology. Didn't trust what it *did* to people. What happened to opening a map and understanding the difference between north and south? What happened to looking outside to see if it was raining instead of going onto the World Wide Web and researching the weather? Even Tommy had been brainwashed by this new electronic age. On his and Lissa's last trip to Maine, they'd given their grandson a Rubik's Cube. The boy had taken it out of the box and sat staring at it, genuinely surprised. Finally he had turned to them, his puppy eyes wide: "But how do I turn it on?"

And of course Danielle was feeling a loss from her mother's death. How could she not? But Danielle had seemed angry with him since Lissa had gone, as if he'd been to blame for not saving her.

That's not it. You are reading too much into it. I'm going to make it right between you.

Fred recognized that part of the problem was that Danielle didn't have siblings with whom to share the responsibility of aging parents. As an only child, she was self-absorbed, a miniature country protected by a stone wall. And he and Lissa were partly to blame, as they'd shielded her from everything. Even when Danielle's childhood dog, Gizmo, a beloved Bouvier des Flandres, had needed to be put to sleep, they'd told their daughter that he'd gone to live with a family in Nebraska. She'd actually believed it, never once even questioning his disappearance or asking to see a photograph of the lame dog in the prairie.

Fred clicked the mouse again, but the screen read CHECK INTERNET CONNECTION. He touched a symbol in the upper-right corner and a box appeared: JOIN OTHER NETWORK; CREATE NETWORK; OPEN NETWORK PREFERENCES.

Things get unstuck, she whispered. *You know what to do. It's not a crime to ask for help.*

Fred opened his desk drawer and pulled out the Seven Oaks residential directory, a sixty-page booklet that also offered general information about covenants and architectural-review guidelines. Four full pages addressed community no-nos. *No recycling cardboard. No riding bicycles on golf cart paths. No keeping garage doors open overnight.* He could look up the number of the main office or someone in the neighborhood to see if they'd lost their connection too.

At one time he and Lissa knew all their neighbors. Once a month, couples on the street would converge at the common area for an evening meal, a picnic with scalloped potatoes and deep dishes of fried chicken. Someone might even bring a Frisbee or a portable radio. But as Fred ran through the names of people in the neighborhood to call, he realized they'd all moved away or died. The only couple he knew on his road were on a two-month South Pacific cruise. Fred used to not be able to get through the grocery store without an extended conversation in the condiment aisle with another Gulfstream associate or one of Lissa's tennis partners. Now when he went, he might as well have been invisible.

After the alphabetical listing came a directory by address. The houses on his street, owned by newly retired couples in a race for their lives to see the Grand Canyon or take a whistle-stop tour of the national park system, were dark at night. But he knew that his neighbor directly across the back woods was usually home. Whenever Fred couldn't sleep, when he'd be sipping hot chocolate at his kitchen table at two a.m., he'd notice the faint burning lights in the nearby patio home on Oak Bluff Lane.

He looked up the name associated with the address. *Ida B. Childs.*

CHAPTER 8

Ida Blue wore an oversize black caftan with creamy pinstripes that ran the length of the fabric, from swoop collar to hem floating above thick ankles. She'd read that vertical stripes were slimming to a full-figured woman. And her new shade of Lady Danger lipstick would draw attention from her ample chin to her perfectly proportioned cheekbones. She'd even tied her waist-length chestnut hair into an elaborate chignon. Though she wasn't going any-where, was just at home watching *Dr. Phil,* she liked to keep up appearances.

The phone rang just as Dr. Phil was doing an intervention with a man who was so obese that authorities needed to break through his walls and use a crane to rescue him. Dr. Phil, who looked like he might have put on a few pounds himself, was always doing that. Getting into other peo-ple's business. Showing up on strangers' doorsteps, rescuing them from whatever he deemed abnormal. *Thank goodness I'm only big boned,* she thought. *He'd never get past security without a guest pass, anyway.*

The ringing phone startled her because she was surprised by the dulcet sound of a sitar, her custom tone for home calls. For a moment, she imagined that Ravi Shankar had sneaked into her living room as she watched Dr. Phil. She rarely got personal calls. Sometimes a pizza man would need turn-by-turn directions to her house as if she were an air traffic controller talking down a disabled plane. And once a Chinese delivery guy had gotten lost with her moo goo gai pan for what seemed like hours.

She reached for the gentle sitar-strumming phone. "Hello?"

"Hello, yes. This is your neighbor, Fred Wolfe." The tingling in her toes started immediately, like the pins and needles one feels when a limb is awakening after an afternoon in a hammock. She was so overtaken by the unusual feeling, she forgot where she was. "What?"

"Your neighbor, Fred Wolfe."

She felt as if someone were holding a heating pad to the balls of her feet, then her ankles. The warm sensation oozed up her calves and over her knees just as it'd felt when she'd been sucked into the green waters of the Okefenokee Swamp once while hunting. "Fred," was all she could think to say.

"Yes, Wolfe. W-o-l-f-e."

As he spoke, an out-of-focus screen seemed to roar to life in her backyard. She spied the gauzy outline of a slightly hunched woman with curly red hair wearing culottes, a golf shirt, and a visor. The muted apparition floated toward the tree-lined edge of her property.

"Is this Ida Childs?" he asked.

"Yes."

"Good. I'm on Jolly Badger Lane in Palmetto Pines. We share the same back woods."

Every time the man spoke, the ghostlike woman floating just above the lawn emerged in greater detail, like the work in progress of a color-by-number picture. The woman drifted toward the back porch while a heat lamp scorched Ida Blue's thighs and abdomen.

"Frrr-red." She said his name slowly, letting it roll off her tongue Eliza Doolittle style, drawing the word into two syllables. "Frrr-red Wooo-lfe."

If she had been in a phone booth, this is when she would have plugged the coin slot with a fistful of quarters so as not to lose this connection. Her whole adult life she'd pretended to have a feeling of extrasensory insight, and here it was, landing on her back porch like a golden goose.

She vaguely remembered seeing this woman walk an enormous dog with black spots around the neighborhood. "You have a Great Dane?" Ida Blue asked distractedly.

"Yes, she's mine. Everyone in the neighborhood seems to remember Sequoia."

She heard him fumbling with the receiver, maybe looking to see if they'd been disconnected.

"Listen, I'm sorry to disturb you, but I think the Internet may be down in our neighborhood. I can't get through to the cable company and the Seven Oaks office goes to voice mail."

With each word he spoke, the woman drifted nearer to Ida Blue's window. If she'd been closer, Ida Blue imagined she could have reached out and taken her hand.

Fred continued, "I'm not good with these computer contraptions. My wife used to handle these things."

The shimmery woman outside pointed to herself and threw her head back with amusement. "The woman with curly red hair? She played golf?"

"Yes, I'm sure you've seen her around. We've lived here for years but she passed in September."

"I'm sorry for your loss," Ida Blue answered, trying to sound concerned but giddy with the magic of her newfound awareness. Like a piano student who, after years and years of stumbling through "Chopsticks," can suddenly perform "Flight of the Bumblebee."

But as was so often the case, Ida Blue became distracted by her own thoughts. Her mind started to take her consciousness captive. As the woman's outfit came into focus — culottes and green shirt — Ida started to slip away. The outline of the older woman floating outside started to dim. Ida snapped the rubber band on her wrist so hard it almost broke in two.

"Yes, I've got it." *Speak slowly and clearly,* Ida told herself.

"An Internet connection?"

The woman outside shook her head and motioned Ida toward the computer. "Wait, stay on the line." *Stay on the line!* Ida Blue felt like a 911 operator. *Keep him talking!* She stood up from the couch. Some bite-size Tootsie Roll wrappers drifted like butterflies to the floor. But once she rose, she couldn't move, paralyzed by the fear that she might lose the connection, struggling like a rusted TV antenna clamped to an aging roof.

She could hear Fred cough and start to say something. Yet nothing mattered but this gift of energy and matter that was flowing through her. She tasted something metallic. Her abdomen was a vacant amphitheater that was suddenly hosting the Golden Globes. *Don't panic,* she told herself. And yet she had to move or she'd lose him. She was a fisherman who had caught the biggest fish of her life, a thrashing marlin, and needed to set the lure by yanking the line in a leap of faith.

She inched toward the kitchen table she used as world headquarters. "Just a moment." She touched the mouse and the computer came alive. The woman outside had turned away to face the back woods. Ida clicked on her email and saw new messages in her inbox: The Ethics of Juggling, Joke of the Day, Mastering the Mermaid Braid. "Yes, my connection is fine." *My connection has never been better in my whole life,* she thought.

"Oh, it must just be me."

"Can I come over?" She said it so suddenly, even she was surprised. Ida Blue could only imagine the connection she'd feel if she were nearer to the energy source, closer to the mother ship.

"Come over?"

"To help. I can reboot it. Check the router."

He remained silent for a moment, considering her offer. "So kind of you, but I'll try to suss things out."

"Please call again." She heard the desperation in her own voice, as if she were the one now having the emergency. *Don't leave me! Don't hang up! Stay on the line!*

"Thank you."

And she heard the line go flat. Ida Blue looked at her phone, then out the window, but the woman in the golf outfit had floated away.

Chapter 9

Catherine and Ralph settled into the outside seating area at the Village Café, the on-island restaurant adjacent to the village and golf cart retailer.

She'd wondered about this new business of specialty stores selling only golf carts or French cheese or flannel bedding. Really? Even downtown the previous afternoon, they'd happened into a place that just sold salt, friendly clerks offering them samples as if they were carriage horses.

"What are you thinking?" Ralph asked distractedly. He was looking at the menu, but Catherine knew *he* was thinking of the marsh view or perhaps even the curve of Audrey's bosom.

A young waitress brought them their iced teas and took out a paper pad. "So, what can I get y'all?" she asked. Her nose was pierced with a single diamond stud. Catherine prayed that Ralph wouldn't mention it.

The previous night, he'd asked the bartender at the 17hundred90 Inn if he'd been drunk when he'd gotten the hammer tattoo on his neck, and Catherine was sure the young man had watered down their drinks in retaliation.

Ralph ordered a turkey sandwich and Catherine a BLT. As the waitress moved away from the table, Catherine called out, "And he doesn't like too much mayo, please. Just one side, light." She couldn't help herself.

Ralph placed his cell phone on the table in front of him. "Honestly, the golf course view is nice but I'm leaning toward the marsh," he said. Momentarily, Catherine imagined him leaning toward Audrey.

"Did you remember to feed Karma?" Catherine asked suddenly.

It was the type of question that might send Ralph into a tailspin. The type of question that married couples ask each other a thousand times during a lifetime: Did you turn off the stove? Did you lock the car? Did you take your medication? Of course he had, and of course she didn't need to ask, but something made her seek assurance. It was solidarity and support she was looking for, a way of asking, "Do you still love me?"

"I don't know," Ralph answered. "Probably."

She was going to have to get used to retirement. The breakfasts, the lunches, the afternoons. It was one thing to speak on the phone a few times a day. *What's for dinner? Do we need anything at the store?* It was another thing entirely to putter about under the same roof. Now Ralph's questions were closer to (1) Where's a paper clip? (2) Can you cut my toenails? (3) Are my eyebrows starting to curl? They'd had friends back in New Jersey who divorced after forty years. "I married for life, not for lunch," the wife said. "Once he retired I got twice the husband and half the time." Ralph sometimes offered to help with cooking dinner or making a bed, yet trying to explain the most efficient way to cut an onion was painstaking. And teaching him hospital corners was like teaching a toddler origami.

Catherine sipped her iced tea and watched as Ralph tried to harpoon the lemon rind that had settled at the bottom of his glass. As he poked at it repeatedly with his fork, she wondered if he'd done the same thing at business luncheons on Wall Street. If anyone had ever suggested a spoon. If the firm had finally found a star investor who didn't impersonate Captain Ahab during client meetings.

"The garage of the last one isn't bad," he said.

She knew he was speaking of the empty space for the golf cart, the side door with a separate entrance. He could pull in straight from the golf course, the equivalent of a ski-in condo at a Colorado chalet.

"I'd be able to work on projects at the bench," he added.

What projects he had, she had no idea. He needed an instruction manual to change a lightbulb. One time he'd fixed a toilet paper holder by replacing an anchor bolt, and the way he'd talked about it for months, you'd think he'd reconstructed the Eiffel Tower. "And Audrey?" Catherine asked.

"Competent, it seems. Knows her stuff."

As it turned out, Catherine was grateful for Audrey and her pathetic flirtation. At the house on Happy Rabbit, Ralph had been so transfixed by her that by the time the two had returned from honeymooning in the backyard, the woman in the closet — Amity — had easily slipped away. Although Catherine felt as self-conscious as if she were wearing a gorilla suit, Ralph and Audrey had hardly noticed her when they came back in. They spoke of property lines and covenants, while Catherine kept silently repeating the phrase, "I like to live other people's lives."

As Ralph sipped his iced tea and checked his email, Catherine tried to envision what it was that Amity *did* in vacant houses. Try on clothes? Cook meals? Read diaries? Steal medication? Catherine had heard somewhere that crooks sold painkillers on the Internet for large profits, but what medication could there be to steal at Seven Oaks? Viagra and cholesterol-lowering statins and blood-pressure pills? Of course, people of all ages lived in the community, but retirees seemed to make up the biggest segment.

The waitress returned and set the plates in front of them. Catherine's sandwich was flanked by french fries while Ralph's had coleslaw and pickles.

"Here," Ralph said and winked as he placed the pickle slices on her plate. "Don't say I never gave you anything."

Across the open courtyard an older man sat eating alone. His white hair was combed neatly to one side. Although clearly in his seventies, he had good posture and strong arms, as if he had been a college rower. He flipped through a glossy newsmagazine, wire glasses perched at the end of his nose. A spotted Great Dane slept at his feet, her giant head resting on his shoes.

"That's another good thing about Georgia" — Catherine watched Ralph thumb his phone's screen with one hand while he held his sandwich with the other — "whether it's a gun or a dog, they let you bring it into a restaurant." She wasn't sure if either part were true, but Ralph nodded, oblivious. Then the older man started coughing deeply and the Great Dane lifted her head until he stopped.

Suddenly Catherine wished Karma were there with them. They had left him locked in the laundry room at their rental, his eyes beseeching them to take him along, but Ralph had put his foot down. "I'm sorry, honey," he'd said matter-of-factly, "but he doesn't have voting rights in this." But, really, Catherine felt that Karma was as much a part of their family as Ralph was. In recent years, while her husband had been commuting to New York, working long hours, golfing with clients, Karma had been the one with whom she'd spent the most time.

If she were alone, as the man and his dog perhaps were, she wondered which house she would choose. Instead of chicken and white rice every other meal, she could prepare salads with things Ralph was afraid to try, like garbanzo beans, shaved almonds, anchovies. She remembered the vague freedom she had before she'd gotten married. Of course she was only twenty-five and living in rural Monmouth County, in her parents' clapboard house, a place as serene inside as it was outside, but there was something to be said for doing only your own laundry.

Then she wondered if Amity was alone. The young woman was pretty and athletic, but Catherine didn't remember seeing a wedding ring. She was probably in her thirties. Perhaps Catherine should have called the police when she'd found her in the closet. Or even informed Audrey. But what would Audrey have done? Gotten security on speed dial to call in the National Guard?

The waitress with the diamond stud returned. "Everything okay?"

"Delicious." Ralph gave her a toothy grin and touched his finger to his left nostril. The waitress didn't seem to notice the implication and so he added, "You've hit it on the *nose.*"

Catherine felt her face flush with embarrassment.

The man in the corner reached down to scratch his dog's head, and the Great Dane snorted gratefully. Then he placed both hands on the chair's armrests and pushed himself up. The dog rose as well.

Ralph's phone vibrated on the table and shook the salt and pepper shakers. He put the receiver to his ear, pursed his lips together, and listened, a million miles away from her. Then he stood and retreated beside a decorative planter.

Stepping slowly, the man walked in her direction, across the courtyard and toward the outside exit. The Great Dane stopped in front of Catherine. "Sequoia," the man said gently. "C'mon." He pushed his wire glasses back on his nose.

Catherine put her hand out for the large dog to sniff. "She must smell my dog, Karma."

The man laughed. "Karma? Fantastic. Do you have good Karma or bad Karma?"

At that moment, Catherine moved her gaze from the dog to the man. In an instant, she looked at his face and saw the most extraordinary blue eyes. The man's pupils were entrapped in a sea of pale turquoise. They seemed to sparkle in the light, a shimmery expanse of hope. She felt as if they had met somewhere before, as if they had been friends for years.

"Good Karma, I hope," the man continued, perhaps mistaking her silence for irritation. "I'm sorry about this." He gently pulled the leash. "Come along, girl." But the dog wouldn't move. The man pulled his hand through his trimmed hair and continued, "Sequoia. Just like the tree — strong, sturdy, and for the first time in her adult life, irrepressibly stubborn."

"What a lovely dog," Catherine whispered.

Embarrassed, the man tugged hard at the leash. "Sequoia!" But still the dog wouldn't budge. She held her head steady, staring at Catherine. Long tail swinging back and forth like a pendulum.

Ralph's voice was low and his back was turned. He spun around and lifted his hand in acknowledgment of the man and his dog, but continued his cell phone conversation.

"My apologies. She's usually not like this."

And just as he said this, with great difficulty the Great Dane reared up on her back legs and placed her front paws on the armrest of Catherine's chair. Without hesitation, the dog started licking Catherine's face, moving her big tongue in wide arcs across her cheek and neck, and Catherine suddenly remembered what it was to be loved.

CHAPTER 10

While Karma remained asleep behind her in his doggie seat, Catherine drove south on I-95, past signs for Philadelphia, Wilmington, the Brandywine Valley. After she and Ralph returned to Short Hills from Seven Oaks, they received a generous offer on their New Jersey home *and* put in a winning bid for the house at One Happy Rabbit Lane. It seemed all stars were aligning.

She and Ralph had hoped to caravan together back to Savannah. They'd even talked about a mooch march, visiting friends near Annapolis or staying a few days with a cousin in Baltimore. But packing had taken longer than expected and they hadn't foreseen the attention needed to the dozen jigsaw pieces that made up their lives: a festive farewell dinner with neighbors; a final cleaning at the dentist; updated vaccines for Karma; and a face-to-face farewell with all their doctors. Ralph left several days before

Catherine to prepare for the closing in Savannah. Meanwhile, she remained in New Jersey, watching tattooed men in puce coveralls cart their belongings into a moving truck as big as Giants Stadium.

As she drove, Catherine became entranced by an audiobook that explained the inner workings of the planets and universe. A client had given Ralph the CD as a retirement gift, but he preferred to listen to *The Zen of Golf* — to learn why his putts weren't straight instead of how the universe worked. So she spent the morning learning about plate tectonics. How even though the world seems stable, it remains in motion, shifting constantly in infinitely small distances until it decides to take a six-inch leap and the resulting tsunami wipes out a distant island nation.

Around lunchtime Karma started snorting, bodily noises making up for his linguistic challenges. Since Catherine needed a break from the highway and the audio, she exited and followed signs to a rest area that turned out to be two sad little gas pumps in front of an Arby's. And she knew she should really call Ralph. She *could* use her cell phone while driving, like every other person on the planet, but she was unfamiliar with the state laws of Pennsylvania, Maryland,

and Delaware and didn't trust herself. She'd read too many articles about cognitive distraction, about how the human brain can't concentrate on two things at the same time. And for a moment she thought of Audrey Cunningham. Could Ralph concentrate on two things at the same time? Could he really be attracted to their Realtor? Or was he just flirting because that's what men *did*? To Catherine, Audrey seemed one-dimensional. Brassy. Impertinent. "All chrome and no engine," as her sister, Martha, might say. Audrey had negotiated a reasonable price on their new house — the house in which Catherine had found Amity in the closet — and had even managed to get the golf cart thrown in to sweeten the pot for Ralph, but her appeal to Catherine stopped at the negotiating table.

Once parked, Catherine pulled Karma out of his baby seat, and he stretched with delight. As she called Ralph, she let her dog pull her in the direction of a hulking green Dumpster.

He answered on the third ring. "Hey, how's traffic?"

"They say sixty is the new forty."

"Are you driving?"

"Why, hello to you too. Yes, I'm fine, thanks for asking."

"I'm serious."

"No, I pulled over."

"Good, I need you here in one piece."

Karma tugged Catherine to a patch of gravelly bone-colored rocks that might have been part of an archeological dig. "How's it going?"

"Good. Lawyer this morning. Insurance agent this afternoon."

"Have you had lunch?"

"Just getting it now."

"Alone?"

He paused. "With Audrey. She's helping sort out the inspection."

Catherine felt her face redden, the blood erupting in a pool beneath her cheeks. She thought of telling Ralph what she'd learned about the zones of convergence and about continental drift. That he walked on an eggshell crust with molten iron teeming somewhere below his spiked golf shoes. Then Karma let out a little yip and Catherine realized the dog had become tangled in the leash, as if he were a lassoed steer ready to be flipped, branded, and sent inside to Arby's. "Well, we're stopping for lunch. I'll call you tonight when I get to the hotel." Catherine thought she heard the tinkle of glass and wondered if Ralph and Audrey were at a fancy restaurant. A restaurant that had embroidered napkins and tablecloths. A restaurant that served steak tartare.

"Okay. Just use your blinker."

"What are you saying?"

"I'm just reminding you to pay attention. And don't dawdle. You're allowed to drive over fifty-five."

After she hung up she cursed him quietly even though she knew he was right about being careful. She was often surprised to find herself in the far left lane, a pace car in front of a pack of impatient drivers at the Indianapolis 500. She'd had three minor accidents in two years, but they weren't technically her fault. The last one — backing into someone at the Super Wawa — had more to do with getting Ralph's melting ice cream home and in the freezer than any sort of criminal recklessness. At an age when their car insurance rate should have dropped, they'd just received an increase.

Ten years ago she would have just laughed at the suggestion of living in a gated community, but as she aged, she felt a growing anxiety. Not about physical ailments — receding gums or middle-of-the-night leg pain — but about being *vulnerable.* She had to start concentrating on things she used to do without thinking. Things like grocery shopping without a list, remembering where she set her eyeglasses, getting out of her car without losing her keys and cell phone. Life, it seemed, was getting hairier.

She spent the afternoon at a steady seventy miles per hour. Cars and trucks passed her as if she were driving a tractor. She made it through three of the CDs, listening to how a giant asteroid had hurtled to earth and struck Manson, Iowa, and left a twenty-four-mile crater in its wake. How it came from nowhere and without warning. Again, Catherine thought how lucky they were for finding Seven Oaks. For moving to the safety of coastal Georgia rather than a condo on the San Andreas Fault or a quaint cabin overlooking Mount Saint Helens. She likened the gated community to retiring to a childproofed play area. No sharp objects. No electrical cords. No glass-top tables. Only Audrey Cunningham to worry about.

Although she felt uneasy about driving alone on such a long trip, she was glad to have the time to herself. Ralph had become increasingly moody since his forced retirement, like a successful greyhound who is forced off the track after a profitable career. And Catherine had been off-kilter for days, at least since the going-away party from her tennis team. Not so much that it was a surprise, for she felt that ten years as an anchor playing number one and then ten years as a floater meant something, but for its sentimentality. Younger women who had happily replaced her on the team roster showed up with heartfelt cards that sounded like they were directed to someone dying of a slow-growing, intractable disease. They wrote *We'll never forget you* and *Stay the course* on ivory cards with serious cursive script. Women who had aimed overheads at her gut and accused her of tight line calls had drawn fanciful hearts with colorful ink messages: *Friends forever, never apart / Maybe in distance but not in heart.* And it seemed every woman Catherine had ever met in her life wanted to take her to coffee and talk about her move. To stop her in the grocery or drugstore and ask how it *felt* to be going south, as if she were embarking on a one-way trip to the moon. One had even asked incredulously: "I mean, do you even *like* shrimp and grits?" as if that were an imperative for relocating south of the Mason-Dixon Line.

After checking in at a roadside hotel in central Virginia and taking Karma for a long walk on a side road, Catherine had a pleasant meal at a Japanese steak house. Pieces of sushi and sashimi arrived at her table on

95

a series of small plates. Because she'd forgotten her book, she kept pushing the ceramic dishes apart and together, trying to visualize what she'd learned about continental drift.

Back in her hotel room, she watched the local ten o'clock news. A young woman with shellacked hair and a strong Southern accent spoke of a recent rash of house break-ins in Albemarle County. She thought again of Amity and her bizarre inclination to wander through strangers' homes. Catherine hoped she would find her again. She wondered what it would feel like to get out of her comfort zone. To stand on the edge of a tectonic plate as it was moving toward something else.

The next morning she woke up feeling a refreshing freedom and realized it had been twenty years since she'd last traveled alone. She'd met Martha in Las Vegas for a girls' weekend and had gotten there a day early. It fell between her sister's second divorce and third wedding, but what she remembered about the visit was not feeling free, but sweating by a crowded pool and feeling proud she was the only woman in the world who had not succumbed to a boob job.

After taking Karma out for a quick walk she went down to breakfast feeling a little giddy. Fake palms framed the entrance to the breakfast nook, an L-shaped alcove off the front lobby. When she walked in she immediately smelled the overcooked sausage and cheesy eggs in rectangular chafing dishes kept at a low heat for hours. Older couples populated most of the tables, as well as a few businessmen traveling alone, reading iPads or newspapers, making notes in Moleskine planners. She ladled crusted oatmeal into her bowl. For Karma, she wrapped several sausage links in a wad of paper napkins and carefully placed them in her purse.

When she sat down she saw the back of a man's head with thick sandy hair. He had broad shoulders and appeared to be in his late thirties, though the farther she got from sixty, the harder it was to tell anyone's age. She wondered who he was and if he had a family. Whether he called his mother every Sunday and was in love with his wife. If she and Ralph had had children when they'd first met and married, this might have even been her son.

At times like this she wished they had tried harder, wished she'd paid more attention to ovulation and folic acid supplements. She regretted thinking that jump-starting a family might be as easy as kicking a motorcycle into gear, naively believing that Ralph would be open to the possibility. If they had, they might have given birth to a child who grew up to sell insurance policies or safety locks or air bags.

After breakfast she moved to the single elevator in the lobby. The floor indicator appeared stuck on three for several minutes. Finally the doors opened and a family of five wheeled out a massive luggage cart as if they'd lived their entire lives in the hotel. Just after she entered and before the doors closed, the businessman she'd been watching walked in too. He and Catherine reached out at the same time to push the floor buttons.

"Pardon me," he said. They pulled their hands back as if they'd touched the same hot stove.

"Sorry," she said.

"Which floor?" he asked.

If she'd had a son, she and Ralph would have never grown apart. A gaggle of nearby grandchildren might have cemented them to Short Hills. They'd have more in common than the same wedding anniversary. "Four."

He pressed the button for four and then hit five, the top floor. She wondered if the hotel had a conference room or cozy break-out area where they could talk. If this had been her son, they could have shared hot chocolate. Of course, he was too old to read to, but maybe she could hear about his job and they could watch the Discovery Channel. They could discuss the big bang theory.

"It's snowing in Boston," he said apropos of nothing, and the elevator started its slow ascent.

"Again?" Catherine hadn't been following the weather patterns or the contour maps of meteorological pressure but wanted to keep the conversation going. It seemed sweet that he was intent on making a connection with her. "I'm glad I'm heading south."

The elevator chimed as they passed the second floor.

"Pardon?"

"I'm moving to Savannah," Catherine said, light-headed with her use of the first-person *I*. As in *I'm alone.* As in *I have my own life.* As in *I never had children, but I can still feel love.* As in *I can start my life over any time.*

"Oh." He sounded disappointed, then turned to take a sudden interest in the elevator evacuation sign. The elevator chimed again.

Catherine noticed his Italian shoes and slacks pressed with a center crease so tight he might have had a personal valet waiting for him. She smelled smoked hickory and momentarily imagined it was his musky cologne. Then she realized it was just the sausages in her purse. "I don't know if you've studied much science, but it's like we're all just floating on icebergs, not knowing where or when they might break and plunge us into the sea," she blurted out. He turned to her and blinked rapidly, an actor in a community theater production who pretends to have something in his eye. The elevator chimed and the doors opened. He put his hand out to hold the door for her.

She wanted to tell him that life is short. That people change over time and without warning. That indecision influences outcome. That roads become slippery when wet. That bridges ice before roadways. That before he knows it, he'll want to retire to a gated community himself.

His hand remained on the elevator door, waiting for her to exit. Another chime, faster and lower and angrier as if the elevator were losing patience. "We're at four," he said matter-of-factly.

"Good luck," she answered as she exited.

When Catherine arrived back at the room she took a long, hot shower. Afterward, she wrapped one towel in a turban around her hair and another towel around her body and moved to the window and the pleated curtain. She could see the back of a strip mall and a discarded mattress rotting in the woods. To the right, cars had started to merge onto an access road that led to the interstate. In the parking lot below, a woman led an anorexic greyhound to the far corner, where he sniffed the ground excitedly and peed. And then the man — the man who might have been her son — emerged from the building rolling a small overnight bag, a serious briefcase resting atop it. She put her hand up to the window. Felt the cold glass against her palm. As she pulled it away she saw the outline in the shape of a turkey. She considered tapping on the window to wave good-bye to him, to tell him to be careful driving in the snow and to remember to call his mother.

But she knew he wouldn't hear. They were all in space. Her future and her past spinning away from her. Thirty-eight years of marriage. She went back to the bed, gave Karma the sausage from her purse, and that's when she started to cry.

CHAPTER 11

My cheaters. That's what Lissa called them.

There was nothing particularly memorable about her eyeglasses, just oval tortoiseshell frames that she used for perusing restaurant menus, admiring photos of Danielle and Tommy, and completing daily Sudoku puzzles. For years they hung from a jeweled strap and rested on the quiet place between her collarbone and breasts. But as Fred went through the dozens, really hundreds, of Lissa's personal items that needed to be sorted, it was the glasses he kept coming back to.

Of course he saw the symbolic significance. He didn't need grief counseling to understand that he was somehow transferring his attachment from his wife to her glasses. After all, in a literal way, they were how she saw the world and how the world saw her. They were on the bedside table when she went to sleep and around her neck by the time she'd found her slippers in the pink morning light.

On the night Lissa had died, Fred removed two things from her neck: the glasses and a gold necklace he had bought for her in Istanbul. It wasn't an expensive piece, and perhaps wasn't even gold at all, but she'd admired it as they'd wandered the narrow halls of the Grand Bazaar, which could have passed for the Mall of America had it not been for the piquant smell of cardamom. On the shiny surface of the pendant an Arabic engraving had been translated loosely as *Patience and compassion.*

After the funeral, Lissa's sister swooped in and took care of the scented moisturizers, eye makeup, and bath salts. All manner of feminine widgets — hair dryer, hot roller set, foot spa — went into a deep cardboard box for the Humane Society thrift shop. Meanwhile, Lissa's friends dropped off her dress shoes, pantsuits, and abundant collection of Gucci silk scarves at the women's shelter. Fred hoped a few of her possessions would live a new life of their own. He was heartened by the idea of children in Effingham County playing dress-up in Italian neckwear.

Most of her belongings would probably

be tossed. Fashions changed. Technology improved. No one needed an orange floral jumpsuit anymore, except at a costume party, and there was only a distant possibility anyone would find a use for her Presto popcorn maker. He knew that, as with a disappearing rabbit in a magic trick, perhaps it wasn't so important where the items went, just as long as they were gone.

As he sat at his desk, running his fingers along the bridge of Lissa's eyeglasses, he felt the deepening curve to his shoulders. He hadn't gone to the gym in weeks, maybe months. He'd even resigned from his tennis group because he'd had to deal with so much — the required minimum distribution of Lissa's IRA, the unpaid hospital charge for oxygen, the notification of a lifetime's worth of distant schoolmates. He spent most days at his desk, except for the hour he took Sequoia to the dog park, so perhaps he was depressed. He'd seen the commercials. How could he not? It was as if the ads were produced just for him, as they played on every late-night channel he watched. Fred recognized the symptoms: decreased energy and irritability. Certainly he had trouble concentrating. But that was only natural. As Hunter might say, "An appropriate grief response."

Fred looked out toward the open screened window and wooded tangle behind his house. Beyond a disordered clump of over-grown hickory and palms, he could see the outline of patio homes on the adjacent street. He knew one of the distant windows belonged to his neighbor Ida B. Childs, whom he'd called about computer service. After he'd talked to her, he'd found himself humming the melody "Ida, Sweet As Apple Cider," an old vaudeville tune his mother had favored and one he hadn't thought of in years. Coincidentally, Comcast had reset the computer connection shortly after their conversation so he hadn't needed to follow up, yet he'd kept her number on a pad by his desk. She seemed pleasant and friendly.

And he might need to contact her again. When his computer did act up, he was never sure if it was his hard or soft drive. He didn't understand the modern way people connected and communicated. The last time he was in the grocery store, a man ahead of him in line wore an earpiece strapped to his head and spoke in a low, serious tone, as if he were manning a NASA space mission while picking up a six-pack of beer.

After paying a few bills, Fred fiddled with the computer mouse. In the center of his screen was a small spinning circle of color. He punched in Command-Shift, Command-Control, Command-Option. All the things his wife once recommended. He even typed in SOS, thinking maybe the computer programmer had a sense of humor. No luck. Fred was imagining the pinwheel as belonging to a lost child at a carnival when the phone rang.

"Hello?"

He heard the muffled voice of Danielle, who seemed to be on another call. Then his grandson, Tommy, chirped in the background, his nine-year-old chipmunk voice easy to recognize.

"Danielle?!" Fred kept calling her name, louder each time, and eventually she answered.

"Dad?"

"Hi, honey."

"Is everything okay?" she asked.

"You called me."

She laughed. "Sorry. I must've butt-dialed you."

"Pardon?"

"You know, called you with my butt."

Fred felt the weight of Sequoia's head on his slippers. Lately the Great Dane had hardly touched her food, and Fred wondered if the dog was just mirroring the exhaustion he felt. "I see." He'd made progress processing his grief, then felt overwhelmed that he couldn't remember his wife's voice.

Don't be so dramatic. I'm right here. It'd been almost a week since he'd heard from Lissa.

"Dad, listen, I'm in the car."

Tell her to pull over. Tell her not to talk while she's driving.

"Be careful," Fred said. Then he heard Tommy again. He imagined the boy strapped in the backseat, air bags ready to deploy at the first sign of uneven pavement. When Fred was a child, his brothers and sisters had been sardined into the back of their Chevrolet sedan. His mother had had a cigarette in one hand and a highball in the other. They didn't need reinforced nylon safety belts to go to the end of the driveway. "So where are you off to?"

"Soccer, then Augusta. I've got a few errands and our local store is out of free-range eggs."

Fred wanted to remind Danielle about marketing. About how a chicken was a chicken. It didn't need a PhD and a gym membership to produce edible eggs. About how dairy-free yogurt and vegetarian pork rinds and cruelty-free carrots were just elaborate merchandising.

Don't do it, Lissa warned.

"I see," Fred said. "How's the weather?"

"Coolish, but not too bad. I think you might enjoy living up here." He heard the sound of a blinker. "What about you? How's Sequoia?"

"Sequoia is fine." Fred might have mentioned his dog's moodiness. Her tail used to thump the floor whenever he reached down to stroke her from his desk. Now it just fluttered momentarily. Dogs couldn't just pull themselves up by their bootstraps as people could, and he wondered if Sequoia might be suffering from clinical depression. The good news, Fred thought, was that a visit to the Seven Oaks dog park was the canine equivalent of attending a support group.

"I told you Tommy had a scrimmage last weekend. Did you watch the video I sent you?"

Just tell her yes.

But the truth was Fred hadn't checked his email for several days. And he probably wouldn't have watched it anyway. The last time his daughter had sent a link, he'd been directed to a six-minute video of dogs playing water polo. "I've had some problems with my Comcast connection." It was the truth, after all.

"Do you even *know* how to open a link?" she said. Had it not been for Lissa's shadowy presence, Fred might have pushed back or responded with something constructive. He might have suggested, once again, that a photograph and brief note would suffice. What happened to the concrete simplicity of sending two or three glossy pictures? What made her think he needed to sit through twenty minutes of footage of nine-year-olds chasing a ball? He felt this email-linking business was the modern equivalent of the chain letters he used to get as a kid: *This letter originated in Africa and has gone around the world twenty times.* He just didn't have the energy anymore.

"Dad, he scored a goal."

Tell her you care. Tell him you are proud.

Lissa's ethereal instructions reminded him of the party lines on telephone wires when he was growing up in the Berkshires. If his mother picked up the phone and asked, "Is it icy by the Turnpike?" she'd get a half-dozen road updates.

"We're so proud!" Fred blurted out, immediately sorry he'd said *we* instead of *I*.

His wife used to take care of these things. She was the cheerleader. She waved the grandparent pom-poms. The last time Fred and Lissa had been to Lewiston, Tommy had led them up to his bedroom with a sticky hand. At the top of the landing, they turned right into his room and Fred had been disconcerted, even embarrassed for the boy. Medals and ribbons and etched acrylic awards lined the bookshelves. On the walls hung team photos of a dozen or more small boys wearing identical uniforms looking like Lilliputian soldiers in a comical army. There were framed citizenship citations and even an award that read MOST CHEERFUL. Statuettes of boys in mid-motion — kicking balls, throwing Frisbees, swinging bats — crammed the bedside table. The child had won an award for every breath taken.

"Tell Grandpa about your goal," Danielle directed her son. "He wants to hear all about it."

And then Fred thought he heard Tommy say: "No he doesn't."

Tell him you do.

"Tommy!" Fred shouted. "Can you hear me?"

Danielle came back on the line. "Dad, he's in the backseat, not Siberia."

Fred took a deep breath. "Yes, Tommy! I want to hear all about your goal! Your big, big goal!"

Silence filled the phone line and Danielle

replied, "Sorry. He just put his earphones on. He's watching *The Hobbit.*"

"Oh." Again, Fred caught himself. He might have mentioned that a car ride could be a good time to read a book or even look out a window. Fred and his siblings used to count cows that resided in the wide meadows of Berkshire County. It might be an appropriate opportunity for Danielle to speak to her son about school or even teach him a song, something Lissa had done for Danielle.

"He thinks you don't care."

Fred was suddenly very tired, as if he hadn't slept in months.

Just try, Fred. Humor her.

Fred remembered Tommy had a girlfriend. "How's Tiffany?"

"Brittany, Dad. Her name is Brittany. Nice try."

Fred fell silent.

"Mom used to send him a dollar for every goal he made."

"Oh?" And then the lawyer in him perked up. He wanted to help the way he knew best. "And what does Mr. Chicago do? How is *he* figuring into all this?"

"Please don't start another fight. We are just fine without him."

Sequoia lifted her head and listened to an

111

invisible squirrel outside the window. "Just so you know, I'm going through some boxes of your mother's. I've been trying to clear the attic."

"You're throwing out things? Without me?"

"Letters mostly." *Correspondence,* he might have said. Something people used to do. *Thank you for the Lego set. Thank you for the skateboard. I appreciate the donation for my class trip. I'm sorry we couldn't come visit over Christmas.*

"Letters?"

"Nothing of value." Mail. The United States Postal Service. It was a way people used to communicate important things. Something people once did as a kindness. *Get well soon. We're sorry for your loss. We will miss her greatly. Thank you for giving me Mom's gold necklace. We wish we could make you feel better.*

"Nothing that you think I'd want?" Danielle asked, her voice rising.

Patience and compassion, he heard.

"Like you can just throw out Mom's whole life?"

Fred didn't know exactly where his daughter's hostility came from, since he and Lissa were reasonable and forgiving, to a fault, perhaps. As a child she'd been so agreeable, but as a teenager she'd gotten and stayed angry with him. He remembered it co-incided with his brief separation from Lissa, but when he returned to the house it was never really the same. "We've got so much stuff here. I've got my own letters that you shouldn't have to be burdened with when it's my time to go."

"Oh, and now you're planning on leaving me too?"

Like he had a choice in the matter. Like it was a play in which he could decide whether to stay front and center or exit stage left.

Don't engage her. She's just like you. You two need to work this out since I can't do it anymore.

No, you can't, he thought sadly.

"Listen, we just pulled into the parking lot at the field so we'll chat next week, shall we?"

Before he could say something smart — something like, "Sure, just butt-dial me" — the call disconnected. He placed the phone back on the charger and took a deep breath.

After a few moments, he instinctively reached for Lissa's eyeglasses. He held them lightly in his palm as if holding an irreplace-able glass figurine. He stroked his fingertips across the lenses, which were streaked with a light film of oil. He held them as he had every day since his wife had died, but now saw something he hadn't noticed: a long brown eyelash that was caught in a tiny screw. An eyelash that had once belonged to his wife and framed how she had seen the world. With great deliberateness, he took his thumb and index finger and carefully picked it from where it had been trapped. A whisper of his wife. All that was left. He held it carefully in front of him, between the tips of his fingers, kissed it gently, made a wish, and then blew it toward the open window.

CHAPTER 12

Catherine brought the cordless phone and a cup of coffee out to her back deck. At the property line she saw her neighbor, Old Man Callahan, with his rosy cheeks and serious potbelly, like a character actor in a waggish sitcom. He poked at something with his cane. No doubt he was checking for broken sprinkler heads, trying to find egregious errors they'd made to report to security. Putting their garbage out too early, not sorting their recycling, hanging a clothesline.

As she settled into the cushioned wicker chair, she felt the cool wind against her face, coming fast and low from the southeast. Even the heavy bird feeder by the kitchen window swayed back and forth, a hypnotist's watch.

As the whitecaps formed in the shallow reeds of the marsh, Catherine, alarmed by the weather, felt panic rise in her throat and wondered if she and Ralph had made the right decision in moving to Savannah. Perhaps they had been too critical with their first impressions of other, possibly safer, places they'd visited — the nasally twang of Nashville, the three-pointed hats of Williamsburg, the aging hippies of Asheville. Once they'd even discussed retiring to a sailboat in the calm Caribbean, but then they saw *The Perfect Storm*. If George Clooney couldn't make it out alive, neither would they. And if she were being perfectly honest, she'd just wanted a sailboat so she could give it a fanciful name: *Cirrhosis of the River* or *Freudian Sloop*.

They'd discussed the possibility of storms, but the issue hadn't been a deal breaker, as they'd assumed Atlantic hurricanes that moved up the seaboard would skirt the coast, preferring the easterly areas: Myrtle Beach, Charleston, the Outer Banks. Savannah was directly under Cleveland, after all. During their sales presentation, Audrey Cunningham had mentioned it might be difficult to get a tee time on Saturday mornings, but not that their living room could fill with sea turtles.

And then there was the threat of Tropical Storm Audrey disrupting their lives. Catherine wondered if Ralph had considered a dal-

116

liance with her. *An affair,* she thought. *Call it what it is.* God knows she'd seen him flirting with Audrey, but men did that. It was to be expected. And maybe Catherine would do a little flirting herself if she had the opportunity, if she ever met someone new who didn't remind her of Ernest Borgnine.

She sipped her coffee and thought of her science CDs explaining the laws at play in the universe, fission and fusion and centripetal and centrifugal forces. Lately she'd felt like she was living in zero gravity, trying to keep things from floating away from her. Her car keys. Her cell phone. Ralph. In New Jersey, she'd thought a garage, a retirement plan, even a dog, would hold them in place. But things had changed. And if she didn't have Ralph, what *did* she have? Who *was* she?

As she watched the roiling water, she knew it was time to call Martha. Even though none of her sister's three marriages had stuck, she had experience in matters of the heart. At least her sister knew how to make a decision. In the eighties, when Martha decided to get pregnant, she followed the old wives' tale that eating garlic would bring about conception, so for a year she walked around smelling like an Italian restaurant. Coincidentally, her grown son now owned a successful pizzeria in Seattle.

The phone rang five times, but much to Catherine's relief Martha finally answered. She was always so busy at the Villages — she'd joined a dragon boat group, a platform tennis league, even the Red Hat Society — so Catherine cut right to the chase.

"Something's going on with Ralph."

"Ralph." Martha said his name slowly. There'd always been a quiet resentment between them.

"We're just not getting along. Seeing eye to eye. He's got this whole new life here and I'm just . . . floundering."

"Details, please." Martha didn't like to beat around the bush.

"You know, he joined a New Neighbors golf group and that led to a regular poker game. There's a whole fraternity of senior men here who won't sit still. After he retired and we were in New Jersey I couldn't get rid of him. Now I don't know where he is."

"Sounds like the perfect husband."

"No, really. He'll leave in his golf cart and be gone all day."

"Ah, the old Chinese proverb: Give a man a five iron and he golfs for a day. Teach a man to golf and you'll get rid of him for the weekend."

"And I don't trust our Realtor. I saw

Ralph's Porsche parked next to her black Mercedes at the clubhouse last week." Rearview mirrors almost touching, she remembered.

"Doesn't, like, everyone there have a black Mercedes?"

Martha was right. Catherine hadn't been sure it was *hers,* but still. "We like Seven Oaks, and downtown, from what I've seen of it, is beautiful, but I'm just not connecting." *I'm floundering,* Catherine thought again, and imagined a dull gray fish thrashing in the bilge of a Boston Whaler.

"You could take up golf. Didn't you try a nine-and-dine a few years ago?"

"You know Ralph isn't what you'd call *patient.*" Catherine remembered nine endless holes of Ralph instructing her to keep her head down and hit through the ball. "And besides, our sex life fell off the back of the car as we drove down I-95."

"Ah, now we're getting somewhere."

"I mean, until just a few years ago we were" — she wanted the right word — "amorous."

In the background Catherine heard laughter. "Where are you?"

"The pool."

Catherine pictured Martha on a wicker ottoman, a wide-brimmed straw hat tilted jauntily to one side of her head to protect her button nose from burning. "Are they bobbing for apples in the hot tub again?" It sounded more sarcastic than she meant it.

"Don't be rude."

"I'm not."

"We're playing Marco Polo."

"As in *Mar-co? Po-lo,*" Catherine warbled.

"It's an icebreaker event for the Bocce Club."

An icebreaker is for third graders, Catherine thought. She heard more laughter and a splash, then shuffling in the background.

Then Martha whispered, "I've been seeing a new guy from Ohio. And can I tell you something about Midwestern men? During sex, there's a reason women shout out *Holy Toledo!*"

"Holy Toledo," Catherine echoed, trying to find some enthusiasm. In some small place inside, Catherine wished she were more like Martha. Outgoing. Brave. Game to join a wingsuit club and jump off the edge of the Grand Canyon on a moment's notice. She breathed deeply and felt a salty heaviness to the air.

"Okay so what do you *want*?" Martha asked.

"I want to *matter.*" Then she added: "I'm going to the gym. Maybe losing a little weight will spark Ralph's interest."

"Okay, and try Kegels."

"Kegels or kugels?"

"Seriously?" Martha asked. "K-e-g-e-l-s. Rhymes with *bagels*. Or pole dancing," Martha added. "That's what I do on Wednesdays. It's fun and it'll firm your core."

"You have pole dancing classes at the Villages?"

"We have everything at the Villages. Trust me. And if you don't start working out, you'll wake up one day as an ostrich, with a bird neck and winged flaps where your triceps were. You'll never be able to fly away."

Catherine pulled into the Seven Oaks fitness center and found a place to park between a BMW coupe and a new convertible. It felt good to take action, although she felt intimidated, as even the cars outside the building looked athletic. In her frenzy of setting up the house — painting rooms, arranging furniture, displaying artwork — she'd successfully avoided the gym since they'd moved. Finding a local car wash or lighting store might occupy an entire morning and leave her exhausted.

Before going in, she rolled up the windows

and turned off the radio. In the passenger seat she saw two flyers she'd found the previous afternoon after shopping at Piggly Wiggly. Whenever she parked there, marketing elves deposited messages under her windshield wipers. One advertised an upcoming lecture about storm surges, the other hawked pet psychic services. *10 minute Session! FREE Consultation! Call NOW!*

Catherine didn't believe in chakra alignments or exorcisms, Ouija boards or séances. But she and Ralph *had* chosen Savannah. She couldn't deny that she was intrigued by the ghost tours around downtown's historic squares and stories of the local Gullahs and their magical powers. Even when she'd taken Karma to Bonaventure Cemetery she'd felt an otherworldliness and the crush of past generations. While standing at Johnny Mercer's grave beside a husband-wife duo humming "Moon River" and slapping away sand gnats, she noted the spanish moss overhead, draped like memorial bunting at a funeral. And although she knew there was no such thing as ghosts, she could see how an area or even a person living in it might have advanced intuition. It wasn't a stretch to think that someone with psychic powers in Savannah might have an edge over a psychic in, say, Short Hills.

So as she sat in her car and wondered why psychics didn't get serious jobs at the National Weather Service, she felt her rising panic again and glimpsed a vision that one day, if she didn't do anything, her thirty-eight-year marriage would be found stranded in a tree.

Catherine grabbed Ralph's gym bag from the trunk. She had repossessed the old duffel after he'd bought a new one — a sleek Nike model that smelled vaguely of cologne and had wide exterior zip pockets.

The fitness center's front glass doors opened to a wide atrium that offered couches and a do-it-yourself coffee bar. There were a half-dozen conversation nooks where a whole community might chat, read newspapers, and let blood pressure return to normal. Yet they were empty. The lobby had the feel of a regional airport. People waved to each other as they passed, but everyone seemed on a tight deadline, holding yoga mats instead of carry-ons, rushing to make group fitness classes as if late to boarding gates.

She'd been here once before, when Audrey had taken them on an introductory tour, but she hadn't remembered the details of the building — the Astroturf-style carpeting and dry-erase boards filled with class listings.

"Hello!" The young woman behind the counter gave her a toothy grin. "Welcome!"

Catherine smiled, feeling the woman was far too enthusiastic for whatever hourly wage she was earning.

"Is this your first time?!"

"Yes. How did you —"

"It's my job!" The woman looked as if she'd just gotten off a treadmill herself. Her ponytail swayed back and forth as she spoke. "Please sign in, just till we get to know you!"

And so Catherine wrote down her name and club number. Behind her, body-hugging merchandise hung on shiny clothing racks. Several toned women walked by in tight nylon tops with built-in bras and clingy capri workout pants. Catherine felt suddenly self-conscious in her shorts and T-shirt.

She grabbed a towel, strode to the far side of the lobby, and took a right down a glass-sided hallway. To the left was the free-weight area and a wall with hooks to hang towels and car keys and cubbies to stow gym bags and magazines. It reminded her of a kindergarten classroom. Catherine turned right into the cardio area. Stairmasters and ellip-

ticals and rowing machines filled the cavernous room. Most of the machines were taken
and everyone looked vaguely similar, as if
they could all star in the same Zumba
infomercial. All the activity made her think
of a spoof on "The Twelve Days of Christmas" — *five bikers biking, four rowers rowing, three runners running* — and it seemed
sad to Catherine that everyone ended up
exactly where they started. *Wherever you
go, there you are.* Why had she thought her
relationship with Ralph would be better just
because they'd moved?

She wandered over to one of the empty
treadmills, deciding that that machine had
the least potential for sudden death, and
that's when she saw the woman on the Ex-
ercycle, her long brown hair secured in a
tight fishtail braid. She knew immediately
who it was. The woman had earphones on,
so Catherine strode over to her and just
mouthed the word. "Amity?"

The woman slowed but continued pedal-
ing.

"A-mi-ty?" Catherine whispered, exaggerating each syllable as if teaching at a
school for the deaf.

The woman sat up, unhooked one side of
her earphones, and smiled halfheartedly, as
if to say, "Do I know you?"

"You *are* Amity, right?" It was more a statement than a question. Catherine would have identified her in a police lineup. She remembered Amity's thin frame and clear complexion. The woman nodded. Before Catherine could lose her nerve she said, "One Happy Rabbit Lane. The closet."

Amity's face went ashen. "Yes. But what —"

"We need to talk." Catherine said it as if she'd never been afraid of anyone or anything in her whole life. "As soon as you're done, we are having coffee."

It's time to fly, Catherine thought.

CHAPTER 13

The way Amity figured it, she had three choices. First, she could cut her losses and run — explain to the woman in the gym that she must be mistaking her for someone else. Deny, deny, deny. Politicians did it. Professional athletes did it. Husbands did it. And maybe by withholding the truth, she could even reshape history. Maybe fate had intervened to help her realize that skulking around this gated community wasn't an effective coping mechanism. Time to get on with her own goddamn life.

The second option was to confess. *Yes, it was me. Yes, I have a little obsessive problem.* But she could explain she had decided to quit. It was simply the last episode in a bad habit that had gotten out of hand. Habits can be kicked, right? Look at alcoholics and junkies. Maybe there was a twelve-step program for slinkers. But realistically, she wasn't ready for that. Just stopping would be unfathomable, as if she could just stop breathing. It was her passion. It's what gave her a sense of belonging in the world. In the same way other people save whales or recycle soda cans, she explored living rooms and broom closets. She flipped through photo albums and listened to CD collections. She wore strangers' hats and sat on wide settees that faced the sunset.

The third option was to be honest. But she wasn't even sure what that meant anymore.

The white-haired woman was waiting for her at a far table in the gym lobby. She faced the glass-plated entrance, perhaps so she could catch Amity if she tried to slip out. Amity waved awkwardly and strode to the coffee bar. She poured herself a cup, not because she wanted one but because it simulated what she'd seen other women do when they met friends at the gym. She had toweled off in the locker room but still felt hot and clammy. And relieved in a way that she'd finally been caught. Maybe that's what her husband had felt too, when his secret meanderings were finally exposed.

Over the past few months, Amity had wondered if she'd ever see the woman again. Since she hadn't, she'd assumed she and her husband were just another older couple looking for a place to retire. Kicking tires of communities with Tom Fazio golf courses and cities with virtual colonoscopy centers, but ultimately heading south down I-95 and getting a golf course villa in Florida like so many other Americans.

Amity took a seat across from the woman, whose shoulder-length hair had been pulled back from her full face in a shiny headband. She wore a T-shirt and shorts and didn't look like an athlete. Amity now recognized her from their brief encounter in the closet.

Amity sat down and tried to smile, not at all sure what the woman wanted. An awkward silence hung between them. The woman watched her carefully, looking at her as if she were a specimen in a science experiment. Her emerald eyes had a hard intensity to them.

"Thanks for coming. I'm so happy we ran into each other," the woman started, as if greeting her at a cocktail party. "I know I was a little blunt earlier and this is a little random, but I was really struck by you when we met."

"You were?" Amity felt complimented in some backhanded way.

"Yes, Amity, I was."

Amity liked that the woman used her name, as though she knew her. "But I don't know *your* name."

"Catherine."

"Look, Catherine." Amity steadied her breathing. Her yoga teacher liked to say, *Take a moment to set your intention.* "As I think I told you, it's just this habit I have. This *thing* I do. It's not malicious. Your community is safe but —"

"Stop!" Catherine said sharply. She held up a stiff hand, like a traffic cop. "Just stop. Please." Catherine closed her eyes tightly and ran her fingers through the ends of her hair. She seemed distracted. " 'My community'? You mean you don't even *live* here?"

"Not exactly." Amity could feel the movement of people behind her, athletes who had finished workouts and were heading off to prepare meals or water gardens. People who lived their lives with a routine of familiar exertions. "Say, are you okay?" Amity was a little concerned by Catherine's red face.

"Listen, I want you to know that I promise, I *promise,* that I *didn't* tell anyone about you and I *won't* tell anyone."

"So what is it you want?" Amity hoped the woman wouldn't report her to security. Her own experience told her promises weren't always kept. *I promise to have and to hold from this day on,* her husband had told her.

"We ended up buying that house. Not that it matters, but that's where we *live.* It's our *home.* It just seemed remarkable when I found you there."

I found you. Something about those words made Amity soften.

Catherine continued. "Ralph — that's my husband — Ralph and the real estate agent, Audrey Cunningham, came back in but didn't suspect a thing. Naturally. Why would they? They really had no inkling, but maybe they had other things on their minds." She laughed nervously and leaned in. "I wonder if you happen to know any of the Realtors here? Do you know Audrey? You know, actually, that's a different story. What's important is that you know your secret is safe with me. I just can't stop thinking about what you said. I need you to share what you do."

Amity might have considered some sort of exit plan, but she felt comforted. *I need you,* Amity heard loud and clear. *I found you.*

Catherine looked down to Amity's hand. "Are you married?"

"Not anymore." Then she felt the weight of the silence between them. "And I used to be an English teacher, too. Used to follow rules," she added.

"Okay, so I just need to know about this *thing.*" Catherine stopped to sip her coffee. "This breaking and entering? Visiting? No. It feels deeper than that. But you don't *steal* anything, do you? I'm a little unclear."

"Of course not."

"Right. I didn't think so. Forgive me. So it's *cruising* or *drifting* almost." Finally the word came to her: *"Creeping."*

"Creeping?" The word reminded Amity of *creeps.* Men who cheat on their wives. It reminded her of her husband.

"For lack of a better word, let's call it that. Anyway, I'd like to know what it *feels* like."

Catherine seemed sincere, not distracted by the herd of women passing through after their Awesome Abs classes. Amity noticed the chatter of conversation, but Catherine was focused on her, as if she were the only one in the world who mattered. "Okay. Listen. When you are in a grocery store, do you ever pick up a magazine that you have no intention of buying?"

"Like *Time?*"

"No, not the newsmagazines. The fancy ones. *Travel and Leisure* or *Elle Decor.* The ones where celebrities sprawl across plush velvet couches or frolic in infinity pools. The ones that show farmhouse kitchens and feathered king-size beds and candlelit, bubble-filled slipper tubs."

"Sometimes."

"And flipping through the pages, you are transported. For a moment you are *gone.*"

"Gone?"

"Somewhere else. You're a countess at a stone villa in the Loire Valley. You aren't just standing in line at Piggly Wiggly waiting for the woman in front of you to find her coupons."

"Uh-huh." Catherine nodded as if beginning to understand.

"You feel *different.* You are somehow *changed.*"

"And you lead someone else's life for a moment?"

"Yes. That's it. That's what it's like. I don't *hurt* anyone, but I feel what it's like to *be* them. I *am* them." *And I'm not me anymore,* she added to herself.

Catherine's face opened up. Amity liked the freshness about her, like an old-fashioned stage actress who had just taken off her makeup. "I understand."

I understand you. I found you. I need you. "My husband left me rather suddenly. We transferred here last year for his job, found a place to live downtown on Tattnall Street, and one day he just decided to take off. *Voilà!*" She snapped her fingers. "He'd 'had

133

enough.' " Amity made air quotations with her fingers. "He hooked up with his high school sweetheart on Facebook and moved out of state. Out of state! She lived in Iowa City, for god's sake. They somehow had this whole life going on that started on the Internet. A virtual life. A life based on a lie." She could feel herself getting worked up. *Breathe into the pain.* "I don't know, but that's when the creeping started."

"I'm not following."

"One day after he left, I saw an ad in the paper. I was looking for a teaching position but there it was. Open house. Marsh views. One phone call does it all." She might have said it was also the abbreviated *language* that struck her (*HW thruout, W/D HKUP, EIK, SOHOA*), a private patois as if everyone on the island were part of the same tribe, but that would have gotten her and Catherine off track. "So once I got to the gate and waved my circled ad, the guard handed me a guest pass and a treasure map of for-sale houses and waved me right through." *I hope you find what you're looking for,* he'd even said. "I went from one open house to two to four. Every weekend I returned. And as I stood in strangers' living rooms, with *their* books and *their* photos and *their* cats, I felt a freedom. Like I'd taken custody of a new history. Like a fresh start. Eventually, I just did it on my own."

Catherine smiled. "I see. But aren't you afraid of getting caught?"

"I'm more afraid of being alone."

"And this creeping, this fresh start, it *works*?" Catherine asked.

"Like a charm."

"Please. I promise I won't tell. Just one time. Take me with you."

"Just once," Amity said firmly.

CHAPTER 14

Ida Blue jumped at the sound of her barking cell phone. She'd been enjoying a quiet afternoon on her couch watching *The View*. "You're barking up the right tree at Ida Blue's pet psychic line." She enjoyed varying the way she answered the phone. She liked to be a little edgy. Today that included a double waterfall braid that cascaded down her back.

"Yes, hello, I found a flyer on my windshield and see you have a ten-minute free trial."

Finally, Ida Blue thought, *someone who can read.* She'd been surprised that the entire city of Savannah hadn't jammed her phone line. "You bet I do."

"But I'm a little cynical. Are you *clairvoyant?*"

"I'm an animal communicator." Sometimes Ida Blue liked to say *com*-moo-*nicator* just for fun. "I can't tell you the future, only what your pet is *feeling,* like Google Translate. So all I need is a name."

"I'm Catherine. My dog is Ralph."

"R-a-l-p-h. Am I right?"

"Yes, that's correct."

It's all about bagging *yes* responses. Ida Blue had read a *Reader's Digest* article that explained five *yes* answers could close any deal. "I'm getting a strong feeling that he is male. Am I correct?"

"Of course."

Two yeses. A gold-medal performance.

"You see, I've had him for quite a while and need advice. I mean I don't know if you really have a connection . . ."

A connection? Ida Blue thought. She was six months behind on her Comcast bill, and the personalized notes from the billing department had gone from *Kindly Pay Your Bill* to *You Are* THREE MONTHS *Overdue* to *PAY NOW OR SERVICE WILL STOP!*

Catherine continued, "You see, I don't know if he's happy or even what he *does* when I'm not with him. You know, if other dogs wander into the yard."

What he does? Ida Blue wanted to ask. *He farts. He scratches. He sleeps. He's a dog.*

Ida Blue had a feeling about people who gave their pets human names. Maybe owners were using their dogs and cats as child substitutes. *Helloooo, Dr. Freud.* But she didn't want to scare away a first-time caller, so she imagined the only Ralph she had known, her mother's brother, who had left her enough of an inheritance to buy this condo. Her uncle was a pock-faced man who liked to drink beer out of a size-twelve ceramic boot and had been married four times, twice to the same woman.

"I'm getting a message." Uncle Ralph had adopted a potbellied pig named Otis and kept him behind his grizzled trailer. Otis drank as much beer as he did. "I get the sense that Ralph is a rescue in need of being saved. Am I right?"

"Not exactly. Ralph is just, I don't know, not *expressive.*"

"The word *indifferent* is coming to mind. Is that accurate?"

"Yes."

Three yes replies. Hell's bells. She hadn't had three *yeses* in the last five years.

Ida Blue looked to the back porch. It was almost a reflex now, to see if the ghostly older woman would appear from nowhere, to see if she could feel a connection to something greater than herself. All that was out there was an overgrown camellia bush that needed pruning.

"Okay, so I'm feeling Ralph's been abandoned on some level. In psychoanalysis we call it *displacement.*" Ida Blue didn't know if that was exactly right, but she knew what she felt and sometimes it even sounded good. "His insecurities will be *transferred* to other things. In a word, he will *misbehave.*" Her uncle had once dressed up Otis as Princess Diana, in a white gown and a glittery tiara, and paraded him through the trailer park.

"Misbehave?" Catherine asked softly.

"Act out. He's thinking he is the alpha dog now, so go ahead and let him make mistakes. If Ralph makes a run for the Invisible Fence with his new doggie friends, don't call him back before he gets zapped." Ida Blue didn't need to be telepathic, or even tele-*pathetic,* to sense skepticism in Catherine's silence, but giving people something to believe in wasn't any more of a scam than Dr. Oz advising patients to lay off the salt.

"Can you put Ralph up to the phone? I need to feel his *essence.*" Ida Blue was ready for heavy panting and a slop of saliva. She took her braid and twirled it excitedly.

"He's not here right now."

"Maybe he's in the yard with the neighborhood poodle?" She laughed at how easy this was.

"Yes, maybe he is."

Four yeses. A new client would pay to keep the lights on and the TV humming. It would pay enough to keep her behind the gates and safe from an intervention by Dr. Phil.

"So stay connected to him. And to me. Next time prepay on PayPal. Call me once a week." She took her sweet time and reapplied her lipstick to orchestrate a dramatic crescendo. "Two more things Ralph wants you to know."

"Go ahead."

Ida could hear the caller's breathless anticipation, as if she were going to reveal other animal mysteries like what the Loch Ness Monster had eaten for lunch or whether Bigfoot vacationed in Oregon or British Columbia. "He likes company, so find a dog park."

"Okay. Sure. And the second thing?"

"We only have a few minutes left."

CHAPTER 15

"Safety never takes a vacation," Amity told Catherine as they power walked through the Greenleaf Park section of Seven Oaks.

"I've heard that before." Catherine nodded with excitement, a bobblehead doll, her sunglasses moving precariously down her nose.

"Pardon?"

"It was our motto at summer camp. The head counselor told us that just before he broke both legs on the high dive."

"Oh, right. Sure." Amity had lost her train of thought. She'd been thinking Catherine seemed a little needy, the type of woman who shouldn't ride alone on a merry-go-round. "Concentration and awareness. You need to be aware of your surroundings and take care of things that need attention."

"And you bought a commercial guest pass? You just drive right on through the gates? That doesn't seem right."

"It's amazing how far a clean driver's license, tutoring business card, and a hundred bucks will get you."

"But what about getting into the actual houses?"

To her surprise, Catherine had asked a series of good questions, which kept leading Amity off track: *How do you choose a house? How long have you been doing this? Are you ever afraid?* "A fake rock. That's one of the things you can look for."

"Interesting. But what about alarms? Or motion sensors?"

"Here? Where someone getting locked out of a car makes the front page of *The Oak Log*?" Amity was being facetious, but still. No one needed yet another layer of safety with the security team and twelve-foot perimeter fence.

"It just seems too easy," Catherine answered.

"It is."

Despite herself, Amity was rather enjoying the company of the woman who'd found her in the closet, then cornered her at the fitness center. The woman whom Amity had agreed to take *creeping,* only so she wouldn't be reported to security and ruin the one activity in her life that made her feel something, even if it was just the *sensa-*

tion of leaving herself. *Some women play golf,* she thought. *I break into houses. Big deal.*

"So what's your backstory?" Catherine asked.

Amity appreciated her interest but was beginning to feel like a guest on an afternoon talk show. "Used to be an elementary school teacher. Loved kids. Loved rules. *'I before e except after c'* and all that."

"How about 'A dog has claws at the end of its paws. A comma's a pause at the end of a clause'?"

Amity had never heard that one but she liked it. Maybe she'd get to use it when she found a full-time position. "I'm a substitute teacher. Have had three interviews with the Savannah-Chatham school district but they're not hiring until late spring. Fortunately, I've got some savings and alimony."

"Good for you. I'm beginning to think it's important for a woman to have a plan B."

After they had agreed to meet, Amity didn't really believe Catherine would show up. She would probably get a better offer from the New Neighbors group to tour Old Fort Jackson or visit a macramé workshop at the Savannah College of Art and Design. But when Amity drove into the community center parking lot that morning she saw a single blue car and Catherine. Early. Doing trunk rotations with arms extended as if they were meeting for Jazzercise.

As they continued down Seven Oaks Way, Amity realized she hadn't taken an interest in anyone or anything in months. When she wasn't subbing, which was most of the time, her days consisted of distracting herself, logging miles on the gym treadmill or around unfamiliar neighborhoods or doing laps in the pool of a stranger's three-bedroom house, then sleeping for twenty-four hours. Weep. Creep. Sleep. Her life could be the basis for lyrics in a pathetic country-western song.

Catherine touched Amity's elbow, then pointed to her untied shoelace. "I said, 'Be careful.' "

Amity stopped and crouched to tie her sneaker, then noticed Catherine's ancient tennis shoes with rubber soles and fraying mesh sides. Part of a white sock peeked out of a small hole. "Wow. You've put some mileage on those puppies."

"Yes I have."

"I played as a kid. Was going to join a Bacon Park league when we moved here but things just didn't work out the way I thought." She might have mentioned her new, unused tennis outfits and credit for clinics. In fact, maybe Catherine would like her graphite rackets. They hung in her front hall above a wire hopper filled with dead, graying balls. Amity double-knotted her laces and grabbed Catherine's extended hand as she rose. "Thanks," she said, and they found their rhythm again.

"I played a lot back in Short Hills. Even won a few club championships if you can believe it. But I haven't hit lately." Catherine rolled her shoulders back and started pumping her arms to match their steps. "I haven't really *looked* for a team yet, but maybe I've found my new sport." She smiled at Amity.

"There's a blurb in *The Oak Log* about a tennis meeting next week. Maybe you could go."

"Would you come with me?"

"Remember, I don't even *live* here."

"And how many people have noticed?"

Amity let the question go unanswered. Maybe Catherine was right. After all, sometimes Amity *did* feel like a cultural anthropologist who'd never quite assimilated into a protected island nation. Maybe she *should* try to change things up — there'd been a time when she had a spectacular drop shot — but she couldn't quite get out of her own way lately. Then she remembered the thread of their previous conversation. "So here's the thing. You know where most keys are hidden? Under front mats. Unbelievable. Makes me think all humans are idiots."

"Unbelievable," Catherine echoed. "But maybe that'd help Ralph. He has trouble remembering our garage door code." Then she added sadly, "Even though it's just our wedding anniversary."

"Anniversaries are always problematic," Amity said, thinking of her own.

"Still, July 8, 1978. Seven-eight-seven-eight. How hard could that be to remember?"

"You know, I saw you and your husband as you stood outside the front door that day you surprised me. I thought you looked happy."

"At one time, we were . . ." Catherine trailed off. "But getting back to *this*" — she wiggled her finger between them — "you said you don't *steal* anything."

"Right." Amity waved her hand across her blue Lycra leggings and matching top. "Do I *look* like a criminal? Half the time I'm doing owners a favor and try to clean up. It's not so bad with houses on the market, but the rotting fruit, the dead flowers, you have no idea the things people leave or forget when they go away. The *carelessness.*"

Catherine drew to a stop as they passed a

blooming bougainvillea. "Just look at this!"

Amity watched as Catherine brought her nose toward the bush, then wiped away a stream of sweat that had run down her forehead, underneath her sunglasses, and onto her cheek. She realized she'd set a breakneck pace in her excitement and told herself to calm down. *Peace and light, peace and light.* Generally Amity didn't notice fragrant plants along sidewalks — she wasn't interested in perfume or scented candles or milled soap — but today felt different. Seeing her world through someone else's viewfinder, she found everything a little more interesting.

"So where are we going?" Catherine asked, as if they were window-shopping on Broughton Street.

"Not far. Fletcher Lane. Quiet street. No intersecting golf cart paths. Flyers piling up in the mailbox. A few of the nearby houses are vacant so there shouldn't be any traffic."

"Okay. Quiet, flyers, vacancy."

"And this one isn't on the market. I learned my lesson." Amity saw Catherine's face brighten and so she added, "*You* taught me my lesson."

"And what lesson was that?"

"You are never safe." Amity pulled a leash

out of her fanny pack. "Sometimes I use this as a prop. People are empathetic to the plight of a missing dog."

"I'm not following."

"You know, you see some random woman who's looking for her dog and you feel bad for her but won't question her. Missing dogs give people permission to go places they wouldn't normally."

"Why haven't you ever gotten a real one?"

"A real dog?" The thought had never occurred to her. "My husband was allergic to them." *At least he said he was, but he said a lot of things.* "And he hated them besides."

"Who hates dogs? That's like hating Santa Claus. But if you ever want to borrow one . . ."

"A husband?" Amity asked.

"No, a dog."

Amity couldn't imagine bringing a dog creeping. A dog couldn't be controlled or might start barking or leave a mess in someone's yard. And dogs needed constant attention, didn't they? They had to be monitored lest they get into trouble, just like husbands. There were a hundred reasons not to have a dog.

Catherine continued, "I mean, you're the expert, but a dog lets you stand in front of someone's house for hours. Particularly at night. Observe neighbors load the dish-washer. See what they enjoy on TV or cook for dinner or what time they go to bed."

"Oh?"

"There was this one couple in Short Hills. She'd do the dishes, he'd watch TV. Every night it was the same. Sometimes she'd fold laundry and watch *him* watching the TV. Once in a while she'd talk on the phone. You could tell she was talking about him because she always moved to another room. It was the saddest thing I ever saw. Such unhappiness. Every single night."

"You used to *watch* them?"

"We all have our habits, I guess. But you're young. If you want to get a dog, you still have time."

"That's what my husband told me when we tried to start a family."

"Like your uterus is a jar of mayonnaise with an expiration date, right?"

"Well —"

"But it's true. You *do* have time to get a dog or start a family. Or whatever. You know, you get to be my age and your options dwindle. It's hard to start again. Or fall in love. Or even just pack up and *go* somewhere." Catherine said it like she'd been stuck in the same room all her life.

"But you just moved here. You *have* gone

somewhere."

"Yes," Catherine answered. "I suppose I have."

"Didn't you just relocate a thousand miles with everything you own?"

"Except for my toboggan. Ralph made me get rid of that. I ordered it online. Of course we didn't really *need* it. Ralph was out of town and we had this little hill in the backyard. It sloped from the patio to a wide meadow. I had this idea that one day my Boston terrier and I would ride it down the hill and just keep going."

Amity liked the visual, the idea that someone could just will themselves away when the time was right. She'd had that desire herself lately.

At the next road they took a sharp right onto a dead-end street. The houses were quiet. No one cutting a lawn or sweeping a front walk. At the end of the cul-de-sac, slightly off to one side, they came to a long tabby driveway leading to a house with a full magnolia tree by the front door.

Catherine whispered, "This is it?"

"This is our baby."

They strode forward, past a pile of grass clippings and over several fallen palm fronds. After following the brick path to the front door they stood rather awkwardly side by side, as if at the end of a blind date.

Catherine cracked her knuckles. "Aren't you going to knock?"

"No, never knock. Dogs half a mile away will start barking. And besides, nobody's here. Look at this place." She pointed to a leafless Easter lily by the front door, a plastic pink rabbit head hanging on the dried stalk. "This is what you came for, so go ahead and give it a whirl."

Catherine moved her sunglasses to the top of her head, and Amity saw her fear and excitement. The edges of her lips curled into a smile. "You're sure?" Catherine's voice wavered as if she were standing on a fixed wing and about to skydive.

"They say your first time is always the best."

Catherine looked under the mat and two planters, then around the adjacent palm to see if there were any fake rocks. Within a few minutes she found a key attached to a nail behind a shutter. Proudly, she held it up. "Ta-da!"

"You are going to make a fine creeper."

"Now what?"

Amity tilted her head toward the front door. "Have at it."

Catherine put the key in the cylinder, and with just a light twist the door opened. They stood transfixed, peering into the entryway, a full-size mirror on one wall and an upholstered bench on the other, but after stepping forward they suddenly both stood still again — paralyzed, confused.

It was Catherine who moved first, bringing her cupped hands up to cover her nose and mouth. "Oh my god," she whispered, as they took in the smell of rotting flesh.

CHAPTER 16

"Jesus, let's get out of here." Catherine stumbled back onto the brick steps.

Amity grabbed her elbow. "Oh no you don't. You can't just leave."

"What if someone died?"

"Nobody died. It'd smell a hundred times worse." She pulled Catherine forward, hard. "And get in here. Someone could see you."

Catherine hadn't considered that possibility. Her fear of being booked for trespassing in a crime scene suddenly surpassed her aversion to the stench, something close to weeks-old fish. "Okay, okay." She stepped inside and closed the door.

"Hello? Anyone home?" Amity called out. Silence.

Catherine looked around the room and felt sadness for whoever lived there. Several slats from half-drawn venetian blinds hung like flat, broken bird wings, and a dozen Beanie Babies sat along the couch.

"You start over there." Amity pointed Catherine to the left, to a room that appeared to be a den. "I'll take this side."

"I can't believe we are *doing* this," Catherine muttered, but then heard the pathetic sound of her own voice. She was the one who had begged Amity to take her creeping. She was the one who had wondered about this for months. She'd fantasized about creeping the way she'd once thought about Ralph's retirement, back when she'd naively imagined moving to a gated community could be a project that they undertook as a team, in the same way other retiring couples rode cruise ships or took trips that involved friendly African elephants or Indian ashrams. She imagined creeping would be easy.

"Catherine, you've got to stay focused," Amity said, suddenly appearing before her. "I'll check out the kitchen, but get going."

Time to jump into the deep end.

Pinching her nose, Catherine stepped carefully toward the Barcalounger and big-screen TV. She tiptoed forward, making her way through a minefield of doll catalogs that had somehow found their way to the carpet. The odor didn't seem as strong in the den, so whatever smelled was on the other side of the house. Eleven-by-fourteen photos on

154

the bookshelves displayed images of babies and families and weddings. Mother of the bride. Mother of the groom. Grandmother with baby in a sky-blue carriage. Generations with the same crescent nose and landscape smile.

When Catherine had been in her late twenties, after she and Ralph had settled in New Jersey, friends started presenting their babies at early dinners like plush toys they'd won in crane vending machines. At the time, Catherine and Ralph had both felt the same, that infants were like piglets — cute in theory but a general nuisance to the neighborhood. In her early thirties she remained open minded about whether she and Ralph would have a family. She didn't encourage him one way or the other, hadn't had the *need* to replicate herself like other women her age. But as she reached thirty-five and beyond, something inside her softened. She even stopped taking birth control pills to see if fate had anything to say in the matter. She should have pushed harder when her clock was still ticking. Amity still had time. Audrey Cunningham probably still did, too. Her own clock had timed out.

"Catherine!" The urgency in Amity's voice suggested it wasn't the first time she'd yelled for her. Ralph sounded like that too whenever he was about to lose his patience.

Catherine rushed down a hall to a guest bedroom, where she found Amity standing over a furry, bloated corpse about the size of Karma. "Is that what I think it is?"

"Raccoon. Smart enough to find an open window. Not smart enough to get back out. Looks like he sure tried, though."

"Poor thing." If it hadn't been for the extended belly and terrible smell, Catherine might have imagined that the raccoon was just napping, his little paws outstretched and slender pink tongue partway out of his mouth. It reminded her of the way Karma slept. On the far side of the bed she saw a shredded pillow and several shattered picture frames. Crosshatched scratches ran along the length of the baseboard. Then she had a clear vision of what would happen to Karma if she were gone and Ralph were in charge. If he left for a weekend getaway with Audrey, he might forget to hire a dogsitter, and her Boston terrier would surely perish in their laundry room.

Amity grabbed a wooden hanger from the closet and touched it to a front paw. The raccoon didn't move. She pushed it, harder this time, and its whole arm lifted up. "Stiff. Probably been dead a day or two."

Catherine, slightly nauseated, wondered if this was what morning sickness felt like. "Since the mystery is solved, *now* can we get out of here?"

"Leave? It'd rot here all spring." Amity shook her head. "And with the summer heat, god knows what it would become by fall. With creeping comes responsibility. This isn't just trick-or-treating."

Catherine imagined finding a shovel and digging a shallow grave. Who knows what they'd smell like by the end of the day, and how she'd explain it to Ralph? But Ralph probably wouldn't be home before her, so she'd have time to wash up. And even if he were, seeing how little interest he'd taken in her lately, she wasn't sure if he'd even notice. But then Catherine had a brainstorm. "Look, I know how to take care of this without either of us getting caught."

"You do?" Amity seemed genuinely relieved and surprised by Catherine's initiative.

"One phone call does it all."

157

CHAPTER 17

Men. Can't live with 'em, can't castrate 'em, Audrey Cunningham thought.

She had just returned to her desk from her weekly sales meeting. The office manager, Dick Moran, had spent a good part of the last hour leering at her breasts as if they were the Doublemint Twins and he had to decide between them.

Audrey watched Leona, her shih tzu, run back and forth on the grass outside her window. In general, Audrey didn't fawn over dogs, but hers was especially adorable and served her purposes. When Audrey brought Leona downtown, to stroll the wide sidewalks of Forsyth Park or just sit at a sidewalk table at the Pink House, passersby invariably struck up conversations. *What's her name? How old is she? Where'd you find her?* Tourists mostly. Out-of-towners who were quietly wondering how they could sell their house in Podunk, Indiana, and move to picturesque Savannah. She'd made more than a half-dozen sales that way. It was like shooting fish in a barrel.

Yet Leona wasn't the smartest dog in the show. The poor dear had recently taken an interest in Mr. Peabody. She'd had a solid two weeks of electric shock treatment before she understood that it was not a good idea to get too close to the white flags of the newly installed underground fence that bordered the lagoon. After receiving a warning beep that should have alerted her to stand down, she'd been zapped a number of times, her white fur ears flying up and little body leaping skyward in pain. Although Audrey felt sorry for the fur ball, and a little guilty she hadn't had time to train her properly, it was more entertaining to watch than she wanted to admit.

Audrey wanted an electronic collar for coworkers, to zap them every time they suggested some half-baked marketing idea or whatever moronic thought drifted into their heads. At today's meeting, someone suggested ditching the usual chocolate chip cookies and bringing smoked sausage from Sandfly Bar-B-Q to open houses. As if the whiff of hickory sauce and sight of frilled toothpicks would compel potential buyers to fling open their checkbooks.

The intercom buzzed. "Audrey. Call on line two."

It took her a moment to come to life. She'd been intent on watching Mr. Peabody sun himself on the island, his long spiked tail half in the water. It was horrible, but she'd been wondering if Leona would taste like chicken. She pressed the button to reply to the front desk. "Who is it?"

"Nelson Rockefeller," came the deadpan answer. "How the fuck should I know?"

Bitch. Audrey closed her eyes and cleared her throat. Game time. She punched a button and spoke into the receiver. "Hello, Audrey Cunningham speaking. May I help you?"

"Yes, good afternoon," said a raspy voice. "I saw your photograph in the paper."

The new marketing had paid off. Simply from her ads showing her standing in front of a sign that read SOLD! instead of FOR SALE, her phone inquiries had increased 200 percent.

"Saleswoman of the month," Audrey answered and turned to make sure her six trophies were still in one piece on the bookshelf behind her. When she was out of the office, the other salespeople sometimes sneaked in and arranged them in compromising positions on top of one another.

Once someone had unscrewed all the gold figurines from their marble bases and scattered them across her desk like a scene from Jonestown.

"I have a house in Seven Oaks and am aware of your fine rep-u-ta-tion." The caller enunciated each syllable, which struck Audrey as odd.

"Oh?"

"It's time to sell."

"Excellent idea. First, I'll need to know where you're located."

The caller hesitated. "West Coast."

"Pardon?" Although the caller's voice was strong like a man's, it was high enough that Audrey imagined it could belong to a woman with a two-pack-a-day habit.

"Cal-i-for-nya."

"No, no, your *house.* Where is your house?!"

"Twelve Fletcher Lane."

She knew just where it was. Off Seven Oaks Way. Near the community playground. She plugged the address into the MLS system, and only one homeowner popped up. "So you are Mr. Edouard Kaminski?"

"Yes, that's me. Call me Eddie."

Kaminski. Was that German? Austrian? Austro-Hungarian? Were they different countries? She didn't know geography or languages. She knew tax benefits, mortgage rates, and property lines. She knew that tourists sipping Savannah Breezes at the genteel Brice Hotel were better prospects than those chugging foamy drafts at World of Beer. And she knew body language, so she reminded herself to straighten up. A confident posture would translate into a confident voice. "I'll need to review comparables in the neighborhood. Perhaps find equivalent properties in town, too."

"I'll leave the key under the mat."

"You won't be there?"

"No. You go."

Audrey clicked through old photos of the last time the house was on the market. Dark wet bar, run-down potting shed, sun room, vinyl exterior. *Oy.* "And let's find you a *new* home too. You can't forget about that." The other brokers were forever blowing the next step. Always acting like a herd of cloven-hoofed sheep in high heels, scurrying from one open house to the next, forgetting creative ways to make another sale. As the interior shots downloaded, she prayed to god that someone had set fire to the mauve wallpaper. "What a captivating home. I'd be happy to help." Leona ran around in figure eights on the lawn, chased by an invisible predator.

"Take a good look and see what it needs."

"Where can I reach you?" she asked, then wrote down a ten-digit number whose area code she didn't recognize. Malibu? Pasadena? Fresno? "I'll get back to you in a few days and give you my thoughts and a marketing plan. We can get the contract signed and the house on the market by the end of the week."

"You'll know what to do, I'm sure."

"And you say you were referred to me by my advertising?"

"Photo. I like your photo. Pro-vo-ca-tive."

And the phone went dead.

CHAPTER 18

"Sorry I'm late," Catherine whispered as she sidled up to Amity in the back of the unfamiliar living room. "What have I missed?"

"Pin the tail on Rafael Nadal," Amity said, flatly. "There's no telling where the fun will end."

In front of them, a sparrow-thin woman in a coral-and-teal Lilly Pulitzer dress finished handing out schedules. More than a dozen seated women about Amity's age, most of them wearing seaside pastels, perched on the wide couch, the piano bench, the frilled poufs. Catherine felt rather out of place in her dull beige pantsuit.

Lilly Pulitzer tittered in place before a large oil painting of herself. Her high heels clicked on the hardwood floor as she placed her hands on hummingbird hips. "So here's our tentative tennis calendar, which you'll also find on the website." The women shuffled the papers from one to another. "And for those of you who missed tryouts, we'll see you in the fall."

"In the fall?" Catherine leaned toward Amity. "But it's only April."

"I know, right?" Amity finished what champagne remained in her plastic flute and set it on the side table next to a large aquarium.

Then in consolation Lilly added, "But don't forget — you can always attend clinics and sub in games." The audience clapped weakly, as if anything harder might splinter a fingernail, and a general conversational hum rose, signaling the end of the meeting.

"Well, Catherine, apparently we've missed the boat."

"Ralph *does* like to tell me I'll be at the airport when my ship comes in." She looked out the picture window, saw a splash in the large lagoon, and wondered if a squadron of bored alligators lurked just under the surface.

"Consider yourself lucky. At least you missed the icebreaker." Amity swept her long hair behind her shoulders and Catherine saw her name tag. Instead of the usual HELLO . . . MY NAME IS sticker, it read HELLO . . . MY OCCUPATION IS, then, in preprinted type: CAT HOARDER. Catherine thought of Martha and her recent ice-breaker. Perhaps she'd call her later and tell her she was getting out of *her* comfort zone. Progress, not perfection.

"It could have been worse. Believe me," Amity added.

Catherine heard a flatness to her friend's voice and wondered if she were coming down with a cold. "Are you okay?"

"I'm tired." Amity pointed to the aquarium. "Like these guys."

They both stared at the brilliantly colored fish. It seemed to Catherine they might just be floating in air, untethered by gravity. Catherine grabbed a glass of champagne from a passing waitress. "Well, I have good news. I took care of the raccoon situation."

"Really? Thank you. Sometimes even my creeping feels sloppy."

"And I'm late because I was shopping for lingerie. Ralph gets one final opportunity to prove he finds me irresistible." She laughed, but she wasn't kidding.

Amity nodded listlessly. "Say, do you mind if I sneak out? I've had about all the fun I can muster for one afternoon."

"Of course." As if they'd been tennis partners for years, Catherine leaned over and hugged Amity. She felt the bones in the other woman's shoulders and wondered if she'd lost weight. "And eat something, would you?"

Amity half-smiled and disappeared out the front door.

As Catherine turned back to watch the fish, Lilly Pulitzer approached.

"Sorry you missed our meeting . . ." She hesitated.

"Catherine."

"Yes, Catherine. I'm Dixie. Team captain. I was just explaining to some of the new girls how we finished tryouts last week. We like to get our rosters set early. It's all about building team spirit."

Catherine noticed that Dixie had lost one large round earring. It reminded her of a missing hubcap on a Jaguar. "But I played USTA in New Jersey. I'm really not so bad."

"As I said, we'll get you to tryouts and *hopefully* onto our roster in September."

Catherine fantasized about launching her drink into Dixie's face, the kind of dramatic move she might see in a daytime soap, but she couldn't damage her future chances with the team. "I like your fish," she said, apropos of nothing, and wondered if the champagne had gone straight to her head.

"We brought them down from Hartford six years ago. The kids left, the dog died, but the fish remain. I thought they'd live a year or two but we've had them for fifteen. No predators. No way to get out. They just wait for food and swim around the castle all day. At least they stay in shape." She smoothed down her dress. "So are your children pleased you've moved here?"

"We never had children."

"Oh, so sorry. You probably have some tragic tale to tell and I've just ruined it."

"Don't be sorry." Catherine looked to the fish. "I'd be the type of mother who shouts: 'Don't get too close to the surface! You'll drown!' "

"I see." Dixie grimaced. "Well you can have some of ours. I've got four, George has five." She smiled as if she'd just won a rally with a sharp-angled overhead.

"That was a lovely dinner," Catherine said to Ralph as they headed up the stairs from Alligator Soul. Catherine held Ralph with one hand and her doggie bag with the other. She had saved a perfectly marbled cut of steak for Karma. "It's nice to get downtown, beyond the gates."

Once at street level, they navigated the rough sidewalk. She felt his craggy fingers, calloused from holding golf clubs, and even imagined she could feel the indentation from his wedding ring, which he'd gotten out of the habit of wearing. As they followed Barnard Street to the crosswalk, they heard the rhythmic hum of two guitars.

"Let's go," she said, pulling him toward Telfair Square. It was not something she would normally do, but she felt invigorated by the steady beat and the potential in the night around them.

Sitting on a wooden bench, two young men with ironic facial hair and vintage T-shirts strummed a song Catherine couldn't quite place.

"Dylan," Ralph told her. " 'Hurricane.' "

They watched as several couples, mostly tourists with comfortable walking shoes and green-and-red trolley stickers still stuck to their shirts, swayed to the music. Catherine started to move too, to find the song's beat, but was having trouble and wondered if it were the musicians or just her. If it'd been too long since she let herself go.

"Would you like to dance?" she asked, suddenly.

Ralph looked at her as if they'd just met, then shook his head. "Rotator cuff," he explained. "Tweaked it on the long tees today."

After the song ended, Ralph dug into his pocket, found a few dollars, and put them into the half-full tip jar. "Thanks, guys," he said. "Nice job."

They followed the brick path, the tapestried spanish moss above them, toward their car. A tanker moaned somewhere on the Savannah River.

"So what do you think *this* would set us back?" Ralph had stopped in front of a block-lettered FOR SALE sign attached to a cast-iron railing. He peered into the lower-level apartment of an old Federal-style brick building. "Five hundred? Maybe six?"

Just as Catherine was going to joke about him planning a move, getting a pied-à-terre for watching football games or hosting poker nights, a pickup truck barreled by and backfired. For a microsecond, in the time it takes for an atom to split or a supernova to collapse, Catherine imagined a drive-by shooting and envisioned Karma's bacon-wrapped beef in a pool of blood on the sidewalk.

When they reached their car, Ralph scurried to open the passenger door. He could be almost charming when he put his mind to it. While she shuttled the doggie bag to the floor, Ralph started the car and pulled forward. The Jepson Center, three stories of incongruous glass, loomed before them. Catherine thought of Dixie's fish living safely in an aquarium but never seeing the world, never swimming in the expanse of the Forsyth Park fountain or even a freshwater lagoon. Living to a ripe old age of fifteen or twenty years — however long goldfish lived — but eating synthetic pellets their whole lives.

Instead of heading toward the Truman Parkway, Ralph continued around the square.

"Where are we going?"

"I just thought we'd explore," Ralph said. "See what type of foot traffic there is downtown on a Saturday night."

"Foot traffic?" On any other occasion, Catherine might have questioned him further. What did *he* care about foot traffic? But all evening she'd been careful not to criticize, even holding her tongue when she saw alligator fingers on the appetizer menu — like alligators had fingers dainty enough to slip into a lady's opera glove. Now traveling in the opposite direction from which they started, they passed the restaurant to their right. "I mean, do alligators even *have* souls?"

"To have a soul you need to be able to self-reflect, Catherine." He sounded as if he'd studied these things. "No animal can do that."

Catherine thought of Karma, probably

curled tightly in his dog bed and wondering where the hell his steak was. She knew Karma had a soul, but she wasn't going to start a fight. She just wasn't sure if souls extended to cats or hamsters or down the food chain to reptiles. "You don't think Mr. Peabody self-reflects?" Right away Catherine regretted bringing up anything related to the real estate center.

"They sure do some great marketing selling Seven Oaks, don't they?"

At a stop sign, a horse-drawn carriage carrying a bored family clattered by. A teenage boy threw what looked like peanuts at the horse's head while his parents talked on their cell phones. Catherine hoped to change the subject. She wanted to move as far away from Audrey as she could. "So I went to an informational tennis meeting." She needed him to know she'd been trying.

"You're joining a team?"

"Any day now." This wasn't the night to explain she'd missed tryouts.

"You need friends," he said, forgetting she'd told him she'd gone walking with Amity.

Ralph pulled the car around a crowded double-decker hearse with visitors on a ghost tour of the city's supposedly haunted houses. Catherine rolled down the window and heard the driver reference the recent sighting of a Union soldier in full uniform, with a Prussian blue sack coat, haversack, and leather cartridge box.

"How about getting involved with the dog park?"

"Maybe."

At the wide expanse of Ellis Square, traffic came to a standstill as a bachelorette party with young women in matching glittery tiaras spilled onto the crosswalk. The one in the lead wore a pink BRIDE sash. Catherine remembered her own bachelorette party, a potluck dinner followed by strawberry margaritas at Martha's walk-up apartment where they discussed conspiracy theories regarding Bob Crane's death.

"Look at all these people," Ralph said, breathless.

It took nearly ten minutes to reach Bay Street as they dodged pedicabs and groups taking selfies. There was even a threesome who appeared to be on a scavenger hunt, carrying several palm fronds and a life-size cardboard cutout of Paula Deen.

Once they reached Bay, the traffic picked up. Taking a deep breath, Catherine thought she'd smell salt from the river or perhaps flowering honeysuckle. Instead she got a heady whiff of sweet pralines. In front of the last bar on the street, Catherine watched as a group of rowdy men in cowboy hats and jeans exited. She thought of an old Western movie, the outlaws emerging through swinging doors. Each man held a large to-go cup. "I love Georgia, but an open-container law *plus* an open-carry law seems like a bad idea," she said, thankful they'd never had any need for a gun.

Once back at the house, Ralph went to the kitchen while Catherine took Karma for his final walk of the evening. As was their routine, Ralph turned on the dishwasher while Catherine implored their dog to have a bowel movement. Ralph moved to the master bath to floss while Catherine stood with Karma on a patch of grass outside their house. She imagined that everyone else's dog was capable of scooting out the back door, doing his business, then returning without a Medal of Honor.

"Hurry, hurry, hurry," she repeated, hoping their secret code word might focus his attention. But he ignored her.

Maybe it's all my fault, she thought suddenly.

Had she been too protective of Karma? When he was a puppy, she'd hardly ever let him off leash, never allowed him his independence. Even now she hovered, a textbook helicopter mom. Maybe if he'd had a little freedom, he'd be more demonstrative and know he was loved. Although she'd tried to teach him simple commands over the years, he never fully grasped what was expected. Sit. Stay. Speak.

Speak, she thought again.

Long ago, Catherine might have told Ralph that she needed more. She needed a real family and a place to belong. She needed to be adored and appreciated and listened to. Just before her fortieth birthday, she'd brought up the idea of children. Maybe it wasn't too late. But he'd told her that their indecision *had* been a decision. They'd chosen free weekends and disposable income over Little League and college tuition. They'd chosen recreation over *re*-creation. She regretted not pushing back, finding a voice for what she needed. For now, though, she needed to know if he still found her desirable.

Without delay, Catherine yanked Karma's leash, harder than she ever had. His little head jerked toward the house. He gave her the stink eye as she pulled him back toward the front steps, but she didn't relent. She needed to make things happen.

It had been more than seven months since she and Ralph had had sex. She vaguely recalled the missionary position and a cursory orgasm during the heat of the New Jersey summer. They sometimes joked about how long it had been, mostly as they watched television ads for little yellow pills — commercials featuring gray-haired models ogling each other in separate claw-foot bathtubs. But fear had stopped her from articulating one crucial question: *Is there any magic left between us?*

Once inside the house, Karma settled on his bed in the laundry room while Catherine retrieved her pink-striped Victoria's Secret bag. Peeking out the pocket door, she could see only Ralph's legs splayed across the bedspread. A funereal TV newscaster reported a domestic disturbance within one of the sturdy brick homes in Ardsley Park, a neighborhood rich with Craftsman gems yet plagued with break-ins. Without delay, she removed the new lacy lingerie from the bag, careful to snip off the plastic price tags. As Karma eyed her suspiciously, she brushed out her hair and remained committed to her plan.

Without disturbing Ralph, she slid the laundry door open and stepped across the hallway to the walk-in closet, the same closet where she'd found Amity, who had opened up a whole new world for her. She quickly undressed, then scooped her breasts into the black push-up bra, plumping them up as if they were sacks of settled flour. Then she pulled on the matching black thong and lifted her full buttocks so they settled between the single tendon of material. It felt several sizes too small.

Thinking of the tennis ladies in their high heels, she found the sexiest strappy slingbacks she owned — a pair she'd bought for one of Martha's weddings — and slipped them on. Standing in front of the full-length mirror she felt a little ridiculous but not embarrassed, for she thought of the bountiful curves of Raquel Welch or Sophia Loren, role models for her generation, women who had embraced their ample bodies. But then Catherine imagined Audrey, with her exuberant breasts and long legs. She would have chosen a pink satin baby doll with ruffles, and would have *owned* her sexuality. And so Catherine did just that.

She backed up so that her shoulders pressed against Ralph's golf shirts, then breathed deeply and straightened up as she took several long steps forward, hips swaying, as if she were a lithe Angel on a catwalk. It was time.

Before losing her nerve, she spun around and stepped out into the hallway and took a few steps to the bedroom. "So what do you think?" she started to say, but then saw Ralph's head fallen to one side of the pillow, mouth open, eyes closed. "Ralph?"

He snorted awake and blinked at her a few times. "Oh my." He sat up enough to grab his glasses from the side table.

"What do you think?"

"I think that's an adorable getup."

"A *getup*?" Catherine pulled the thong out of the crack in her buttocks.

"Come here." He shifted on the mattress and patted a spot next to him.

She doddered over on her high heels and sat. She felt ridiculous, like someone who arrives at a Halloween party *en costume* only to realize it's come as you are.

"I've always admired your enthusiasm," he said.

"You have?"

"Of course I have." He cleared his throat. "But we walked eighteen today and I'm not quite sure I can get up for the celebration, if you know what I mean." He took her hand. "Can I take a rain check?"

"Of course you can," she answered, thinking of the few rain checks they'd collected from postponed night games at Shea Stadium, unused tickets that had sat for years in a crowded utility drawer. Then, thinking of Audrey, she added softly, "But no substitutions or exchanges."

CHAPTER 19

"He is a liar. I just don't know what the lie is yet," the television voice said.

Ida Blue pressed the remote control and powered off the rerun of *CSI: Miami*. She usually admired Lieutenant Horatio Caine, with his peach cobbler–colored hair and his creative tactics for solving crimes and collaring perps. He was like a race car driver on an icy highway — prepared, focused, and always on the edge of danger. Yet lately she'd been feeling bored with network TV and fictional mysteries when she had her own.

She remained splayed across her old couch, a can of flat Diet Mountain Dew resting on her stomach. Outside she saw the leaning trees that bordered Fred Wolfe's property and recognized that she'd felt a little unzipped since she'd spoken to her neighbor, since she'd experienced a pulsating aura that must have been very close to real psychic energy. Maybe the phantom old woman hovering on her deck was a key to another dimension. If she could tap that wellspring, she could attract new clients or develop a radio show. Even an Internet webinar. Embracing Your Oracle. Secrets to Good Karma. Vibrational Energy Enlightenment. Maybe she could compete with the likes of Celebrity Animal Communicator Sonya Fitzpatrick, who surely had no better connection to the inner thoughts of pets than anyone else, just the spicy pull of a British accent.

Ida Blue had to quit pretending that word of mouth would grow her business. That clients would fall into her lap like pecans from a tree. That wishing would make a phone ring. If she was to keep her house and continue to live in Seven Oaks, she needed to expand. She needed to *do* something. As Lieutenant Caine would have said, holding dark sunglasses between the tips of his fingers: "The only thing that matters is the evidence." And the evidence was that she was going broke.

If Ida Blue could pay off her bills, she could work on building an empire. She imagined hosting a heartwarming show about animals finding love. She'd originally conceived it as a sort of matchmaking business for dogs, but she knew such a powerful idea couldn't be restricted to one species. Perhaps the universe needed a dating service for cats, ferrets, turtles, even silverback gorillas. The primates were endangered, after all; the World Wildlife Fund might be a viable sponsor. And what *didn't* she know about love? Ida Blue had done her research and watched all the latest episodes of *The Bachelor* and *The Millionaire Matchmaker*. Courtship rituals were fairly straightforward. In the wild, male birds presented sticks, flamingos danced, and cockroaches stroked antennae. In humans it was equally obvious. Don't order the most expensive thing on a menu. Say thank you when complimented. Don't go to second base on the first date. Never vomit in a Jacuzzi.

Although it had been years ago, she *did* have firsthand experience. Nothing long-term, but she could still speak from her heart. In high school she had had a boyfriend for a few months. McSweeney was a slender senior in the AV club who smelled of maple syrup. Sadly, she'd lost track of him once he'd moved to Las Vegas to pursue his dream of becoming a ventriloquist magician. But maybe one day, when Ida Blue got herself back on her feet, she'd throw her own hat back into the dating arena. If so, she'd need to be careful. She knew she'd come across as intimidating on a first date. *Yes, I'm a career woman. Yes, I run my own successful business out of my home.* And she wasn't sure a husband was really a good thing to bring into a house. It seemed an ironic coincidence that the breeding of farm animals was known as animal *husbandry*.

On several occasions in the last week, Ida Blue had been tempted to call Fred Wolfe to try some sort of psychic reconnection. If she did, she could ask him if his computer was running, just as he had asked her: "Is your Internet working?" She used to make prank phone calls, before caller ID put the kibosh on a little neighborhood fun. *Is your refrigerator running? Is your air-conditioning running? Is your computer running? Well, then go catch them!* But calling him out of the blue felt a tad aggressive, and the last thing she wanted was to scare him away. She feared smothering the source, like an Eskimo who has lived his entire life in Arctic darkness throwing himself on top of the first Weber grill he sees.

But given her financial pickle, Ida Blue knew it was time to get closer to Fred, as if he were a sort of human Wi-Fi connection. So it wasn't hard to will herself off the couch. After setting the TV remote and Diet Mountain Dew on the coffee table, she maneuvered around a mass of empty pizza boxes tilting dangerously to one side. *The Leaning Tower of Pizza!* Inside her walk-in closet, she slipped off her housecoat and selected a sundress with brown vertical stripes. Oprah had worn a similar outfit on her recent vacation with Stedman. The dress seemed a little tight and she wondered if it had shrunk in the spring humidity. After choosing a pair of wide red flip-flops that would accommodate her bunions, she congratulated herself on putting the smart outfit together. She might even offer fashion advice on her matchmaking show. *A V-line neck will give the illusion of a slender torso. Long necklaces bring attention away from wide hips. Let your smile be your umbrella.*

She moved back into the living room and out the sliding doors onto the deck. Cobwebs hung from the eaves, and she waved both hands in front of her head to get through them. Moving down six steps, she arrived at the flagstone patio. Dollarweed thrived in the fissures between broken slate where she hadn't been in several months. She saw her single chaise longue with a missing armrest. Of course, it had come with the house, but it didn't look as uncomfortable as she'd remembered. Perhaps she'd even sit outside one day, if she could find the time.

Fred Wolfe's house was practically within spitting distance, but Ida Blue didn't dare wander through the half acre of tilting trees. She'd watched too many episodes of *The Crocodile Hunter,* Steve Irwin wrestling an alligator, calming a stingray, or mugging it up with a Komodo dragon. He'd told her about rattlesnakes and copperheads and cottonmouths. About how the venom from a single bite could cause hemorrhaging and sudden, painful death. And look what happened to poor Steve! Of course, she was a large woman, so it would take the Arnold Schwarzenegger of the reptile world to really give her a run for her money, but still.

As she walked out onto the lawn, she noticed that a large clump of lemony daffodils had taken root at the far side of her giant oak tree. From her vantage point on the living room couch she had never noticed the cluster, and it surprised her that flowers so vibrant could grow untended. She moved farther to the property's edge, where a thick band of pine straw separated the lawn from the tangled undergrowth. It was burnt orange, like dull police tape. Probably like Lieutenant Horatio Caine's hair before a little Hollywood highlighting. "Slowly step away from the crime scene," he might tell her. The pine straw was a visual break from the green grass to the dark thicket of woods. From manicured suburbia to savage wilderness.

As she approached the edge, birds began to call above her, and she thought she heard the snickering of a raccoon. She could even see Fred Wolfe's breakfast alcove, a curtain pulled halfway across one of the windows. As she watched, she hoped she might catch a glimpse of him. She lifted one leg, dangled her foot above the edge of the property, and felt a tingle move from her toes to her ankles. She didn't dare step closer lest the venomous snakes appear, but she knew she had a connection to the old man she needed to explore.

Although Ida Blue used her car only for weekly trips to the grocery store and occasionally downtown to promote tourism, she knew it was an appropriate time to splurge on a few unwarranted miles. This was about getting a connection, investing in her business and maybe even herself, so she padded back across the lawn and climbed the porch steps one at a time. Like most patio homes on the street, her house was single story but raised eight feet above sea level, as the housing code required. Her knees were thankful she lived in a low-lying city like Savannah and not San Francisco or Machu Picchu.

On her way to the garage she stopped at the pantry, her shelves filled with AA batteries and drinking water and duct tape, supplies for any apocalyptic incident. Though she couldn't be sure of the coming chain of events, she figured she might need some quick energy. Dr. Oz always said that dark chocolate was loaded with nutrients, so she grabbed several chewy-chip granola bars and congratulated herself on a healthy choice. She would take the snacks just in case. Justin Case. Justin Time. *Is Justin Time home? No? Well, when he gets back tell him he's late.* She snapped her rubber band.

The garage was a mess; always had been. Almost from her first week in the condo, she'd collected neighbors' knickknacks on dump days. Even though she hadn't had a *need* for slanting chairs or stained comforters, she hated for perfectly good hand-me-downs to be carted to the incinerator.

Wood rot had created several gaping holes in the garage door, so Ida Blue's car sported a thin layer of bright yellow pollen, as if Rachael Ray had sneaked into Seven Oaks and sprinkled curry powder across the hood. In order to sit down, Ida Blue had to move several empty bottles of diet soda and the manila envelope that held her pet psychic flyers. After opening the door and backing into the road, she pulled the car forward to the stop sign. *Journey's Greatest Hits* was stuck in the CD player.

It was time to take immediate and positive action. "Bag it and tag it," Lieutenant Caine would say. At the main road she turned left. This wasn't rocket science. In fact, the adjacent neighborhood looked vaguely familiar, since earlier in the week she'd used Google Maps to make a virtual journey to Fred Wolfe's house, to see if she felt a connection from the computer screen. She hadn't.

In a quarter mile she reached Jolly Badger Lane and took another left. Just as she pulled onto the road, a surge of electricity moved up her spine. Of course, the Seven Oaks homeowner code didn't allow any last names on mailboxes, no reflective letters that spelled WOLFE, but as she approached number four, a fiery spark ignited in her stomach, like the start of inflammatory bowel disease.

Fred Wolfe's house was a traditional Low Country home with a covered, wraparound porch, black wooden shutters, and two third-floor dormers that seemed to eye her suspiciously. His neighborhood was fancier than her own, but it offered the same wide streets and neat sidewalks. As she drove past his mailbox, she felt as if she'd just lit a Fourth of July sparkler on a dark night. But she had to keep driving. She couldn't just stop and draw attention to herself and her car. She couldn't just roll up to his house like some sort of lost relative. Or lost niece. *Do you have Aunt Jemima in a bottle? Well, let her out!* As she continued past the house, the electricity faded. In two hundred yards, the road ended in a wide cul-de-sac. Several real estate signs identified the undeveloped marsh lots for sale. She pulled around the circle, rolled down the windows, and turned off the engine.

From this spot she could see Fred Wolfe's property. There was no car in the driveway, no Great Dane on the prowl, no one sweeping the front walk or watering the bushes. A coiled hose hung from a metal hook by the side of the garage. *Is your hose running? You'd better catch it. May I speak with Mr. Hugh Jass?* "Stop it!" she shouted, her voice reverberating in the small car. She had to keep focus. Couldn't panic. Couldn't get all worked up about what she didn't have — a steady income, a plan for the future, a connection to psychic power. She had to focus on what she *did* have, and right now it was hope. Hope that she could connect to an energy and a matter greater than herself, if only through her neighbor.

She knew that if someone saw her idling outside Fred's house, he might think she was a nutcase. A stalker. *What did the celery say to the vegetable dip? I'm stalking you!* But Seven Oaks was too safe to harbor stalkers. She wasn't some sort of psychopath who jumps out of Martha Stewart's pantry or Alec Baldwin's pool house. She was just inextricably drawn to him to get a link to another world.

The longer she lingered, the greater was her longing. She felt an invisible pull, a giant magnetic horseshoe drawing her car closer. After five minutes, she could barely take it anymore. The amount of effort she was putting into *not* driving up onto his lawn and throwing herself at his feet was exhausting. She'd never lifted weights or been to an aerobics class but imagined this was what exercising felt like. And as she sat, she felt a rise in her blood pressure and a lightness to her chest. It reminded her of McSweeney and the first time they'd tried Boone's Farm Strawberry Fiesta wine. They'd been parked on a dead-end street

190

and had left their senior prom early. He'd been showing her a magic trick that involved taking a joker out of her ear. "Just wait till you see where the jack is hiding," he'd said. As she sat in the car by Fred Wolfe's house, she remembered the cool night and the tickling in her throat and carbonated rush to her head. The feeling that anything was possible.

The memory made her think of missed opportunities and roads not taken. It'd been seven years since she'd relocated from the cragged Georgia mountains, but it was now time to be proactive again. To make the universe aware that she was willing to make an effort on her own behalf. She took the manila envelope on the passenger seat and pulled out one of her pet psychic flyers. She grabbed a pencil from the carpet before realizing it was just a dried french fry. She threw it out the open window and found a pen. The nib was clotted with dirt so she ran it in small circles until a ragged line of ink appeared. She didn't want to scare her neighbor, but she needed to get her point across: *7 OAKS CITIZENS . . . 1st Call FREE!!!* And then for added emphasis she wrote: *LARGE dog special!!* As she sat there, she had the sensation of looking down at herself from above. Willing Fred Wolfe to appear before her, half-expecting him to come out of his house, arms outstretched, light emanating behind him.

With a plan in place, she turned on the engine and slowly moved her car forward. With each advancing moment, her heart beat faster. At last she was in front of Four Jolly Badger. She parked the car, sat back, and reveled in conscious completeness. Just as on her half-dozen dates with McSweeney, she felt fully alive, at one with her body and the universe. She caught her breath and grabbed the flyer. She would just roll it up, step out, and place it in Fred Wolfe's mailbox. Nothing could be simpler. She looked ahead of her and behind her, and no one was on the street. No one was walking a dog or pushing a baby carriage. No one was delivering mail or trimming a hedge. The world had stopped for a moment. All the noise in her head was suddenly and uncharacteristically quiet. As she unfastened the seat belt and opened the car door, she looked one more time at the house. And that's when she saw it.

In the wide living room window, an indistinct figure. It might have been a reflection on the glass, her eyes playing tricks. But as she stared, the lacy white curtain fluttered. Ida Blue was so surprised that she felt paralyzed, as if a lightning bolt had struck her.

Unsure whether to get out, stay put, or race away as fast as her car could carry her, she remained still. Then, as if in answer to her question, the curtain fluttered again. This time a willowy arm pulled the fabric away and a red-haired woman peered at her. The woman moved her face toward the window. As she did, Ida Blue spied a golf visor and knew immediately, in the same way a mother can identify her newborn child in a crowded nursery, that it was the very woman from her patio the previous week. Ida Blue refused to move, could barely breathe, but the woman pushed her face even closer to the pane. It seemed her head might have even passed through the glass. Then, slowly and deliberately, the woman brought her arm toward the car, fingers cupped together, and beckoned Ida Blue inside.

CHAPTER 20

"And the dog park committee?" Fred was just trying to make conversation with Ernie. Trying to pass the time as he got his dog and himself out of the house. Hunter had stressed the importance of *routine,* so here he was at the park again.

"We're working on some very important issues." Ernie lowered his voice, as if the NSA were listening. "You know, implementing some new rules."

"Like?"

"No digging, no humping, et cetera." He stopped to let Fred catch up. "And did you know dollarweeds are infiltrating this joint?"

"Not really." Fred didn't notice and didn't care. He cared that his wife's boxes of letters and unfinished crochet projects crowded his living room coffee table. He cared that he was beginning to feel like a curator in some sort of perverse theme park. Not Dollywood but Lissaland.

"It's not the Pentagon, but we do discuss nuclear waste." With no response, Ernie repeated, "Nuclear *waste!*"

Fred pushed out a mock laugh because it was probably what he would have done before Lissa's illness. But that seemed so very long ago, and he could barely remember what it was to feel normal. To act normal. *Fake it till you make it,* Hunter had told him, and so he tried now.

Lulu, Ernie's terrier, had struck a play position in front of Sequoia, hind legs up and chest to the ground, but Sequoia was having nothing to do with her. "Sequoia still in a funk, huh?" Ernie asked.

"Comes and goes, just like me. Maybe she's just getting old." Then the Great Dane lifted her watermelon head and blinked rapidly, the first real movement she'd made in the last half hour. Sequoia turned toward the front gate and both Ernie and Fred followed her gaze.

In the transition area to the dog park, the enclosed space between the front gate and the six-acre enclosure, a woman stood as her dog, a brown-and-white streak, ran back and forth excitedly. "Calm down!" she said, laughing. The woman opened the interior gate and the dog tumbled through it, rolled on the ground a few times, then took off.

195

"Looks like we got a live one," Ernie said. They both watched her with interest. Fred saw her pull her left hand across her forehead, then stop to take in a big breath, then exhale. He studied her as Ernie turned his attention to her dog. "A Boston terrier, looks like. Look at him go."

But Fred was studying the woman and thought she looked vaguely familiar. During his last visit to Lewiston with Lissa, they'd played Simon Says with Tommy. *Simon says take a big breath in. Simon says breathe out. Simon says take a big breath in. Simon says hold it. Now breathe out.* But he could barely breathe watching the woman and her dog. Something inside him wouldn't let him catch his breath.

Stop with the drama, he heard Lissa say. *You're fine.*

The woman picked up a tennis ball where her dog had dropped it at her feet. She brought her arm back and then threw it in a heady parabola.

"Not a bad arm, either," Ernie said.

"You are sure right."

Ernie looked at his watch. "I gotta go anyway, so I'll be the bad cop. You be the good one. You're better at that." With one hand on the arm of the bench Ernie raised himself and walked slowly toward the woman. Lulu and the new dog eyed each other, then took tentative steps forward until they met, sniffing with delight. The woman had turned and was looping her leash around one of the hooks.

Although Fred couldn't hear their conversation, he knew Ernie would lead the woman through the protocol for entering the park. With his top-secret committee clearance, Ernie made it his business to introduce himself to all new members and make sure rules were followed. Was she aware of the registration procedure at the Seven Oaks office? Did her dog have up-to-date vaccinations? Did she understand the parking rules? She must be a patient woman, Fred thought, for she nodded dutifully and laughed again. Shortly, Ernie collected his dog and leash and left.

Fred suddenly noticed a change in the air. Slate-gray clouds had gathered in the west. The wind picked up, and dried leaves skipped across the grassy expanse. The woman walked halfway across the park, closer and closer to Fred. She wore comfortable dark shorts with a flowery short-sleeved shirt, and had a toned, shapely build. Meanwhile, her dog made wide circles around the park.

She turned toward him and smiled. "Hellooo," she called shyly and waved.

"Well hello to you," he replied, and heard a surprising playfulness in his own voice.

The Boston terrier found his tennis ball and placed it at the woman's feet again. "Okay, here we go." She picked it up and threw it over the natural rise in the center of the park and, although he couldn't see it, he imagined it rolled down to where the grass met the pine straw and overgrown cedar trees. Her throw was solid, the ball going farther than Fred expected. He imagined she must be an athlete and almost unconsciously noted the curve of her hips.

To Fred's surprise, Sequoia pushed herself into a standing position, stretched, and trotted to where the woman stood. He knew most people would be fearful of the dog — Great Danes didn't have the natural smiles of Labradors and goldens — yet the woman knelt to eye level and patted Sequoia's head. "Hello again, gorgeous," she said.

"She's friendly," Fred called to her.

"Yes, I know."

There was something about the woman. Perhaps they'd played together once in a golf scramble, or maybe she'd been an acquaintance of Lissa's, someone he'd met at her crowded memorial service.

"Sequoia, right?" she asked, smiling. The

woman's white hair was pulled back into a youthful short ponytail. As she approached, he could see her bright green eyes.

"Yes. But I'm embarrassed. Have we met?"

"The Village Café. Almost three months ago."

And then Fred remembered. "Of course. How could I forget? She practically climbed into your lap. My apologies."

The woman neared the bench and Sequoia shadowed her, step by step, as if they'd been training as a team for Westminster. "No need to apologize. I liked the attention." She stopped and looked out to her dog, who had taken an unbridled interest in a patch of dull grass. "I mean, Karma isn't the most loving dog in the world."

"Karma?"

"You know, as in 'Good Karma!' 'Bad Karma!' "

Fred laughed, vaguely remembering the name, but didn't really know anything about karma. As with a slow cooker, he understood what it was but not how it worked. It was something rather magical — *alternative,* his daughter might have corrected him — having to do with luck and fate.

The woman sat next to him, and Sequoia sat too and rested her large boxy head on the woman's lap. "Well, I see you haven't lost your charm with her."

"Bathing with Gravy Train is my dirty little secret."

When Catherine stepped into the park and first saw the harlequin Great Dane, she remembered her from the restaurant. How could she not? She'd never seen an animal as colossal and gentle. Like a small horse. And she liked the name: Sequoia. She even remembered the gentleman — handsome and tall with a wide forehead and good posture. He reminded her of a broadcaster on the six o'clock news. Someone you could trust. He might have been a little over-dressed for the setting, in a light wind-breaker, blue button-down shirt, and khakis, but she liked his kind face and sweet smile.

Karma raced up to Sequoia and skidded to a stop in front of her. He pawed at the ground. Sequoia looked up at Catherine, seemed to smile, then placed her head back on Catherine's lap.

"Sequoia's eight," Fred explained. "She'd like to play, but she might have forgotten how."

"I don't think anyone ever forgets how to play," Catherine answered. "They just lose interest." She was thinking of Ralph. How in the first few weeks of getting the dog, he'd taken Karma on walks in the woods or brief errands but quickly abandoned the excursions. What with the bags and the leash and the treats, he felt it was all a bit too complicated.

"Is Karma a puppy? He's so youthful."

"Why thank you," Catherine replied, feeling herself blush, feeling complimented in an indirect way. "He's five. I found him at the Humane Society." It had been just before Mother's Day, and Ralph was traveling again. With all the television commercials featuring sons bringing mothers roses and taking them out to brunch and delivering handwritten cards, Catherine felt it was time to have something to love, something that was intrinsically *hers.* It was all rather serendipitous, and it occurred to Catherine that it was sort of how she met Amity in the closet. Good karma, indeed. "What about Sequoia?"

"She was my wife's. Our daughter moved, got married, and had a baby, and Lissa felt, I don't know . . . replaced? She always had a lot of love to go around, and felt like she'd lost Danielle. I wish I'd been more aware . . ." His voice trailed off. She wondered if the man was widowed or divorced. Widowed, she assumed, since he wore no ring and no woman in her right mind would willingly leave a kind, handsome man who loved dogs.

Sequoia stood and stepped back from the benches. She raised her head and looked into Catherine's eyes for a moment as if to tell her something. "What is it, beautiful?" Catherine stroked the dog's broad chest.

Suddenly Sequoia's ears were alert, stretched straight in the air, noting some intangible sound in the distance. The Great Dane drew up her head even higher, her eyes closed, a jazz musician waiting for her turn in a complicated ensemble passage. At once the dog trotted off stiffly to the field and over the rise in the center of the park. Catherine felt sympathy for the animal as she watched her gait. She was beginning to feel that way in the mornings herself, as if she'd turned into a marionette overnight, a slender wooden rod in her lower back.

"Uh, I'm afraid your dog is doing a little business," Fred said.

Catherine had lost track of Karma. "Oh, yes. Sorry."

Rising from the bench, she grabbed a plastic bag from her shorts pocket. *Doing a little business.* She liked that. Ralph would have said "taking a dump."

She reached the center of the park, picked

202

up the deposit, and walked over to the nearest trash can by the water bowls. She was at the highest point of the sloping grass and could look down to where the open space bordered the woods. Although the crowded trees made it hard to see, Catherine thought she caught a glimpse of a redheaded woman in a golf outfit. She thought she saw her bending over to stroke Sequoia, but in the next moment she was gone.

Catherine felt a raindrop grace her cheek, just where a tear might have fallen had she been crying. It surprised her because she didn't think rain was in the forecast.

She moved back to the bench and held out her hand. "I'm Catherine."

"Fred," he replied, taking her hand and shaking it gently. "It's a pleasure."

When Catherine let go she felt a sizzle of excitement, a static shock, as if she'd been wearing wool socks on a carpet.

"So I take it you're new here?" he asked.

"Three months. My husband retired from a job on Wall Street last year."

"How do you like it?"

She didn't know if he meant relocating in general or Seven Oaks or her husband's retirement. Catherine considered telling him the truth, he looked so trustworthy and dependable. She might have told him that

Ralph's retirement had changed everything. "It's an adjustment," she said.

"Life is an adjustment." Fred pulled his hand through thinning hair. "Have you met many people since you moved?"

Catherine might have mentioned Amity. She might have confided that she suspected her real estate agent, Audrey Cunningham, had the hots for Ralph. And maybe, just maybe, the feelings were mutual. She might have said something about trying to go regularly to the gym, but instead she heard herself say, "Now I've met you."

He liked the way Catherine spoke. She had a thoughtful way of hesitating before answering, so different from Lissa, who shared whatever popped into her mind.

Did not.

It was a good thing. You kept me on my toes.

Well, thank god for that.

Fred had met Lissa as a college freshman. A deliberate woman who remained thoughtful and optimistic throughout her life. Two days before she died, she even suggested they book a cruise for the fall. Maybe they could convince Danielle and Tommy to come.

"How is security here?" Catherine asked suddenly.

"Security?"

"You know, are there any cat burglars?" She laughed nervously.

He smiled and considered asking her what there could be to steal. Cholesterol-lowering statins? Viagra? Wraparound sunglasses? "No. It's very safe. The gates keep the crime out. The only thing you've really got to watch out for are the old men at the dog park." He felt himself wink. Felt himself get a little giddy. He hadn't flirted in years, but here he was. What was he doing?

"Don't worry. I can tell Ernie is a bit of a player, but I'm not really attracted to Santa Claus impersonators." She laughed too, and as she did a light rain began.

"Why, this isn't very conducive to our little parade." Fred extended his open hand, feeling the wetness on his palm.

"No. I didn't even bring a jacket."

But the rain was rather refreshing, as if it were floating from a wide wand attached to a kinked garden hose. Neither of them moved.

"First things you learn when you move to Savannah, Catherine: order the milkshake at Clary's; don't miss the Saint Patrick's Day Parade; and bring an umbrella just in case." Fred watched Catherine as she closed her eyes briefly, then lifted her head skyward. She didn't seem in a hurry to rush home. And he certainly wasn't, with Lissa's old boxes waiting for him on his coffee table. He'd promised himself he'd get to them on the next rainy afternoon. And here it was. Yet he felt as if he and Catherine were settled at the closing credits of a mesmerizing movie, like it was time to go, but something invisible was keeping him in his seat. Suddenly he realized Sequoia was no longer by his side. He looked around.

"I saw them head down to the woods," Catherine said.

Fred nodded and laughed. "She's certainly old enough to take care of herself. Even in Afghanistan."

"I beg your pardon?"

"That's what everyone calls it back there. We don't go in because it's too dangerous. Too many IEDs."

"IEDs?"

He leaned over and whispered, "Indelicate extreme deposits."

Again she laughed. She had a girlish way about her, and he liked her pleasant temperament. He wondered if she were the kind of person who woke up in a good mood, like Lissa. His wife would open her eyes and want to know when their first activity started, as if each day were summer camp.

The rain came down more heavily, the garden hose unkinked, and they both stood.

"C'mon," he said and they racewalked to the front gate. By the time they reached the entrance, the skies had opened. Within minutes mud started to pool by the hooks. "Here," Fred said. He grabbed his umbrella and unfurled it. "Please." He opened his hand, inviting her underneath, protecting her from the downpour. Then he stepped away and into the rain, the water seeping into his shirt. "Sequoia! Karma!" He whistled loudly, as if calling a taxi in Midtown Manhattan, as if they'd just stepped out onto Forty-Fourth Street after a late lunch at Sardi's.

"This is so odd," Catherine said. "Karma hates rain."

He called again, but the rain fell harder and louder, and he moved back under the umbrella.

"Maybe they found a nice dry spot under a tree," Catherine said. "I saw Sequoia with a woman by the back gate."

"Back gate?"

"You know, by the nature trail. Afghanistan."

But Fred knew the far gate was kept locked. It was only opened once a week so the public works department could bring in grass-cutting equipment. He'd served on the original dog park committee when the project was initiated. He'd helped design the park. Even ordered the benches, choosing durable metal over more comfortable plastic. Ernie would have made sure there was no deviation from the rules. "Did she have a dog?"

Catherine hesitated. "I didn't see one, but she must have. Maybe Sequoia and Karma are cuddling under the trees," she said, shouting now. Rain pounded on the umbrella, splashing in bursts around them like water on a hot griddle. Their shoes absorbed the runoff from the earth.

Fred tried to imagine it, had a mental image of Sequoia blocking the downpour, his dog's large body curled around Karma to keep the smaller dog dry. "Cuddling?"

"Huddling!" Catherine raised an eyebrow. "I said *huddling!*" He wondered if she were flirting with him, too.

As they moved together toward the dark edge of the park, the wind picked up and the air cooled. Without conscious thought, Fred handed Catherine the umbrella, took off his jacket, and placed it around her shoulders. "You must be getting cold."

She leaned into him. Although they barely touched, for a moment he felt like Gene

Kelly in *Singin' in the Rain,* Debbie Reynolds by his side. They reached the top of the slope but didn't see the dogs. As they continued on, the sweet smell of damp earth came to him. For a moment, he imagined they were a young couple in a Manet painting, strolling along the banks of the Seine.

When they reached the border of Afghanistan the wind stilled, as if the world had stopped rotating. Fred had a fleeting thought about how quickly life can change. Things like weather and health. Love and itineraries. The travel brochures that had sat forever on his coffee table. He and Lissa had had countless conversations deciding whether to cruise along the Rio Negro or spend a month exploring the eastern Mediterranean and Greek Isles. They'd talked about dogsledding in Sweden, maybe even staying at the Ice Hotel, or riding an elephant in India. But in the end, he'd sat by Lissa's hospice bed, reading her detailed advertising copy and showing her photos from full-color brochures, as if she were just a child: *Here's Iguazu Falls in Brazil. Just look at that water. Isn't that nice?*

Their lives had taken a sudden hairpin curve, and cancer hadn't figured into their ambitious itineraries. He and Lissa had once daydreamed that they'd leave the world together, neither left alone to tie up the loose ends of their lives. If it hadn't been for traumatizing Danielle and Tommy, they might have liked to perish softly, in a faulty single-engine plane that glided into the warm waters off the Galapagos, like slipping into a pleasant bath. Or maybe on the last day of an around-the-world tour, their hot-air balloon unexpectedly setting down into the lush Masai Mara.

And as Fred thought about journeys discussed but not taken, scripts written but not acted on, he saw the metal gate. Wide open.

Their dogs were gone.

CHAPTER 21

Ida Blue stood on Fred Wolfe's walkway, somewhere between his mailbox and front steps. She was mesmerized by his house — the line of leafy azalea bushes, the two rocking chairs on the porch, the wide living room window where she had seen the apparition of the older woman. The house was ordinary, the neighborhood familiar. Under other circumstances the home might have been part of a television set for a sitcom about prosperous families leading happy lives. But *The Brady Bunch* didn't have a ghost. Maybe someone had laced her Lucky Charms with LSD.

If Ida Blue had been more cognizant of her surroundings, had only moved her head to the left or the right, she might have seen the dark clouds approaching from the south, like waves rolling in on a rough sea. If she had raised her gaze from the front window, she would have noticed the treetops swaying. But her focus remained on the house. On the window. On the possibilities ahead.

She was so in her own world that when she first heard the roar of rain she mistook it for an approaching truck. Then, with the hard drops on her head and shoulders, her natural reaction was to rush to the safety of the porch rather than back into the storm and toward her car. As she raced up the steps to Fred Wolfe's front door her heart pounded. Once at the top of the steps she stopped for almost a minute to recover. Doubled over, hands resting on knees, she felt her breath return to her, a rubbery helium balloon slowly filling inside her chest.

She didn't know what she would do if Fred Wolfe opened the door to find her there. Perhaps she could have played the role of the concerned neighbor. *Are all your windows closed? Is your Great Dane inside? Did you fix your Internet?* Or even, *Did you know your house is haunted?*

Standing on the front porch, she felt complete. *Full,* as if she had just topped off her tank at a gas station. She wasn't hungry and she wasn't afraid. She just wanted some sort of acknowledgment of why she was there. The ghostly being had beckoned her forward, after all, but then had just as quickly disappeared.

She put her face up to the window and looked in to see a ceiling fan circling slowly in the center of the living room. Then her eyes focused on a narrow sofa, an Oriental rug, a few large cardboard boxes. There was no redhead knitting on the couch, no Great Dane curled at her feet. No evidence that this was anything but an ordinary, if gray, afternoon and an ordinary house.

Then the rain came harder and the wind stronger. Water assaulted her from the side, spraying across the porch. She could feel it seeping into her plastic flip-flops and between her toes. For a brief moment she imagined Cecil B. DeMille perched on the roof, operating a rain machine in some sort of movie extravaganza.

There was nothing left to do but knock. She was tentative at first, tapping her knuckles on the door in three short bursts. But she remembered Fred Wolfe was older; she had heard it in his weathered voice when he had called her, as if he'd been eating crackers all day. And so she rapped harder, slapping the door with an open hand. No answer. Then in a desperate attempt to have the world open up to her she began pounding the door with her fist. "Come out, come out wherever you are!"

she shouted maniacally.

If Ida Blue hadn't been so preoccupied she might have heard the slamming of a car door. If she had turned around, she would have seen the man jogging toward her across the stone path, an oversize golf umbrella protecting him from the downpour. Just as timing is everything in all things dangerous, whether tightrope walking or bullfighting, she might have turned before he reached the wooden stairs. Before he startled her half to death by shouting "Hello!" over the thudding rain.

The suddenness of his greeting pulled her off balance. Her surprise was so violent, she spun around faster than she needed or expected to. Before she knew it, her body had tilted off center, and she tried to put her foot down to catch herself. It skated off the slippery painted porch boards so she attempted to steady herself with her other leg, but that one too flew out beneath her, as if her legs weren't hers at all. They just skated off the wet surface and propelled her sideways over the porch railing. Before she knew it she was falling through the air, arms outstretched to protect her face from the leafy azaleas. She fell downward toward the earth while her legs flew skyward.

"Ma'am?!"

Stuck upside down in the shrub, Ida Blue felt her sundress bunched somewhere by her upper thighs. The rain pelted the stairs like a troupe of tiny tap dancers.

"Ma'am?" he repeated. "Are you all right?" It was not the aged voice she'd heard on the phone. This wasn't Fred Wolfe.

With the umbrella as cover, the man stepped off the stairs and over to her. His work boots were smeared with dirt, his laces loosely tied in a double knot. If she'd been a smaller woman, she might have been able to wriggle free, to jump up out of the bush like a jack-in-the-box springing up into the world, but the weight of her body held her in place. "Help" was all she could think to say.

"Give me your hand." And so she pushed her fists through the branches, felt the rounded leaves scratch the skin along her plump forearms. The man's feet were set firmly, tug-of-war style, left foot settled in front of right. "On three," he instructed. "One . . . two —" And then he pulled. She fell out of the bush sideways and onto the grass. Mud seeped into her dress and a flip-flop disappeared somewhere in the shrubbery. It took her a moment to find her way to a standing position and under his umbrella.

"Are you okay?" Concern crowded his voice.

She looked up at the man, about her age and with bushy red hair. "I guess."

He took her elbow and led her out of the rain and up to the covered porch. It looked as if the storm would stop as suddenly as it had started. "That was quite a fall," he said, then plucked out a knot of leaves from her hair.

He reminded her of the Gumby doll she'd had as a child, a plastic figure with a square head and long, gangly arms. The word SECURITY was embroidered on the right chest of his green uniform, and underneath that a metal tag read RUSTY.

"Mr. Wolfe isn't home yet, is he?"

She shook her head. "Don't think so."

"He just reported some missing dogs."

She nodded, thinking of his Great Dane.

He looked serious. "Have you seen them?"

"Not lately." She'd seen the ghostly woman, of course.

"Well, he seemed pretty worried. Pretty insistent. Thought I'd swing by to take a look."

"Maybe I can help."

He raised an eyebrow.

"I'm a pet psychic." She said it so quickly and confidently it surprised her. She'd never said it to someone in person. Someone who wasn't on a telephone. She said it like it was something that was an intrinsic part of her, the same way she would have said she was farsighted or left-handed. "I'm a pet psychic," she repeated. "My name is Ida Blue."

He looked at her quizzically, his eyes narrowing, and scanned her muddy dress. "Okay. So you're a pet psychic, but what are you *doing* here?"

"Just checking in. He's my neighbor, and elderly." It wasn't a lie.

"That's sure kind of you. But why were you pounding on his door and pressing your face into his window?"

I was getting full, she thought. Maybe under different circumstances she would have felt guilty snooping around Fred's house, as if she'd been caught stealing Funyuns from the supermarket, but she just felt satisfied. "I was *concerned.*"

"Well, you should go on home and get yourself cleaned up," he suggested, as if she had anywhere else more important to go. "This storm has probably caused some damage, so I'll need to get back to my rounds." Rusty turned, furled umbrella in his left hand, and ambled down the stairs. Before he got to his hybrid patrol car, he turned. "Sure was nice to meet you, Miss Ida."

The rain had stopped.

Ida Blue was so focused on her feeling of fullness she barely remembered driving the short distance home. All she knew was satiety, as if she had been the only one at an all-you-can-eat buffet. So when she pulled into her driveway she was disappointed to see that in her haste to drive to Fred Wolfe's house she'd forgotten to close the garage door. But she'd been so distracted, hell-bent on tapping the connection, she wasn't surprised.

After parking, she got out of the car and placed her feet on the cement. Her striped dress was now stained brown and green, but she didn't care, because she felt something. An instinct. A feeling that she was not alone anymore. *This is what intuition is,* she thought. An incredible gut sense of knowing something without seeing it. Like the blind faith that pressing a gas pedal will move a car forward or that a parachute will open in a free fall.

And that's when she saw them. Behind an old pile of tag sale towels and comforters lay two dogs. A small dog with brindle-colored damp fur settled against the broad

chest of a Great Dane. Both were sound
asleep.

CHAPTER 22

By the time Fred and Catherine walked back to the parking lot, the steady downpour had become water dripping from an old faucet.

The first thing Fred did when he unlocked his car was reach inside to find his phone in the center console. When Danielle had last visited, she'd programmed in the numbers she thought he'd need now that he was alone. Savannah Fire and Rescue. State Police. Seven Oaks Security. At the time he thought she was being melodramatic, but at the moment he felt grateful.

He didn't think calling security would bring the dogs home, but the guards were the eyes and ears of the community. So he explained to the gum-snapping woman who answered the phone that the long-standing dog park regulation of unlocking the back gate only for mowing had been breached. That two dogs had escaped and were in danger, roaming the wilds of Seven Oaks. The woman took his information with no more sense of alarm than if he'd reported a bottle of spilled milk in aisle six.

Truth be told, as he stood in the parking lot with Catherine beside him, he tried to sound a little more dramatic than he felt. "A Boston terrier and a Great Dane! There's no telling what harm they could get into!" He really wasn't worried, but his companion was clearly upset, as she kept bringing her hands to her face, resting her slender fingers in the dip of her temple. He wanted to give her confidence in him and in the process of trusting a stranger.

When he clicked the phone off he tried to console Catherine, exaggerating his conversation: "They said they'll do everything in their power to find them."

"Well, we should do something, too." She furrowed her brow. "Would you drive? Then I can keep my eyes peeled."

Fred opened his passenger door, and she climbed in. After starting the engine, he cleared the wet windshield with the wipers on low. The *thwap-thwap-thwap* reminded him of Sequoia's wagging tail. He pulled out onto the main road while Catherine rolled down her window to get a better view of the street and the dense forest that lined the sidewalks.

"Karma is a follower," Catherine said abruptly, apropos of nothing. "He's not the sort of dog that takes off. I'm sure he's just following Sequoia. Just along for the ride." She laughed nervously. "But the thing is, he won't know how to get home. We haven't even been here that long. I kept promising him we'd go on these long walks and all I've done for him in the past three months is throw that stupid ball in the backyard."

Fred remained silent, focusing on the road. After all, what could he offer but platitudes? He'd been given a lifetime of them when Lissa died, and they hadn't helped. *I know exactly how you feel* and *Everything happens for a reason.*

"Where would they have gone?" Catherine said, more to herself than to him. "How will they survive?"

She was acting as if it would be days or weeks until the dogs were found, but Fred figured it would just be an hour or two. Sequoia had more common sense than most people he knew. She seemed to understand the rules of time and the nuances of human character. She knew enough to avoid a snake and steer clear of an alligator. She never walked in the road and wouldn't get near the lagoon. Fred thought she was probably enjoying the expedition with her new terrier friend, even if the walk home would be a little much for her old legs. "Don't worry. Sequoia will know how to get back to the house," he said confidently. "We live nearby, on Jolly Badger."

Catherine shook her head and laughed.

"What's so funny?" He was glad she was lightening a bit, distracted at least for a moment from her lost dog.

"Just thinking of street names. I used to tell Ralph I felt like I always lived on Wit's End or Wild Goose Chase or Backseat Drive."

He and Lissa had done the same thing years ago. *We joked we had a place on Lover's Lane,* he thought of saying, but saw Catherine's hands clenched in her lap.

"Lately it's been more like Divorce Court," Catherine added wistfully. "Sorry."

"About what?"

"TMI." She waited but he didn't say anything. "Too much information," she added.

He felt a little sorry for her. Over the years he'd seen his share of friends, some married fifty years, go through troubling times and fall in and out of love. He and Lissa had had their challenges, especially early on, but

223

he was glad they never reached a breaking point.

I said I was sorry. I'm trying to make things right, Fred.

He heard Lissa but ignored her this time.

From Seven Oaks Way he took a left onto Pelican Retreat. It was the road the dogs would have come out onto if they'd followed the trail directly from the park. Fred drove slowly, not wanting to miss the wisp of a tail, and realized he hadn't driven someone in his car for months, at least since Lissa had died. When his daughter came and they'd visited hospice, she always insisted on taking the wheel, confident now that he was in his midseventies he might crash into a double-parked UPS truck at any moment or suddenly confuse a red traffic signal for a green one.

"Is that too much for you?" He put his hand out in front of Catherine to feel the air blowing through the vents. Even though the window was down, he needed the circulation to prevent the windows from fogging in the damp afternoon.

"No, no. It's fine," she said. Then, "You are a very kind man."

When she turned back to her sentry at the window, Fred unconsciously looked at her well-proportioned legs and thighs. He wondered if she might have been a runner at one point or perhaps just liked to dance.

Fred pressed the knob to the radio and a Dean Martin song came on, one he used to sing in his car when he was driving to work. He knew it by heart: *With soft words, I whispered your name . . . But that was as close as I came.*

Fred wondered if Catherine knew the song. Perhaps she'd danced to it in high school with an older beau. How old was she? In her early sixties? He was probably at least ten years her senior. He imagined a young version of himself, holding her tightly and swaying back and forth to the music. "Sequoia has always been spooked by thunder . . ." Fred's voice trailed off as he forgot the point he was making. It had something to do with finding them, but instead he thought of how during storms Sequoia would jump up on their king-size bed and cower between Lissa and him, burying her large square head under her paws and her paws under the pillow.

Catherine filled the empty space of their conversation. "At least my husband will be happy. He never liked Karma anyway."

Fred was going to make a joke. He never met anyone who didn't like dogs or Dean Martin songs or old movies, but she spoke again before he could.

"I mean it's not like I'm one of those crazy women who treat their dog like their child but . . ." And then she started to cry.

In all the years of their marriage, Fred remembered Lissa breaking down only a handful of times. When she had miscarried shortly after their wedding. When Danielle had walked down the aisle and then, three years later and shortly after Tommy's birth, when their daughter's husband had a change of heart and requested a divorce. Fred hadn't known what to do then, and he didn't know what to do now. Hoping to comfort Catherine, Fred patted her left knee. Perhaps if he'd taken a moment to consider the gesture he might have stopped, but as he touched her skin, he felt heat inside him, the awakening of a long-silent longing.

Since he usually kept a spare tissue packet in the driver's side door he reached for it, his eyes still on the road, but all he found was a hammer-like tool to cut a seat belt and smash a window if he were submerged in water. He held the LifeGuard aloft. "What do you think? My daughter gave it to me for my seventy-third birthday. I asked for a book on the Civil War but she got me this." What Danielle had said was: *You never know when you might careen off that bridge and into the water.* "On the brighter side, I might have a spare handkerchief in that jacket of mine."

Catherine put her hands into the jacket and felt around until she pulled out a business card. She squinted at the small lettering. "You know Audrey Cunningham?"

Fred looked at the embossed green of the Seven Oaks logo and the postage-size photo of a blond woman. "Pardon?"

She read the card aloud. "Audrey Cunningham. Realtor. One phone call does it all."

He thought for a moment. "I think I may have met her once or twice at the dog park over the years, but when news of a widower gets around, Realtors come a-calling. As if it's a crime for an old man to live alone in a three-bedroom house."

"Audrey Cunningham," Catherine repeated, a hardness in her voice.

"I found it in my mailbox. You know, your wife of fifty years dies and everyone has ideas for you." He was thinking of Danielle: *Why don't you just move closer to us? Have you considered assisted living? Why don't I just take the silverware now? It's not like you'll be having a lot of dinner parties.*

Catherine nodded. "It's hard to move.

227

Hard to change."

Fred checked the rearview mirror but there was no one behind them, and he realized they hadn't passed another car since they'd left the dog park. The storm had pushed everyone inside. If he hadn't known better, he might have imagined they were alone on the island.

Fred was glad Catherine had stopped crying, had somehow pulled herself together. He appreciated her sensitivity but didn't want her to worry. He knew it would work out. He could feel it. And he didn't want her to be sad, because he was enjoying the feeling that he and Catherine were on a road trip somewhere. A man and woman in a car with a common quest. Like Albert Finney and Audrey Hepburn in a white roadster in *Two for the Road.* Maybe the dogs just needed some time to explore too, an excuse for an adventure.

Fred thought of the many real estate agents' cards and sympathy notes that had flooded his mailbox in the six months since Lissa's death. "Everyone talks about downsizing but it always makes me think of that old science fiction movie."

Catherine shook her head.

"You know the one." He said it like they'd watched it together years ago. Like they used to share buttered popcorn at Saturday matinees. Like Catherine had always been a part of his life. "With Raquel Welch in the submarine."

"The Fantastic Voyage?"

"Exactly. Like when we all reach sixty and it's time to *downsize* we should all be zapped with a ray gun."

She laughed, and the sound filled the car with life.

"Let's stop," she said suddenly. "We must have circled back to near where we began, no?"

He pulled the car onto a grassy patch and shut off the engine. The storm was over and Fred saw breaks in the clouds. Catherine got out, folded the business card in half, and put it back in the pocket of his windbreaker. She moved to the shoulder's edge. "Karma! Sequoia!" Catherine shouted, cupping her hands to her mouth.

Fred didn't think the odds were good that the dogs would just emerge from the trail, magically appearing like two rabbits from a hat, but he got out too, if only to be helpful. If only for the sake of his new friend. He shouted into the air, into the universe, "Sequoia!" and then "Karma!" but saw no movement. For a moment they stood side by side and stared into the woods.

Once they returned to the car he opened the trunk and grabbed a fresh beach towel that he kept in the back for just this reason, the very real possibility of a sudden spring shower. "Here you go."

Catherine pulled out the elastic in her ponytail, took the towel, and bent down, her head hanging low, her hair still damp from the rain. She rubbed the towel slowly along the pale nape of her neck and through her wet hair. When she flipped back up, Fred imagined they might have been on a European vacation together and she'd just emerged from a dip in the Aegean.

He stepped toward her to grab the wet towel but took her hand as he did.

He had meant to comfort her but suddenly felt hungry, as if he hadn't eaten in months. Without conscious thought he gently pulled her and the wet towel toward him. She looked up and smiled, then started to say something. Fred thought perhaps she was going to ask a question or suggest an alternate route or say it was time to go, so he didn't wait. He leaned over to her. His lips hovered in front of hers for just a moment to give her time to pull away and stop a foolish old man. But she just blinked, a curious expression appearing on her face. She looked at his eyes, then at his lips. He thought he'd detect fear or perhaps embarrassment for him, but what he saw was longing.

The kiss was brief. Not lingering or dramatic. Not the type of kiss that might happen to a time traveler in *The Fantastic Voyage*. It was the soft kiss of two high school students. It was a kiss given on a front porch after a prom date. It was a kiss that suggested a fresh start in the world. He stepped back and took a deep breath. What had he done?

Reluctantly, he opened the door for her and she climbed in, neither of them saying a word. As he walked around the back of the car he noticed that brilliant shafts of sunlight had broken through the clouds, bathing the wet street in bright starbursts. Once settled in the driver's seat he felt the change of atmospheric pressure, as if mission control had pumped pure oxygen into the car while they'd been standing outside. They remained silent for almost a minute. Each facing forward. Fred put his hands on the steering wheel, gripping it tightly.

"So?" he asked. "Shall we check back at the dog park? Do you want me to drop you at your car?"

"No," she said quickly. "Let's just keep driving."

CHAPTER 23

Ida Blue stood in her garage and looked down at the sleeping dogs. She'd watched enough Animal Planet to know the smaller one was either a French bulldog or a Boston terrier. The smushed-in nose and small head reminded her of a monkey, while the compact body resembled a baby hedgehog. The animal didn't look threatening, just tired, with its paws curled under its head, and its breath like that of an asthmatic who has forgotten his inhaler. Though she didn't know much about the breed, or dogs in general if she was being completely honest, this one didn't interest her. It was the Great Dane that caught her attention.

There was no doubting it — the huge black-and-white form lying on the old comforters was the same dog that belonged to her neighbor, Fred Wolfe, and the mysterious old woman who had hovered outside her window. This animal, with its mustached smear of saliva, was her connection to another dimension.

Ida Blue stepped slowly toward the pair so as not to startle them, but neither stirred. She sat down beside the dogs on a pile of towels that had fallen from sagging plastic shelves. She'd meant to clean the garage for years, ever since she'd moved into the patio home, but had never found the time. Never *made* the time. Maybe this was what she needed to kick-start the organized life that Dr. Phil said would bring happiness and success. Maybe this was magic working in her general direction. Two dogs don't appear out of a storm coincidentally. Don't arrive in a stranger's garage without a little push from fate.

She grabbed a towel and blotted her hair and dress, both still damp from her unfortunate swan dive into Fred Wolfe's azaleas. She was sorry she'd worn the rather chic outfit to find Fred in the first place and felt mortified that she'd ended up upside down in a bush with a security guard asking her a hundred questions. She could just imagine the conversation going on back at the gatehouse.

If the Dog Whisperer were here, he'd tell her to be the pack leader, to offer the sleeping creatures water and food. So she went up the back stairs from her garage to her kitchen freezer. A few years ago, she'd bought a package of deluxe pigs in a blanket. At the time, she had a vision of hosting a few new friends at a neighborhood cocktail party, offering appetizers stuck with frilled toothpicks and drinks with unfurled paper umbrellas. Of course, no party or friends ever materialized, so now she plopped some frozen mini hot dogs on a paper plate, zapped them in the microwave, and brought them along with a large Tupperware bowl of water back to the dogs.

When she lifted the water bowl to them they both opened their eyes and stared at her as if they'd been drinking all afternoon. Then she did the same with a hot dog. Again neither moved, so Ida Blue brought the first mini dog to her mouth and made a dramatic show of how delicious it was. "Mmmm," she said, chewing it slowly, really tasting the meaty innards and letting juice squirt over her tongue. She realized she never took the time to chew her food, so she made a promise to do that from now on. "They're magically delicious!" She tore the next pig in two and offered each dog a half. Almost simultaneously they opened their mouths and she dropped the meat inside as if feeding trained seals.

The Great Dane came to life and licked her hand, the large pink tongue moving rhythmically up and down her skin. Ida Blue felt her heart swell. She'd heard that a dog could smell a drop of blood in a swimming pool and wondered if Sequoia could tell that Ida Blue had just returned from her owner's house, could smell Fred somewhere on her clothes or sense she'd been upside down in the same bushes Sequoia had probably peed in since she was a puppy. Ida Blue considered keeping the dogs. Not as hostages — she wasn't some sort of crazed dognapper — but as quietly borrowed confidants. She could give them a good home and a lot of attention. She could spend every day with them curled on her couch, and together they could all watch *Animal Cops* or *Pit Bulls and Parolees*.

She sat with the thought for several minutes, but then considered the old man. Fred Wolfe. He must be very lonely without his dog, and, honestly, she couldn't afford the extra dog food and treats and toys and whatever else dogs needed for a happy life. So she reached her hand out to the smaller dog, lightly patted his head, and touched his collar. Engraved on a silvery bone-shaped tag was KARMA and a telephone number.

"Good Karma," Ida Blue whispered. She felt an invisible connection to whoever owned this dog.

So ignoring the part of herself that wanted to keep them, she used the pigs in a blanket as bait and led the exhausted dogs up the stairs and to her living room. Once there, she stroked the wide back of the Great Dane. She felt stronger, not even realizing she'd been weak, like the last time she recovered from the flu, when her body ached for weeks but she barely knew it until she started to feel better. She didn't see the ghostly woman but had a general feeling she wasn't alone anymore.

CHAPTER 24

Fred and Catherine spent a few hours driving through the neighborhoods of Seven Oaks, over cross streets, by the community softball field, down dead-end roads near the outlet to the nature trail. As they passed certain houses, Fred told Catherine stories of people who had once lived there. Anecdotes about couples, now mostly gone, who had populated their community during its development. Catherine understood that he was trying to distract her from her distress about the missing dogs. Though she found it hard to stay focused, she appreciated his effort.

She considered alerting Ralph to what had happened. At one time in their marriage he would have dropped everything to help her, but already she knew what he'd say: *You're overreacting. You worry too much. That dog can take care of himself.* If Karma still hadn't turned up by breakfast, Ralph *might* offer to rearrange a tee time to help look. She had a vague recollection that he had a poker game anyway, so she let him fade from her consciousness.

By the time they arrived back at the dog park it was after eight o'clock. The parking lot was empty except for her car. Just where she had left it almost five hours earlier. As if nothing at all had happened and the world were exactly the same. Inky puddles reflected the light from a single weak street-lamp.

Fred pulled in next to Catherine's car and they sat quietly for a few minutes, both staring straight ahead. Then she asked, "What next?"

"I'll keep checking with security and let you know as soon as I hear anything."

She nodded slowly, exhausted from the long evening. She pulled her fingertips along her lower lashes, imagining that the little mascara she wore had run down her face with her tears. For the first time she felt self-conscious. She hadn't thought ahead to the end of the evening, to saying good-bye. "Fred" — she said his name out loud, unsure if she'd spoken it before — "I don't know what I would have done without you." She was going to ask if he felt it too — the sense that they'd known each other longer

238

than a few hours. The feeling they'd met somewhere before, not just at the Village Café when Sequoia had licked her face, but during a trip somewhere. Maybe they'd struck up an easy conversation years ago when Catherine had taken a train to Manhattan to meet Ralph for a client dinner. Perhaps she'd been spinning under a crush of Fifth Avenue business suits and had asked Fred, a kind-looking stranger, the way to a steak house. Instead she said, "But you promise they'll be okay?"

She didn't know why an acquaintance's assurance would calm her, but she was relieved when he answered, "I promise."

He turned to her, and for a moment she thought he might take her hand. He didn't. Perhaps she'd made up the intensity of the kiss they'd shared. Mistook it for something else. For a concerned man attempting to comfort a not-quite-hysterical woman.

"Listen," he offered. "I know things can and do go wrong, but you never know. This might have happened for a reason." Just as he said that, the overhead light in the parking lot brightened as if someone had eased up a dimmer switch.

"Yes." Then she imagined Karma. Wet fur. Wet nose. They both watched the glow intensify as if watching a sunrise.

"I've got your contact info" — he patted a slip of paper in his shirt's front pocket where he'd written her telephone number, street address, even her email — "so I'll call you when I hear something." He spoke confidently, as if he made a living out of making promises that he kept. She'd never met a man like that.

"I believe you . . ." Her voice trailed off.

"But are you okay to drive, Catherine?" His tone suggested they'd been sipping champagne at a wedding reception all night.

"I'm not usually like this."

"Like what?"

"Ridiculous. I mean, do you think I'm being ridiculous?"

"Not at all."

"Okay, needy. Ridiculously needy."

"I don't think you are ridiculous and I certainly don't think you are needy." Fred's soothing voice calmed her. A man who said what he meant and meant what he said. Karma was out in the island darkness but not alone. He was with Sequoia. A dog literally four times his own size. A dog who knew the area, like a tour guide, who could escort him to safety. "In fact, you are a wonderfully concerned mother to Karma." He touched her hand.

"Am I too much for you?" The question

emerged from her mouth before it had even formed in her consciousness.

He shook his head and laughed.

Catherine considered moving toward him and letting the night bring them together. She wanted to be stroked, his hand to caress her neck and back, the way she petted Karma. She wanted to be curled in his lap and reassured. She *was* being ridiculous.

"All right then," Fred said, interrupting her thoughts. "Drive safely."

Catherine got out of Fred's car, shut the door, and went to her own vehicle. When she buckled in she saw an old grocery list: broccoli, ham, rice, butter. It felt like years ago that she'd written it. As if she'd been a different person. Before something deep inside her, like vast tectonic plates, had shifted inches.

After pulling away she drove around the Palmetto Pines neighborhood again. She followed the same route that she and Fred had. Her headlights remained on high so she could see a motion in the bushes, anything that would tell her the dogs were all right. And as she peered into the darkness, she considered her exchange with Seven Oaks security as if the dogs had been missing children:

Question: Where was the last place you saw them?

Answer: By the back gate in the dog park.

Question: What were they wearing?

Answer: Sequoia had a hand-stitched needlepoint collar. Karma wore one with blue polka dots.

Question: Did they carry ID?

Answer: Yes, metal tags with names and numbers.

Question: Was there anyone else present when they went missing?

And then Catherine recalled the red-headed woman by the distant edge of the park. By the open gate. Catherine had seen her only briefly but remembered her golf outfit. If Catherine could find her, maybe they could locate the dogs. She'd been too disordered to think of this earlier. Everything had seemed splintered in her mind, like chipped china from an old wedding registry that she'd never be able to put back together.

CHAPTER 25

Amity had hoped to arrive at the house earlier in the day so that she might relax a bit, not feel rushed, but she'd been called in to substitute at a morning study hall, and the afternoon storm had taken her by surprise. Then the rain had stopped as suddenly as it had started. Significantly, she thought, it lasted about the length of a curtain call in a dramatic play. Despite the urgent tweets she'd seen from Chatham County (*Severe T'storm warning til 6PM, Flooding @ Victory, #TurnAroundDontDrown*), the drive from Tattnall had been uneventful, with only a few detours to avoid the orange-and-white-striped sawhorses set in truck-size puddles.

After sliding under the Seven Oaks security gate as effortlessly as a salmon being swept downstream, she drove directly to the Sunset Point lot. Empty, of course. After parking, Amity exited her car and adjusted her fanny pack. She carried her dog leash out of habit, even though Buddy, her invisible dog, remained in his invisible doghouse behind his invisible fence. As she looked out to the gray marsh, she took a moment to appreciate the musky smells the rains had unearthed. The air itself held weight. For a moment she imagined herself scuba diving with a fogged face mask and two air tanks pressing on her shoulders, encouraging her to go deeper. She felt sluggish, as if she'd then ascended from the sea too quickly, forgetting the rules of decompression.

As she followed the street to the driveway she felt a rush of excitement, a nice contrast to the flatness that had overwhelmed her of late. Since the owner was away and the house wasn't for sale, she knew there was only a slim chance of being discovered by a nosy neighbor or confused housekeeper. On reaching the front walk she continued around the garage toward a side fence. Just as it had been the previous month, the gate was unlocked. And why wouldn't it be? This was a safe community.

After taking the few steps up to the deck and back door, she crouched down, reached into her fanny pack, and pulled out a tension wrench, a flathead screwdriver, a rake pick, and a pair of needle-nose pliers. From the blue doggie waste bag she grabbed a pair of latex gloves out of habit. She set the leash down, settled on one knee, closed her eyes, and took a breath. While placing the wrench in the keyhole, she applied the pick. The first order of business was torque. She raked the pick along the cylinders, caressing them, imagining she were tuning a grand piano. The point was to apply steady pressure — strong enough to release the chamber, light enough not to jam the sensitive teeth. By holding steady with her arm but using the tips of her fingers to manipulate the tool, she could feel the lock moving, opening up to her.

This is what it must feel like to be free, she thought.

Once inside the house, Amity noticed the rococo grand piano in one corner and the grandfather's clock in the other. She took a few minutes to admire the impressive collection of early Hudson River School paintings lining the wall. The furnishings, oiled landscapes, and soft pillows could have been props from her own home if she and her husband had stayed married and continued to build a life, something that might last. In the kitchen, she saw what had caught her eye on her previous visit: *OFF TO NAN-TUCKET!* printed in indelible marker across a year-at-a-glance wall calendar. It was clear the owner vacated the premises before the Savannah heat crept around door edges and window casings.

A sad potted plant sat on a porcelain dish on a windowsill. She guessed it was a verbena or violet but really had no idea. Its dull purple leaves lay in rotting clumps, and a single bare stalk reached toward nothing. In the haste of spring travel the owner had forgotten it. Or perhaps abandoned it on purpose to see if it would be strong enough to make it alone. So Amity strode directly to the wet bar and retrieved a large silver wine goblet. She filled it with water and placed the plant on the living room coffee table. Taking great care, she poured half the water into the dry soil, hoping to save it at least temporarily.

Once in the master bedroom she noted the wedding-ring quilt and wide-screen TV. In the master bath she smelled a vague swish of lavender and the sea. She imagined the woman who lived here drinking cocktails by the craggy Nantucket shore and perhaps enjoying a soft-shelled lobster for dinner. It was early in the season, but shedders — sweeter lobsters that had abandoned their hard shells — weren't unheard of this time of year. A white claw-foot tub rested like a polar bear in the corner.

She turned on both faucets until the milky streams ran clear. The rubber stopper fit snugly into the drain, and the tub took several minutes to fill. After pouring in bath salts, she stood in the middle of the room, then pulled her T-shirt over her head, untied her sweatpants, unhooked her bra, and stepped out of her panties. She lowered herself into the water.

Once when they were vacationing in Maine, her husband had asked her, "You ever feel like you're the last lobster in the tank and the waiter is rolling up his sleeve?" She settled into the warmth and let her mind go.

It had been exactly a year — the first week in May — since she and Alex had first moved into the Tattnall apartment. They had just relocated from Cleveland and she'd been outside adjusting an American flag when a neighbor appeared. With a strong Southern twang, the woman introduced herself and welcomed Amity to the neighborhood. She suggested dinner once Amity and her husband got settled. They even exchanged phone numbers. Her real estate agent had said it was a friendly street, had explained Savannah was called the "Hostess

City" for its hospitality. So several hours later when the phone rang, Amity imagined it was her neighbor calling to follow up.

"Hello?"

The woman's voice on the phone was strong and clear, as if she were standing next to her in their bedroom. "Is this Amity?"

"Yes." Within moments she was already imagining the dinner with her neighbor and trying to remember where she'd put her datebook. How wonderful that she'd called so promptly. Maybe they could grab a drink first at the Crystal Beer Parlor. If they made a date for the following weekend, she'd have time to get a pedicure.

"It's about Alex."

Amity heard no drawl. No beating around the bush. This was not the woman from down the street.

Her thoughts immediately went to an accident. A catastrophe. A crash. The span of their ten-year marriage retreated to a few seconds. "My husband?" In case there'd been some mistake she spoke his name: "Alex Higginson?"

"Yes. Alex."

"Who is this?" One moment became two became three became ten. The silence hung between them. An empty laundry line.

"What happened?"

Amity imagined a dented rental car. A bruised Hertz bumper lying on the shoulder of a highway. He'd been traveling for business and could be easily distracted. And he liked speed. He'd even taken a few helicopter lessons, but he could never get the hang of the thrust. There was such a shocking fragility to life; he might have been hit point-blank by a golf ball during one of his outings. They'd known a man who'd been struck in his temple on a par five. He was dead before he hit the tee box. But words barely formed in her mouth.

"Is Alex all right? Is he hurt?"

"We didn't plan it like this. I need you to know that."

Amity sat down on one of the extra-large moving boxes. She'd bought six dozen cardboard containers to relocate books and knickknacks and photos, but even that had not been enough to fit in all the props of their lives.

"Pardon?" She planned to sort the books by genre, not size. Mystery. Romance. Nonfiction. Travel. A new house in a new state warranted a new arrangement. After all their work and planning, they deserved an organized library.

"He didn't want to hurt you."

She liked novels with happy endings. Boy meets girl. Boy marries girl. Boy and girl can't have a family but they have each other.

"We know it's not an ideal time."

Amity noticed the caller kept saying *we*, as if she and Alex had been together for years, a vaudeville team that performed across the country.

"He didn't ask me to call. But I wanted to do the right thing. Before you got settled."

Amity tried to picture the woman. To imagine a face. But she couldn't pull anything into focus. She just thought of an empty call center with a telemarketer sitting with a script before her.

"We feel it's best for everyone. Considering."

"Considering?"

"We're sorry."

"Considering?"

And then, "There's a child."

She remained quiet.

"A son. Our son."

She thought of her doctor visits. Her hostile uterus. His slow swimmers. She might have referenced medical terms if she could remember them. That would certainly clarify the situation, and the misunderstanding could be dropped. She heard the faint chime of music, a tinkling glockenspiel in the background. "I appreciate the phone call, but you've got the wrong Alex Higginson."

But the music got louder and Amity recognized the tune. *Lullaby, and goodnight.* Brahms. As a boy, Alex had even had a wooden music box that played it. He said it was his favorite. *Dwing-dwing dong, dwing-dwing dong.* She could almost hear the lyrics: *May you sleep now and rest / May your slumber be blessed.* Finally Amity heard crying. That's what she heard, crying. A baby's at first, and then her own.

Startled by her vivid memory, Amity sat up. The bathwater had grown cold. It was time to act.

She emerged from the polar bear tub, wrapped herself in a terry cloth towel, and moved to the master bedroom closet. To one side, golf outfits were sorted by color: aquamarine, fuchsia, mint. Scarves and leather belts dangled in the middle. To the right hung an impressive selection of long dresses. Surprising even herself, she chose a red silk gown with brocade running along one side. A gown her future self might have worn to the Telfair Ball had she and Alex stayed married and in Savannah. She stepped into it and pulled up the side zipper, though it was several sizes too large.

It's showtime, she thought.

She sat at an antique vanity table and looked into the beveled mirror. Her puffy eyes and mottled skin surprised her. In the drawers before her she found tools to pluck and tease. She found combs and barrettes and hairnets. She pulled plum lipstick across her lips and black mascara along her eyelashes. She applied buttery eyeshadow and twirled her long, damp hair into a loose bun, clipping it to the nape of her neck. The foundation she discovered was lighter than she would have chosen, but she'd been out creeping so often her skin had become bobcat brown. After taking another good long look at herself, she retreated to the living room. Ceramic coasters from voyages — on the *Rotterdam,* the *Volendam,* the *Zuiderdam* — sat on the coffee table and reminded her of her honeymoon. She and Alex had taken a cruise from Turkey to Italy. Before the ship sailed, they'd had a couples' bath at an Istanbul spa, where bubbles as big as babies floated around them.

Without wasting more time, she took the fanny pack off the table and unzipped it. She placed the needle-nose pliers and key pick on the wooden surface and pulled out four burnt-orange bottles. Hydrocodone.

Xanax. Valium. Ambien. They had all been prescribed and she was just following the labels' instructions. *Take as needed.* She emptied a fistful of pills into her palm then took the goblet, filled with enough water to do the trick.

As she raised her glass in a toast to the dying potted plant before her, she stopped to listen. After a moment she heard it again, the plaintive bleat from the cell phone in her fanny pack, as if someone, somewhere, needed her.

CHAPTER 26

After parking in her garage, Catherine scrambled out of her car and took the steps to the mudroom two at a time. It was just before nine o'clock.

"Ralph?" she called. Then louder, "Karma?!" Maybe her dog had somehow found his way home. Maybe he and Ralph were watching the Golf Channel upstairs, Karma's wet nose pressed into Ralph's thigh, while Ralph pushed a towel under the dog's head so as not to get slimed. Maybe some balding pro was telling them it was all about getting arc on a five iron. Maybe they'd been worried about where she'd been.

As she walked to the kitchen she spied small tufts of wet grass on the floor. Ralph had probably been on the golf course when the storm arrived, and in his rush to get inside, to close the windows or grab a beer, he had forgotten to remove his shoes. The sink dripped steadily, the water hanging momentarily, teardrops falling to the basin. When she turned the handle off she saw the remains of a half-eaten chicken breast, its puckered skin on a plate. Part of a bone sticking out of white meat. *Welcome home,* she thought.

And then on the counter she found the note. Slanted letters, rushed, as if he had a plane to catch: *Don't forget . . . poker night. Back late.* He'd done that more and more. Gone off for the evening to the wood-paneled clubhouse with his new friends. Men she'd never met, but names she'd heard over and over. John. Kevin. Richard. Paul.

Catherine pulled out the chair at the kitchen table and sat. For the first time in three months, since they'd packed up their things and left their friends and gotten Georgia driver's licenses, she felt completely alone. Karma, usually underfoot, wasn't nudging her with a tennis ball. And it occurred to her she hadn't made a network of new friends to rely on in a crisis. Whom could she call? Someone who signed her in at the gym? Audrey Cunningham? Martha, who was five hours away and probably in the middle of a date and shouting "Holy Toledo!"? Fred had already alerted security, and this really wasn't a matter for Savannah Fire and Rescue, so she called the only person she could think of.

The phone rang six times, then snapped off, not even going to voice mail. Perhaps it was a satellite issue. Catherine pressed the number again. It was answered on the seventh ring.

"Hello?"

"Amity?" There was such a long hesitation, for a moment Catherine thought the line might have gone dead again. Maybe the storm had knocked out a circuit. "Amity? Can you hear me?"

"Yes."

"It's Catherine." She considered going into a long apology. Explaining that she understood their creeping was a one-time deal, but there was really no one else Catherine could turn to. Instead of *I found you* she heard herself say, "I need you." She started to tell her about the incident. About how the dogs got out and Karma was gone and that she'd met a kind man at the dog park, but she heard something in Amity's silence. A long exhale of breath. "Did I reach you at a bad time?"

"I was just going to have" — Amity hesitated — "some quiet time."

Catherine recognized the fatigue in Amity's voice. Catherine had felt it herself lately. Her new friend had probably been at the gym all day, going round and round on an elliptical machine. "It's just I didn't have anyone else to call."

"I see."

"Karma's gone and Ralph's out and I'm just —" She heard her voice waver. It'd been such a long day. Her life had come down to this: a broken marriage and a lost dog. "I just don't know what to do." *Floundering.* The word came to her again.

Then Amity seemed to recover a bit. It was the firmness Catherine recognized from their first meeting: "Okay. Take it easy."

"There's no one else I can call. I can't seem to find my way out of this."

"I know the feeling."

"You do, don't you?"

"Yes."

Catherine heard nine deliberate peals from a grandfather's clock and finally Amity answered. "I'll be over in the morning."

After Fred returned home from his adventure with Catherine, he took a quick shower and changed into dry clothes. He couldn't stop thinking of their kiss, envisaging the outline of her body and her sweet vulnerability. He'd wanted to kiss her again when they reached the parking lot but hadn't had the nerve. And she departed quickly, perhaps embarrassed by his actions. Maybe just eager to get back home to her husband, who would promise their dog was safe, who could give her the reassurance that he could not.

He felt as if he'd been away from home for a year or more, like Odysseus on a ten-year voyage. But it had really only been six hours since he had arrived at the dog park at his usual three o'clock slot. He might have been on an around-the-world voyage, passing through the international date line, the imaginary space that separates one day from another. He thought of how far he'd traveled though nothing had changed, except that Sequoia wasn't with him and that everything had shifted in his heart.

Then the phone rang. It was his neighbor, Ida Blue.

"I found your dog. And a smaller one. They're real tired."

"You have both of them?"

"Sequoia and Karma. Says so right on their collars. They just sorta fell right into my lap, you could say." She hesitated. "But I can watch 'em for a spell if you're busy."

Without delay he jumped into his car feeling invigorated, like he'd just emerged from a brisk ocean swim. He hadn't been so worried for Sequoia coming home, but his concern was for Karma and Catherine. After he parked the car he approached the front steps to Ida Blue's home and was a little surprised by the lack of maintenance. Piles of rotting pine straw and overgrown bushes crowded the front walk, and rain had pooled in the broken concrete driveway. He carried a canvas bag and large dog bed and just as he was going to press the bell with his elbow, Ida Blue opened the door. He was taken aback by her linebacker neck and broad shoulders. She wore a tentlike flowery dress, the type of oversize muumuu you might see on a Polynesian island. "Ms. Childs?" he asked.

"Oh my, my, my!" She seemed skittish, like a friendly mastiff that had just been delivered a jolt of electricity. "This *is* a treat."

Fred put down the bag and they shook hands. Her grip matched those of men he had met in business, men with whom he'd negotiated contracts. It took her a while to release her hold.

The dogs came up behind Ida Blue, and he saw Sequoia's head hanging low, Karma just behind her. Fred leaned down to hug Sequoia but his dog let out a brief moan, something she did when her arthritis troubled her. She didn't seem excited to see him, but he understood she'd had a long day.

"So pleased to meet you," Fred said. "You have positively saved the day." She grinned and transferred her weight excitedly back and forth.

"Paw-sitively," she said.

"I'll take the little one right away. Karma's owner is beside herself with worry. But would you mind keeping Sequoia, my Great Dane, just for tonight and perhaps tomorrow morning?"

"Really?!" she practically yelled and held her hands at her chest as if he'd just presented her with an Academy Award.

He had thought this through. Of course he would like to take Sequoia home, but he knew her well enough to know that after giving her the pain pills the dog would just sleep straight through the night, and getting her back into the car, even with the ramp, would be too hard on her. "I'm sure her arthritis is bothering her. I'll take her out briefly now, give her a little food with her medication, then she'll just sleep for fifteen hours. Always does. You see, somehow these adventurers found their way to you all the way from the dog park."

Ida Blue kept nodding, her throat skin jiggling.

"Of course I'll pay you for the imposition." Ida Blue's eyes were so wide and unblinking, protruding out of a normal position, Fred thought for a moment his neighbor might have a thyroid condition. "If it's not okay I can take —"

"I run a doggie day care and dog-walking service!" she thundered, and he looked relieved.

Fred settled Karma into the seat beside him and set out toward Catherine's house. After a minute the seat sensor chimed, so he reached over and pulled the safety belt behind the dog and clicked the locking mechanism, as if strapping an invisible person into the car with them. Without wasting another moment, he drove right to Greenleaf Park and her front door.

Fred wondered if her husband might answer the door with a strong handshake and full head of hair. Fred should have felt guilty for kissing Catherine, but he didn't. The kiss had just *happened.* He decided he would decline if he were invited in for a drink, but it would be nice to catch a glimpse of Catherine and see her happiness at her dog's return.

When Catherine answered his knock she

saw him and Karma before her and in one motion grabbed the dog in her arms and they spun around in tight circles. After a few moments, without saying a word and still holding the dog, she flung one arm around Fred. He felt her face in his neck, her wet tears against his skin. "But Sequoia? Where's Sequoia?" he heard her whisper.

Suddenly he had an idea, a little plan to bring Catherine to him again. He looked up to the sky, silently apologized to whatever force had delivered their dogs safely to Ida Blue, then replied, "I don't know."

"You don't know?" Her voice cracked as she pulled back. "Sequoia wasn't with Karma?" She placed her fingertips from her free hand on his cheek. "I'll be at your house by eight a.m. and we won't stop until we find her."

CHAPTER 27

Ida Blue wasn't getting anywhere with the old dog. While she sat on her mattress on the floor, the Great Dane just stood in the center of her bedroom, staring, as if she didn't know what was expected. "Oh sweetheart, you are so, so very pretty," Ida Blue cooed, patting the space beside her. "Come here." Sequoia blinked a few times in response.

And then Ida Blue had an idea. She padded out to the kitchen, the head on her sock monkey slippers bobbing excitedly, and dumped the rest of the frozen mini hot dogs onto a paper plate. After microwaving them, she returned to the bedroom and gave one to Sequoia just for standing there. Just for coming into her life. A gift of good faith. The second one she placed on the floor, six inches in front of the animal. Then she put others at foot-long intervals, a trail to her mattress. She left the remaining hot dogs on the plate in the center of her comforter, then sprawled out next to the greasy meat and waited.

Maybe Ida Blue didn't really have psychic ability, didn't know what pets thought or what motivated them, but she wondered if she might have a talent for training. After Sequoia ate all the hot dogs, they settled together onto the queen-size mattress and, almost immediately, both fell into a deep sleep.

A few hours before dawn, Ida Blue drifted out of a dream, felt Sequoia's breath on her face, and realized they'd been sharing the same pillow. The Great Dane smelled like a truck driver who ate only bologna sandwiches. Perhaps she was meant to find a husband who enjoyed long-haul cuisine and drove an eighteen-wheeler. Starting with Sequoia's neck, she ran her hand along the dog's short fur and to her chest, feeling the comforting drub of her heart. She could almost imagine what it would be like to wake with someone in her bed. McSweeney the magician had been the only candidate, but they'd never made it farther than a nervous make out session on a rickety Ferris wheel at the Blue Ridge Fair. She wondered what had become of her old boyfriend. Probably he was married. Perhaps he had a few children and had bought an enchanting two-bedroom condo with wall-to-wall carpeting and a garbage disposal. Maybe he'd even followed his dreams, hitting the big time and performing in front of packed birthday parties. Sequoia's unexpected entry into her life reminded her of their courtship. Sudden. Sweet. Unlikely.

After several minutes of increasing restlessness, as if Sequoia were dreaming of starring in a Scooby-Doo movie, Ida Blue realized the pigs in a blanket might have been too rich for the dog. At least she had had enough sense to skip the spicy jalapeño mustard. It might take time, but she could adapt to Sequoia's habits and tastes. She could stock doggie brussels sprouts or carrots or whatever was healthiest. She would ask the old man for a list of preferred foods.

Although Ida didn't have much access to motherly role models — the few times she'd seen her own mother, she'd had a cigarette in one hand and a hunting rifle in the other — she'd learned something from TV. She'd watched Marge Simpson and Carol Brady tend to colicky babies, fix a teenager's kite, and calm Homer or Mike. She wondered if mothering were an innate skill or something that could be taught. Whether you could pretend to be a mother, like you could pretend to be a pet psychic.

Using the faint light from her clock, she rose from the mattress, found her sock monkey slippers, and stepped toward the kitchen. "C'mon. Let's get you outside." Rather miraculously, Sequoia followed. Together they padded through the kitchen and her slippers' shadows bobbed as she walked, almost as if the spirit of the old woman at Fred Wolfe's house were nodding with encouragement. She grabbed a penlight from a wicker basket on the counter and they exited the kitchen's sliding glass doors as she snapped on the outside light switch. Two of the four backyard bulbs had burned out, probably years before. A few large clouds left over from the storm crowded the sky, and there was just enough light to make it down the stairs and into her yard.

"Over there," Ida Blue said and pointed. And then, as if Sequoia had been listening to her for years, the dog retreated to the pine straw off the lawn. "Go potty," Ida Blue instructed with intensity, just as she'd seen on Animal Planet, staying assertive and calm and using a phrase that perhaps the dog would be familiar with.

Miraculously, it seemed, Sequoia crouched into position and did her business. This wasn't just make-believe. Ida Blue was being heard. Ida Blue asked Sequoia to relieve herself and she did. Voilà. With the penlight illuminating the darkness, Ida Blue examined the dog's dropping. *Meadow muffins,* her uncle called them.

Across the woody expanse behind her lot, she noticed the lights in her neighbor's house. Although she sometimes saw the faint bluish glow of Fred Wolfe's TV, she'd never seen it this bright. Every light in the house was on, lit up like a casino ship on the ocean. She wondered what he was up to, dropping off his dog to her, then hosting *American Idol*?

As Sequoia sniffed the overgrown grass, Ida Blue brushed off the layer of hard-coated seeds, berries, and spanish moss from the rusted table and plopped down onto the metal seat, still damp from the big storm. The moist, calm night made her sad that she'd never thought to sit outside to watch the stars. Sometimes just taking a phone call or changing a channel felt like a supreme effort, but sitting here with the Great Dane felt easy.

Sequoia came over to her side. "Sit," Ida Blue said. The dog sat. After a few minutes, and feeling confident that maybe this really *was* her calling, she said, "Down." The dog lowered to the ground.

She *did* have a gift. She could become a dog trainer or have a cooking show or both. Maybe do personal training while cooking pigs in a blanket. *Franks and Planks.* Perhaps Nigella or Sandra Lee was looking for a partner. She would call Judge Judy to start the copyright proceedings.

Sensing Ida Blue's excitement, Sequoia perked up and looked toward Fred's well-lit home. She stretched her neck forward and sniffed the night air. Ida Blue imagined the dog could smell Fred's back deck or even her owner from this distance, as if a nearly invisible fishing line connected the dog and the old man.

The following morning, Ida Blue and Sequoia woke at about the same time. They stayed in bed, blinking at each other. Looking into the dog's eyes reminded Ida Blue of the dark opening of a Magic 8 Ball and a childhood of asking questions of a multi-sided pyramid. *Will I ever leave Pine Straw, Georgia?* SIGNS POINT TO YES. *Is ventriloquism a gift?* IT IS DECIDEDLY SO. *Will I eventually find love?* REPLY HAZY, TRY AGAIN.

It was after ten but, remarkably, Ida Blue wasn't hungry. By now she usually would have had several jelly donuts and watched at least two morning talk shows to see what everyone was up to. On any other day she might enjoy the hilarious antics of *Live! With Kelly and Michael,* with cheery Kelly Ripa, her teeth sticking out into the audience like those of a badger who's just gone to the dentist, or the pleasantries on *Good Morning America,* with George Stephanopoulos looking like he'd taken a wrong turn in the TV studio and fallen into an insane asylum. Somehow, with Sequoia beside her, it didn't seem as pressing to learn the secrets of taking selfies or playing the ukulele.

Today she might even take Sequoia for a walk or teach her a few more tricks, like rolling over or carrying her purse or climbing a ladder. She imagined a future with the dog. If Fred didn't need dogsitting, she would talk to him about renting Sequoia on a daily or weekly basis. She could walk her along the marsh, or they could train for Savannah's Rock 'n' Roll Marathon with sponsorship from the Woof Gang Bakery. She and Sequoia could spend afternoons downtown taking loops around Forsyth Park or window-shopping along Bull Street. They could wander down cobblestoned River Street, with delighted tourists asking, "Is this *your* dog?" She could harness the

Great Dane to a giant green wagon for the annual Saint Patrick's Day Parade while she rode behind, waving to the crowd.

And so she closed her eyes, the dog's wet nose pressed against her collarbone and her hind legs across her calves. She knew this was just make-believe. That they had known each other only a little more than twelve hours, the life span of a mayfly. That Sequoia wasn't her baby or even her own dog. Yet it was more real than anything she had felt in a long time.

CHAPTER 28

He can no more carry a tune than fly to the moon, Catherine thought.

From her stool in the kitchen, she heard Ralph singing in the shower. Something from *La Bohème* or *Don Giovanni.* He must have the bathroom door open. Again. Even after years of her suggesting he keep it closed and remain anonymous until the world was ready to embrace his talent.

Catherine was already dressed in a casual flowered skirt and short-sleeved shirt, her white hair brushed into a low ponytail. Though she didn't normally wear makeup, she had dabbed bronzer on her cheeks, smoothed matte powder on her eyelids, and flicked mascara across her lashes. She'd gotten up early so as not to disturb Ralph and have to review yesterday's adventure with him. When he'd arrived home late the previous night she was pretending to be asleep, eyes closed, lying in their darkened bedroom, thinking of Fred.

And this morning she didn't dare go in to ask about Ralph's poker game and whether he'd won or lost ten dollars. And what if he'd been lying to her about where he'd been spending his time? Maybe he'd been with Audrey, having drinks or dinner or more. But she didn't want to dwell on that possibility, because this morning she felt fresh and clear and invigorated by her adventure with the kind gentleman.

She remembered how the storm had come on suddenly, the rain falling in breathtaking sheets. How Karma and his new friend Sequoia had escaped through the back gate, and she and Fred had driven around in the dark evening. How he had somehow found Karma later in the night and brought him back to her. She couldn't recall exactly what they'd talked about. They'd been in the car for hours, so they must have filled the air with conversation, but it was the kiss she remembered.

Now, in the brightness of the morning, she called for Karma. Her dog sensed they were on the move and was already waiting for her by the door. Before leaving, she scribbled a note: *R: I'm off. Have a good day.* It reminded her of when Ralph worked in Manhattan, when he'd leave early to catch the 6:37 train to Penn Station. Sometimes they didn't really see each other for days, besides sleeping at the same address, their feet bumping into each other under the comforter at night.

Catherine settled Karma in his doggie seat, not bothering to strap him in. She wondered if mothers did the same with children. *I'm just going to the mailbox. I'm just dropping a book at the neighbor's.* She imagined they didn't, but there were just too few opportunities to rebel in this world. The only ways she ever rebelled were ripping a recipe out of a magazine at her doctor's office or eating a few chocolate-covered pretzels before weighing the rest at Whole Foods. And she wondered if her kiss with Fred was a rebellion against Ralph or just something that happened organically. An *outlier,* it would be called in science. Like a distant island outside a tight archipelago.

Though the audiobook about the universe's origins had been intermittently jammed in her car's CD player for months, today it started up right away. It reminded her of her drive alone to Savannah and the young businessman who'd spoken to her in the hotel elevator. It reminded her that there was life outside the gates and that the universe didn't begin and end with Ralph.

She arrived at Fred's house at eight o'clock, just as they'd decided. He lived in the first phase of Seven Oaks, reflected in the older trees and narrower sidewalks with homes that had fewer windows and petite, almost baby, mailboxes. She parked in his driveway and let Karma out the back door. He raced across the lawn, sniffing wildly, his stub of a tail shaking with excitement while Catherine breathed deeply, filling her lungs with the soft morning air. She felt an unfamiliar lightness, as if she'd just been given great news — a free turkey or an extra spin on the Piggly Wiggly discount wheel. Fluffy azaleas lined Fred's front porch. And she thought how sweet the house seemed, similar to what she used to imagine all Savannah homes looked like, a house with a wide porch to relax on while drinking sweet tea and reading *Gone with the Wind.*

Fred opened the door before she made it up the front stairs. He wore khakis and a button-down checkered shirt, his hair damp from a shower.

"Cath-er-ine," he said, pronouncing each syllable as if each part of her mattered. Momentarily, it seemed he was going to lean in to hug her or even kiss her cheek, as if they were at a crowded cocktail party. Instead, he stepped aside and opened the door wide. "Good morning. Come in."

She liked the cozy feeling of his house. It wasn't as open as hers, one room didn't run into another, but the lower ceilings gave his furniture a sense of appropriate proportion.

"Sleep well?" he asked, as if they did this all the time, spent their lives waking up together.

"Yes, thank you. Very well."

In the kitchen he poured her coffee and stopped just before adding cream. He looked briefly out the window, then back at her. "Sorry. Old habits. Do you take half-and-half?"

"Yes, just a splash."

His hand shook a bit as the cream lightened the coffee, and he handed it to her. "My wife did too."

Catherine sipped the coffee, tasted burnt cinnamon or chicory, and imagined the Brazilian rain forest where the beans had been harvested. Ralph wouldn't allow anything but french roast in the house. "Any sign of Sequoia?" she asked.

"Sadly, no. I've called security again and just returned from putting signs around the neighborhood." Then suddenly he asked: "But where's Karma?"

"Oh my!" *What kind of mother am I?* she thought. As if Fred hadn't just gone through all this trouble to bring him home to her. Catherine rushed to the front door and there her dog was, sitting happily on the porch. He dropped a single rubber flip-flop in front of her as if delivering a message about Cinderella.

"Bring him in," Fred called from the kitchen, but Karma had already stormed inside. He raced excitedly around the living room.

Catherine returned to the kitchen. "Maybe he's still hyped up from yesterday."

"I think I might be, too," Fred said. "I thought maybe we could begin at the nature trail, if you'd be willing."

If she'd be willing? "Wherever you'd like." She moved to the refrigerator and fingered an old photo attached to the metal door with a Mount Rushmore magnet. It showed Sequoia as a puppy in the arms of a red-haired woman. Catherine felt moved by the woman's wide smile and deep-set dimples.

"We can take my golf cart to cover more ground, if that's okay."

"Of course."

"Maybe that's part of my confidence in Sequoia," Fred explained. "That dog has been everywhere, lived an exuberant life, and gotten out of scrapes worse than this. She'll be just fine." He motioned to a frying

276

pan on the stove. "But, have *you* eaten? Would you like some scrambled eggs? I've also been known to whip up a mean French toast."

"No, I'm fine," Catherine answered. And she meant it.

Fred had been up late into the night. He'd started with the garage, specifically his golf cart, because he had the idea that if he rode with Catherine, she'd be that much closer to him. He recharged its batteries and wiped pollen from the plastic seats. He removed Lissa's sunglasses and visor from the wire basket and hooked them around her golf clubs, which were still resting against the garage wall as if she might show up at any time for a quick round.

Inside his house he'd cleared a pile of laundry that had somehow accumulated in his entryway, rinsed the dishes in the kitchen sink, and run a vacuum around the dining room. He dusted the living room, mopped the kitchen floor, and threw out the dead plant on the hutch. Who had brought it as an offering for his loss, he had no idea.

He stayed up well past midnight, organizing, recycling, even throwing out rotten food from the fridge. Slimy sausages and brown onions that he'd never noticed. These were tasks he should have accomplished months ago, but he'd had neither the motivation nor the energy. Now, like his golf cart, he felt his batteries recharging.

After Catherine finished her coffee, they walked out to his garage. She called to Karma, who came running out, and the three of them settled on the golf cart, the dog on the floorboard between them. Fred hoped that Catherine didn't notice the emptiness in the garage where Lissa's car had been. To him, it felt like a vacant lot.

"Aren't you going to bring a leash?" Catherine asked. "Just in case?"

"Of course." How could he be so careless? He stood, reentered the mudroom, and grabbed the spare leash from the side hook. "And treats," he whispered to himself. He felt like a prom-bound teenager who had forgotten a corsage. It had been only twenty-four hours since he'd met Catherine, but his world had been shifted upside down. On its axis and inside out.

They pulled out of the driveway and to the end of the street. He turned left, away from where Ida Blue was keeping Sequoia. He had tried not to think too much about his Great Dane. He knew that after the dogs' long journey she would just sleep until noon. It would be good for her to rest. And

278

the professional dogsitter, although a little odd, would certainly know how to handle anything that arose. He would retrieve his Great Dane after he had spent the morning with Catherine. He would bring Sequoia home that afternoon to check the pads of her feet and give her extra glucosamine. He would make sure she had a nice dinner of chopped steak or chicken strips. He would make it up to her.

Fred stroked Karma's boxy head. "So how's he doing after his adventure?"

"I think he's happy to be here and be able to help look for Sequoia. To have a purpose."

"Yes, we all want that."

"He likes to hang out alone, but it's good for him to have a new friend. To get to the dog park and socialize. To get out of the box."

Tell her! Fred heard his wife's voice. *It's a perfect opening: "To get out of the box!" Mention your crossword puzzles! You do Sundays with your eyes closed. Why not do one with her this afternoon? God knows you have a pile waiting. You could sit together on the porch! She might even know opera or pop culture. Go ahead! You always just guess at those anyway.*

The golf cart path ran parallel to the road

279

and was empty, golfers already at tee times or enjoying Mulligan omelets at the clubhouse. Fred and Catherine followed the main road to reach an arm of the nature trail. Once midisland, they stopped at Seven Oaks' single traffic light.

"There should be a word for this," Catherine said.

"What?"

"Waiting at a red light. You know, that feeling you get just before it turns green."

He understood exactly what she meant. Lissa had taught him dozens of foreign words that translated into entire situations.

Catherine seemed embarrassed by his silence. "I don't know, I'm just running on, but like when you buy something at the grocery store just before it goes on sale?"

Tell her the words we like!

Fred thought of *schadenfreude,* and the word he and his wife had made up — what was it? — for an indentation in a couch after someone stands. He wondered if there were a word to express an unintended silence between two thoughts.

The light turned green and they crossed the intersection. "Yes. I believe German has lots of those words." He tried to sound interesting without appearing arrogant. "My favorite is *wanderlust.*" He pronounced the *w* like a *v* just the way Lissa had taught him.

"Vanderlust," Catherine repeated.

"Technically, it's the *impulse* to go traveling, the *desire* to experience something new. People hear it and think it's just a restlessness, but it's much deeper." *Not unlike the excitement I'm feeling today,* he thought.

It's a start, Freddie, but you're running on at the tooth.

"I'm sorry," Catherine said. "Your wife passed?"

"It's been nine months. Sometimes I can still even hear her."

You damned coot! You are starting to bore her, and me, to tears.

"You were happy?"

"She was a wonderful woman." He wanted to lie, maybe get a tad melodramatic to elicit sympathy. Or even mention that they had separated once, but he wasn't sure how that would reflect on him and knew Lissa was listening anyway. "It's like the movie's ended and I'm the last one in the theater. I've still got a bucket of buttered popcorn but no one to share it with." He stopped, not wanting to make Catherine uncomfortable. "I don't know how to say this, but you are a beautiful woman."

She looked at him. "Really?"

There it was. He'd said it. He wasn't

thinking of her husband. Wasn't thinking of where this was going or why they had been brought together. He wasn't planning the next step, any kind of seduction, just speaking from his heart. He used to play in tennis tournaments. But as he got older he'd moved from ending up in the finals or semis of the main draw to the consolation and finally the last-chance round. This was it — his last chance.

As they drove, Catherine thought of all the things that are invisible yet still felt. Static electricity and gravity and wind. She felt like she were falling into a black hole. All that mattered in the world could be packed into a hatbox.

"Look, I'm sorry about what happened last night," Fred said.

"Sorry about what?" she asked, playing dumb.

"I don't know what came over me."

"No need."

"Pardon?"

"I kissed you back, I believe." There. It was the truth. "Let me ask you this . . . how did you keep it alive?"

"What?"

"Your marriage. For fifty years? How does that work?"

"It wasn't work. We had our little issues at first, but once we got past those there was nothing difficult about it."

He said it with such confidence. As if it were a thing that was built so solidly that it could be sat on like a finely crafted divan. And then she thought of her marriage to Ralph. How every day was like going to a factory, a conveyor belt of grass-stained laundry and golf anecdotes.

Once at the start of the nature trail they headed east, but the thick trees and foliage blocked the view inside the forest. After several minutes of driving, Fred pulled to one side, parked the cart, and got out. "Let's see if we can get Sequoia's attention," he said. "Cover your ears," he warned, then pressed his tongue against his teeth and made an O shape with his mouth.

He turned away and made a piercing and commanding whistle. A noise that demanded respect and would stop a cab driver in his tracks. Then Catherine thought of Ralph in New York City. He would stand in the rain for twenty minutes with a single hand held high, as if he were the Statue of Liberty in a bad mood.

They both waited and listened to the birds and the hum of the forest.

"Sequoia!" Fred called into the universe.

He turned back around. "Sorry," he said to Catherine. "Just one more." This time he placed his index finger and thumb in his mouth and whistled again. Three times in rapid succession.

Then Catherine imagined traveling with Fred. Of visiting cities across Europe where they could use his whistle. Get a pedicab in India or stop on the edge of the Grand Canyon, just to hear the echo. Just to see if they were really there.

Karma moved from his seated position on the floorboard and onto the trail. He looked back and forth, from Catherine to Fred, as if waiting for something to happen. So Catherine stood too, to stretch her legs and get closer to Fred. To discuss their next step. But as she stepped forward she felt a force pulling them into one another, something as simple as a magnet drawing to a refrigerator.

Before she knew it, he touched her arm and turned her toward him. She looked into his blue eyes and felt momentarily lost. Then he moved toward her and delivered a feathery kiss. Like cotton candy, it melted away the moment their lips touched. She started to speak but he brought his hand up slowly. He placed the tip of his index finger on her lips. "Shhh . . ."

She remained still and felt a heat flowing from her hips, to her pelvis, then her stomach, and finally to her breasts. A helium balloon let go at a carnival. She became aware of every part of her body and smelled the pine trees and his aftershave. She heard the twit of a songbird and felt his soft cotton shirt in her hands. She moved into him with an intensity that surprised her. *It's just a kiss,* she told herself. Their second and final kiss. This one must last a lifetime.

They stepped back for a moment. Absurdly, she thought. As if they were actors on a stage who needed to let the audience keep up with the action. Catherine noticed the wrinkled outer edges of Fred's mouth, like he'd spent his entire life smiling and laughing. As if he'd never regretted a thing. "What are we doing?" she whispered.

He considered her question. "Looking for Sequoia."

"No. Right now."

He brought his hand to her face and ran his fingertips from her forehead, across one side of her temple, down her cheek, and to rest on her chin. "Right now, I'm hoping to find what I've lost." His eyes held her.

Catherine felt like she were watching a complicated magic trick. If only she could view it in slow motion or from above, then maybe she could figure it out, could deconstruct the mechanics of what was happening.

"I don't know how to explain it, but I feel like I'm waking from a very sad dream," he continued.

Fred moved forward again in slow motion. His hand brushed the small of her back, and her hips pressed into him while the rest of the world spun around her. Her skirt had ridden up on her legs so she pulled it down and laughed. "Look at me," she said, an embarrassed schoolgirl.

She'd stopped worrying about Sequoia. Something in Fred's voice made her believe that his dog would be okay. She didn't want to spend these moments someplace else. She owned them.

They spent almost ten more minutes in an embrace. *Making out,* someone might call it. But making out was just mild entertainment for teenagers in the backseats of cars. This felt real, as if her whole life were coming into focus.

After a bit, they stopped, as if coming up for air. Karma trotted to them, barked once, then hopped up on the golf cart. It was time to continue. Without saying a word, they returned to the wide seat and drove to another break in the trail. It led to the Seven

Oaks community area, with a slide, swings, jungle gym, and seesaws. Despite a few parked cars in the lot, the area was empty.

Fred parked the cart and they all got out. Though Karma ran ahead, the local leash law was the last thing on Catherine's mind.

"Let's go," Fred said and took her by the hand.

"Where?"

"For a ride." He pulled her toward the playground and, once there, stood behind the middle of three swings, offering it to her. "Madam, your chariot."

She sat down into the swing and was surprised at how strong and secure it felt, the plastic seat wrapping around her buttocks. If things had been different, if Ralph had wanted children, she'd be pushing a grandchild in a swing by now. Spending her days here. "I haven't ridden one of these in forever," she said, laughing.

"It's like a bicycle." Fred pushed her gently at first, his hands on her shoulders. "Don't forget to pump with your legs."

As she accelerated she rose higher and higher and Fred's hands fell to her middle back, then to the sides of her waist. She felt stronger and younger than she had in years. As if she could simply will herself off the swing and into the cloudless sky. As if she could find Sequoia and have the strength and the determination to leave Ralph. As if she were free.

CHAPTER 29

After returning the gown to the walk-in closet and wiping the makeup from her face, Amity collected her prescription pills and fanny pack and left the house, moving out into the inky darkness. Instead of abandoning the plant to endure a slow and sure death, she took it with her, cradling it in the crook of her arm. Not having anticipated a return trip, she hadn't brought a flashlight, so she stepped carefully into the night, being sure to lock the back door on the way out.

Clouds skittered across the sky as if eager for daybreak. Though light from the half-moon helped, it was difficult to make out what was ahead, so she kept her bearings by shuffling along the hard driveway. She used the edge of the tabby pavement as a compass, taking careful baby steps, one at a time.

After finding her car and driving out past

the bright security booth and the community's electronic sign (HURRICANE MEETING TUESDAY . . . STAY IN THE KNOW FOR THE BIG BLOW), she followed Diamond Causeway over the Intracoastal. She might have taken the Truman Parkway to the Henry Street exit, the fastest way home, but decided it was time for a change and headed northeast on Ferguson Avenue toward Sandfly, then left on Skidaway Road.

The scenic route, Alex might have said.

She passed a Chicken and Waffle House, strip malls, and low apartment buildings. Once on Victory Drive she noted the dark expanse of Daffin Park. After miles of unsynchronized stoplights, Amity decided "Slo-vannah" deserved its nickname. In contrast to how lost she'd been just an hour earlier, she felt herself perking up, the English teacher in her bristling at egregious signage — HARD HAT'S REQUIRED, DIRT4SALE, and several examples of DRIVE THRUS. *Whatever it takes to get back to my old self,* she thought. As she crossed the invisible line from Ardsley Park to Midtown, she rolled down the windows and could almost taste the wet earth in the air, as if the rain had washed away all the pollen and dirt and dark debris from the past so the world could come alive again.

In the historic district, she found a convenient parking space on Tattnall and felt exhausted, every muscle in her body spent. She considered leaning back her car seat and settling in for the night, but she willed herself forward, if only for the sake of the poor plant beside her. Instead of going upstairs to the guest bedroom, where she had slept since her husband left, she went directly to the master suite on the main floor and collapsed on the bed in her clothes. The sheets had been stripped and thrown out long ago, but there she remained undisturbed on the bare mattress until the next morning.

It was after nine o'clock when the sunlight streamed through the windows and awakened her. She was shocked that she'd slept so well without the assistance of Ambien or meditation CDs. The first thing that came to her was relief that she hadn't gone through with her pathetic exit plan. She felt indebted to Catherine as she considered the ironic timing of her phone call. *Karma is gone. Can you help look for him?* For months Amity had had the overwhelming feeling of being attached to the railing of a sinking ship, a reluctant passenger on the *Titanic*'s sunset cruise. Today, just by the simple fact that she was needed — not just once in a while by a slow-moving school district — she felt as if a lifeline of hope had been thrown her way.

Without wasting any time, Amity dressed in yoga pants and a T-shirt and drove directly to Seven Oaks. At the gatehouse, Rusty waved her through while giving her a thumbs-up, and she headed straight to Catherine's house, where she and Catherine had found each other in the first place. There was little traffic, residents already in tennis matches or pickleball games, doing whatever it was that people not strapped to sinking ships did.

As she approached Catherine's street, she saw a man in a golf cart pulling out of Catherine's driveway, his clubs strapped into the bag holder like a child riding pig-gyback. She recognized his salt-and-pepper hair blowing in the wind and vaguely re-membered Ralph from the day she'd met Catherine. It seemed he hadn't cut his hair since then. Amity had seen it a million times. Men who have post-midlife crises and grow their hair long, buy a convertible, or have an affair. *Manopause,* she'd heard it called.

Amity parked her car in Catherine's driveway. Whereas three months ago she'd sneaked into the yard and jimmied the lock of the side door, today she rang the doorbell, proud that her presence had been requested. *I need you.* She heard the correlating chime somewhere within. In the entryway she noted a small ceramic gnome, a lucky horseshoe, and a sign by the front door. WARNING: KILLER BOSTON TERRIER ON DUTY. The cartoon dog wore a pointed polka dot hat. Amity felt momentarily disappointed in Catherine. She should know better than to joke about security.

In her fantasy, Amity hoped that Catherine would throw open the door and greet her with a giant hug. *You're here!* she might exclaim. *What would I do without you?!* It was the type of relationship she'd seen while having coffee at the fitness center, in a world where women cared about each other.

With no answer and no barking, she knocked. Three times. Louder with each. Knocks that said, *Open up! I can help!* Then she tried the knob. Locked, of course. And that's when she felt a familiar pull. The feeling came upon her before she recognized it. The feeling an alcoholic must have after a certain period of sobriety — that one sip of wine would be nice — shortly before swan-diving into a vat of tequila. Amity hadn't brought her fanny pack that contained her

293

tools, of course. But before she knew it she was at the garage door, punching in the numbers of Catherine's wedding date. The date Ralph could never remember — seven-eight-seven-eight.

The house seemed smaller than she remembered, as if she'd been just a little girl when she'd last visited. But Amity recognized the view and feeling of openness. On an intellectual level she understood that she shouldn't be doing this, shouldn't be snooping around Catherine's house, yet another part of her reasoned that Catherine had asked, had *pleaded,* for her help, and that she was simply answering the call of duty. And Amity felt indebted to her for contacting someone to remove the raccoon corpse without getting them both booked for trespassing. They could have left it there to rot for months, but it was the neighborly thing to do.

Walking into the living room she shouted, "Helloooo!" as a real estate agent might.

No answer.

Again, without conscious effort, she became an archeologist at a dig, just as she'd done in dozens of other houses. In the living room antique golf clubs lined the wall, and on the coffee table sat photo books with glossy covers featuring jarring names like

Fifty Courses to Play before You Die. "Hel-loooo!" Amity called again.

If for some reason Catherine was in the house, just stepping out of the shower, Amity would explain that the garage door had been left up. That Catherine's husband must have left in a hurry. Every wife would understand that sort of recklessness. Amity would tell her she was here to help find Karma and was sorry she'd been delayed but had slept better than she had in her entire life. She would thank Catherine for the well-timed phone call, not bothering to explain that she'd decided to give this business of living another chance. Amity might have worried about Ralph returning to find her standing in their living room, but she knew a man holding a golf club on a pleasant day was like a teenager with a key to the fun house. He would be gone for hours.

Amity moved into the kitchen and saw that someone, probably Ralph, had spilled milk and several chunks of granola on the granite counter, so she wiped up the mess with a dishrag. While there, she put what she presumed was his cereal bowl into the dishwasher and turned off the dripping tap. A folded Savannah newspaper, open to commercial real estate listings, and a half-drunk cup of coffee sat on the kitchen table.

Amity picked up the mug, still warm, and held it in her cupped hands before taking a sip and rinsing it out.

On the first floor was an office, clearly Catherine's. Thick books promoting power aging lined the bookshelves. Amity thought it remarkable and a little pathetic that someone Catherine's age could still believe that a little virgin olive oil or static stretching would keep her young. An antique planter held fresh flowers, and an old tennis racket, painted pink, hung on the wall. Terse notes were clipped to the strings: *Martha BDAY; Find Dentist; Dog Food.*

On Amity's previous visit, when the house had belonged to someone else, she hadn't had time to explore, hadn't seen the stairs that led to the second floor. So up she went, confident that Ralph was by now on the first tee and Catherine was somewhere with a pound of raw bacon trying to locate her dog. Amity felt a little guilty not leaving to join her, but there were a dozen places Catherine might be — the walking trails, the marina, the narrow sidewalks of Palmetto Pines. If she'd had her cell phone she might have called Catherine, but she'd forgotten it in her fanny pack and, besides, maybe she could do more good here.

After passing two guest rooms she came

to an enlarged skylit alcove overlooking the living room. Clearly it was where Ralph had taken up residence. A brown swivel chair sat in front of a desktop computer. As if he were ten years old, clear Lucite trophies for business-deal closings lined the top of his lateral file. Amity's ex-husband had kept the same things on his desk, along with framed photos of her, now presumably replaced with images of his son and new wife. To one side sat books on finance and fishing and an engraved stone that read NOTHING IS EVER ETCHED IN STONE. Above Ralph's desk hung a Civil War map identifying Gettysburg, Antietam, Shiloh. She felt sorry for Catherine, trapped in the world with a man who celebrated the bloodiest war in US history.

As if Catherine were a naive older sister, Amity felt protective of her and angry that Ralph had departed with his golf clubs, clearly not available to look for their dog. Her experience had proved that men kept secrets, and wives needed to be informed. There were falsehoods hidden in plain sight everywhere, from fake rocks to pretend marriages. And so she started looking.

She began with the dozens of small containers scattered around his office — a commemorative golf pencil caddy and rusted brass tin and felt-lined valet box filled with coppery coins as if Ralph might need to feed parking meters in Europe someday. Then she opened two carved wooden boxes — the first filled with specialty golf balls, the second with cell phone and iPad chargers. She ruffled through the manila files labeled *Mortgage, Flood Insurance,* and *Battlefields to Visit.* She couldn't find anything remarkable. No love letters or hidden receipts. No pornographic VHS tapes or angry letters from the IRS. It took every bit of fifteen minutes, but she knew it was there. Every man had something he kept secret, part of a covert operation of living.

Finally, in the back of the lateral file, behind dozens of hanging folders and under several back issues of *Fortune,* her fingers hit upon something hard and cold.

A gun.

Amity wasn't going to take the weapon. That would have been absurd. She had never even actually held a handgun and had no more use for one than a bald man had for a blow dryer. But she surprised herself by bending down and lifting it out of Ralph's filing cabinet.

It was heavier than she'd imagined. All her life she'd watched actors grab handguns from holsters, spin them around their index fingers, and sling them to compatriots in dusty shoot-outs. She'd assumed they were lightweight, like Frisbees, but this was decidedly dense. Using both hands she held up the gun and looked through the small metal sight at the end of the barrel. It was exactly how she'd looked at Alex on their honeymoon — through the viewfinder on a camera. Whenever he held his hand up in mock irritation or sidled out of the frame she'd told him in a deadpan voice: "Don't move or I'll shoot."

Feeling the rough grip, she passed the gun back and forth between her hands as if handling a hot, unwieldy lead potato. Then she cocked her elbows and posed breathlessly for a moment. A year ago, Amity might have had reason to borrow the gun, to stuff it in her yoga pants and get on with the job. To shoot her husband and his girlfriend as they emerged from the Bohemian Hotel or as they shared crème brûlée at the Mansion. *Say your good-byes, suckers.* But at the height of her anger she preferred to dwell on more dramatic instruments of revenge than something as simple as a pistol. She'd imagined tying Alex and the Other Woman to hard-backed chairs and torturing them with one of the thoughtful gifts from her wedding registry, gifts she'd hardly had a chance to use, even after ten years of marriage, like the electric turkey carver or handheld blender.

Amity wasn't all that surprised that Ralph had a gun. This was Georgia, after all. She'd crept in several houses with elaborate gun racks. She'd seen shotguns and BB guns and pistols displayed behind thick glass like dangerous fish in oversize aquariums. Most weapons were locked into metal bars, but Amity knew that like anything else in the world, all you needed to steal something, whether it was a gun or a husband, was a little enthusiasm and a plan.

She wondered if Catherine knew about the gun and decided she didn't. Amity couldn't imagine Catherine being comfortable with a weapon in her house, and besides, why would her husband need to keep it hidden in the back of his file cabinet?

She'd been in the house more than an hour and realized Catherine or Ralph might return unexpectedly, so Amity placed the gun back where she'd found it, behind the hanging folders of mortgage papers and tax documents. As she turned to leave she became distracted by all the boxes in Ralph's office. The round and rectangular shapes were askew, awry, and askance. It hadn't bothered her earlier, but now she noted all the edges out of alignment. She had an undefined feeling that something would happen if she didn't straighten things. Not to Ralph, someone she hardly had any feeling toward except disappointment, but to Catherine or herself. And so she started straightening, which gave her the vague feeling of being in control, at least for the moment.

After she placed the boxes at regular intervals along his desk and bookshelves, she grabbed a fistful of pencils from the leather caddy. One by one she rearranged them so all lead points faced up. Next she took Ralph's reading glasses from his desk, where they'd been lying upside down and splayed with one temple straight, the other bent, like a man with a broken leg. She folded them and placed them in their hard case.

Now Amity understood why Catherine had seemed so intent on creeping with her, getting out of her own life for a bit. Maybe her friend sensed that she was in some sort of danger. Maybe Ralph was even planning to harm his wife. If so, Amity wondered how she would be helpful. She was uncertain if she could ever really use a gun if needed, but promised herself that she'd try.

CHAPTER 30

Fred handed Catherine a glass of tap water as they stood in his kitchen. He would have offered her ice cubes, but he'd forgotten to replace the ones he'd used from his old freezer. That had been Lissa's department. Make the ice cubes, make the bed, make the reservations. Despite his anticipation of Catherine coming back to his house, he hadn't worked out the details of her visit. It reminded him of a complicated chess game in which he could plan only one move ahead.

"Have you ever used one of these?" Fred motioned to a shiny Keurig machine on his counter.

"No, never."

"We won it in a raffle a few years ago but our daughter shamed us out of using it. She's worried the plastic coffee capsules will go into a landfill and be there for a millennium." Catherine sipped her water and slowly nodded, so he continued. "Can you imagine?"

"A millennium," Catherine repeated.

She brought the glass to her lips, and he noticed her long neck. He wondered if she'd ever been a dancer. Maybe she had taken ballet or jazz. He was about to make a point but had lost his way. Something about recycling. "She's thinking a thousand years down the road. Not even a hundred or ten. I mean, what happened to tomorrow? At my age, I don't even use long-term parking." It was an old joke, but Catherine smiled.

To pad the room with something other than his own voice he turned on the old radio that rested next to the coffee machine. It occurred to him that the electrical gadgets, side by side, were sort of like him and Catherine. The plastic-veneered old receiver next to a shapely chrome appliance. She was probably only ten years younger than he was, but he felt the difference. He wondered if her husband was part of the broad-shouldered troop that jogged around Green-leaf Park in the mornings, then stopped to chug kale milkshakes at the Village Café.

He turned the radio dial to bring the deejay's voice into focus the same way he'd focus a camera. When he was growing up he could find dozens, maybe hundreds, of radio stations to listen to. Today he got exactly one. The station broadcast from somewhere out of South Carolina and the raspy-voiced deejay sounded as if he were chain-smoking in his carport, but at least it was an oldies station. "But I'm being impolite. You must be famished."

"Just a bit." She took another sip of water and refolded the kitchen towel he'd left on the counter.

"Let's see what we can do about that." He opened the pantry hoping to find a selection of water crackers or a tin of mixed fancy nuts. Maybe, just maybe, there'd be a jar of artichoke tapenade or even some chocolate-covered toffee. He'd read that dark chocolate could be an aphrodisiac.

Then he heard Lissa: *An aphrodisiac? Really?*

Really.

He knew he was jumping way ahead of himself. They had shared only a few kisses. They'd done less than Audrey Hepburn and George Peppard had on a crowded soundstage, but he couldn't help it.

Inside the closet he found a six-pack of strawberry-flavored Ensure that Danielle had bought him and three bags of pretzels. "Hidden bachelor treasures." He emptied the pretzels into a bowl. "Welcome to my world."

"I think I like your world," Catherine said rather suddenly.

"So shall we retire to the living room?" He immediately felt regret. *Who says retire anymore?* It was something his father or, even worse, Hugh Hefner might say.

"Sure," Catherine answered, and they moved past the mirrored bar to the living room couch. He was glad she had kept smiling at him, so he didn't feel as much a fool as he might have.

They sat on the couch that faced the fireplace. If it had been winter, perhaps he would have built a fire. He knew a foolproof way of crisscrossing wood so that the flames torched upward and the embers stayed strong. If they'd been in an Aspen snow lodge they might have spent the afternoon huddling together, reading novels.

Cuddling, not huddling. This isn't football. Haven't you two been through this before?

This isn't so easy, you know. I have no idea how to do this. I feel like a fool.

You're adorable. Just be yourself.

He needed to focus on Catherine.

"So what's our plan?" Catherine asked.

For a moment he thought she meant tonight: *What's our plan? Pizza or pasta?*

Movie or music? Seafood or Mexican? He could pick up Sequoia at Ida Blue's house and they could celebrate her return. The four of them, he and Catherine in the front seat, Karma and Sequoia behind them. They could drive downtown and park along Wright Square. He could point out Chief Tomochichi's granite monument and dazzle her with historic stories. Maybe they could relax on a bench as the sunlight slanted through the spanish moss, then he'd present her with a gift. He didn't know when her birthday was, but he'd like to buy her a necklace that accented her emerald eyes.

"I'm sorry," Catherine said, interrupting his reverie. "I shouldn't be so presumptuous. It's *your* plan. I mean, I want to be helpful, but I just throw myself into situations sometimes. Just stop me if I get annoying."

"Annoying?" He hadn't felt anything so refreshing in years.

Catherine laughed a little. A tender, girlish laugh, he thought. "I mean, I just want to be supportive. To help bring Sequoia back to you."

Sequoia. His dog. What was he *doing*? Had he really not even checked on his dog all morning? When they'd returned from their golf cart ride he could have made a

306

quiet phone call to Ida Blue from his office, could have made sure she'd held down breakfast. "Don't worry. I've got some friends keeping their eyes out. And I just *know* she's fine. In fact, I just read about a dog in Florida who returned to his owner after more than six months and a hundred miles. And think of monarch butterflies. Generations can migrate thousands of miles just by the earth's magnetic signature." He could hear himself talking, but couldn't seem to stop the rush of words, a corroded pipe that had come unclogged after years.

Catherine stood as something behind him caught her eye. She moved to the piano to examine the photos displayed on top. "Your daughter?" She held up a faded photo of his once little girl dressed as an astronaut, wearing a white jumpsuit and a diving mask to represent a helmet. They'd just been to a fair.

"Yes. That was taken here. In Forsyth Park. We'd just moved in. Hasn't changed much."

"Your daughter or Forsyth Park?"

"My daughter, Danielle." As he said her name he realized he hadn't spoken it to anyone besides Hunter for months, maybe since Lissa had died. Perhaps to Ernie in passing at the dog park, but nothing like he used to. Lissa had spent hours obsessing about their daughter and her divorce and their grandson. *What do you think Danielle is up to? Is it too early to call Danielle? Do you think Danielle will get Tommy a puppy?* "I thought she should have been a princess, but she had to be an astronaut. She's still a pragmatist, I guess."

"How so?"

"She keeps telling me to come visit. She's got ideas about what I should be doing with my life." He thought of her insistence that he move to Maine. Her idea that he was getting too old to take care of himself. "She's always had a mind of her own. Nothing's changed." But what was he saying? It'd been thirty years since the photo was taken. Everything in the world had changed. His daughter. Savannah. Seven Oaks. The only thing that hadn't changed, perhaps, was the one thing that doesn't. The impractical exhilaration of new love.

"And this is your grandson?" Catherine pointed to another photo, a candid shot Lissa had taken of Tommy three summers before. Before Danielle had allotted every moment of his days to music lessons or soccer practice or math club.

"That's Tommy. I always assumed he was named after Saint Thomas Aquinas. I found out last year that my daughter chose the name because she craved English muffins during her pregnancy."

"He's cute."

"He looks like my wife."

"Maybe. But he's cute like you too."

Fred felt suddenly flustered. Had it been that long since someone besides Lissa had flirted with him? Since before the Carter administration, he guessed. Maybe even before Apollo 11. Lissa was the one who'd done the flirting. *The operator,* he'd called her. She worked a cocktail party like a pro, twirling her hair, touching strangers' elbows, sitting down to drinks with Jack Klugman.

Then Fred heard Lissa's voice: *I was just having fun.*

I know, he thought sadly. *You were always just having fun.*

And I wasn't obsessed *with Danielle. I just wanted the best for her. And to make sure you two would be okay together after I was gone.*

What are you saying?

You two are exactly alike. Stubborn. That's the problem.

And then the deejay stopped talking about the weather and a patio furniture sale and baseball results, and a familiar song came on the radio. Fred immediately recognized the instrumental opening and Louis Armstrong's crooning about a wonderful world. It was a song he and Lissa used to dance to. Maybe it was time to have some fun himself. He went over to Catherine, still at the piano, and spun her around.

She laughed, as if relieved he finally got there.

With that green light he put his right hand on her hip and his left in the air. Without hesitation, she accepted his hand and pressed against him and they started dancing in rhythm. Head to head and toe to toe, they moved through his living room. By the piano and couch. In front of the wide picture window that looked out to the backyard. He was at a gymnasium dance on a Friday night with streamers and balloons and a hand-painted sign that read GO INDIANS!

But his mind was jumbled, as he wasn't sure what to do next. Was she just humoring him, a lonely old man with a lost dog? Though at this moment, he realized, he was neither.

He hadn't read many articles in the AARP magazine about seduction. Was that what this was, anyway? A seduction? Maybe it didn't matter, because he felt young and excited, a boy hosting show-and-tell at his house: Here's my espresso machine. Here's my family. Here's my bedroom.

Your bedroom?

Our bedroom. It was our *bedroom.*

I'm kidding. It's your *bedroom now. Get on with it.*

Catherine was married, of course, but that wasn't his concern. What did he have to fear? A jealous husband tracking him down? Would anyone feel anything but sorry for an old man wanting a little companionship? Nobody would believe he could seduce a woman like Catherine. People would assume he wanted someone to share soup with or to remind him to take his blood-pressure pills.

And so he bent his head even closer, feeling a pull along his arthritic neck. His chin rested on the top of her head, and he could smell her lemony hair. But when he opened his eyes again a movement surprised him. Across the wooded lot he saw the unmistakable lumbering figure of Ida Blue, with Sequoia on a leash, walking laps around her yard.

Fred had taken her by surprise by offering to dance, but she admired his confidence and graceful movement. Ralph was a terrible dancer. He didn't know how to lead,

311

and when it came to freestyle, he was always snapping his fingers and cocking his head as if he'd been stung by a bee. Fred gently pulled the small of her back toward him to go forward and pushed her gently as he spun her away.

At one point, Fred pulled her rather urgently away from the expansive window and they sashayed by the leather ottoman and heavy shelves filled with guidebooks. They slid by the coffee table and brick fireplace. For a moment her heart dropped as they moved toward the front door. Was he going to nudge her out? Was this the way he would say good-bye? She felt as if she might cry, as if Fred had realized she was not a princess at all, just a woman from New Jersey with nothing to offer but an obstinate Boston terrier.

But just as quickly he spun her again. The music quickened and their dancing became more urgent. She could feel her heart beating, her palms sweating. Momentarily she felt a pang, a feeling that had been sitting in her gut all morning. Should she be doing this? But then she considered what Ralph would have done had the circumstances been reversed and it had been Audrey Cunningham who'd been choreographing the dance. She knew exactly. So when Fred opened the door to his bedroom, her decision was as simple as following Arthur Murray shoe silhouettes directly to his king-size bed.

CHAPTER 31

Once in the bedroom they danced in circles, a whirlpool of excitement. At this distance, Catherine couldn't hear the song from the kitchen, just the occasional slap of a cymbal, as if meant to bring her back to this moment and not to worry about what was to come. Once they reached the side of his bed, Fred stopped. He dropped her right hand while he kept his arm wrapped around her waist. He looked down into her eyes and smoothed away a tendril of hair from her cheek.

"Dear, dear Catherine," he said. "I don't know where you've come from but I thank my lucky stars you've arrived." Then he pulled her closer, surprising them both that it was even possible. The only thing that separated their bodies was their light spring clothing. With her head pressed into his shirt she smelled lavender, as if he'd put too much detergent into the washing machine.

Then she thought, *If I were gone, Ralph would need a docent just to find his way into the laundry room.*

Catherine stepped away and, a little light-headed, sat at the edge of his bed.

"Stay right there," Fred said. "I'll be back in a minute." He left the room and she took a deep breath, feeling as if they'd spent the last twenty-four hours in a jitterbug contest.

She took note of her surroundings and of the moment. This sort of thing didn't happen to her. Sometimes she caught a shoe sale or parking place just right, but she didn't simply end up sitting on a stranger's king-size bed. She didn't meet a man in a dog park one day and feel overwhelming desire the next.

A framed photo of Fred and his wife perched on a side table. Judging from their collared shirts and the green expanse behind them, she figured the photograph had been taken in the middle of a golf game. They stood on a small bridge that looked no bigger than a canoe, a fairy-tale bridge that a tiny troll might live under.

Fred returned carrying a bottle of white wine, two long-stemmed glasses, and a corkscrew. He placed the glasses on the side table and sat down next to her.

"That looks like fun," Catherine said,

motioning to the photograph.

He looked up at the frame as if he were surprised to see it there. "Oh, I thought you meant the wine."

"Well, I suppose wine is fun too."

Fred removed the bottle's metallic collar. "Yes. That was Swilcan Bridge on the Old Course."

"The Old Course?"

"Saint Andrews," he explained gently. "In Scotland." It wasn't the pejorative tone that Ralph used when he mentioned golf courses he thought everyone should know. Pine Valley, Cypress Point, Shinnecock. "Do you play golf?"

"No," she said, "but I'd like to try."

"You would?"

"Yes, I think I would."

Fred set the screw into the cork. It took several tries before the spiral worm caught and he could twist it. "God, I haven't done this in a while. I think the same guy who invented the wine bottle invented childproof medicine containers. Why can't there just be a little Velcro for an old fart like me?"

Catherine found her hand on his forearm. "Could it be they just don't trust old farts like you?"

"Well, they should. Everyone should. My intentions are pure." He pulled out the cork with a flourish. After pouring the wine into the glasses he passed one to her and held up his own. "To a new friend," he said. "To getting to know each other."

"And to Sequoia coming home." Immediately, Catherine regretted mentioning the Great Dane. Fred looked confused, as if he'd forgotten why they'd spent the day together in the first place. "But I'm not worried," she added quickly. "Because you told me not to be. Because you said everything will be okay. Because I trust you."

"Certainly," he said. "Trust is important."

Catherine needed to change the subject. She didn't want him distracted by his missing Great Dane. She didn't want him to suggest they race back out to the nature trail. She took a long drink from her glass and was surprised to find the wine so cold. "Delicious. What kind is it?"

"Sauvignon blanc from the Loire Valley. It was a toss-up between this and a Californian Chardonnay. I thought this suited you. It's a little more adventuresome."

Adventuresome? She'd never been called *that* before, but she liked the idea of it. "And you've chilled it and everything."

"I had high hopes you'd stop by after a morning of looking."

"May I?" she asked and tilted her head

sideways.

"Please."

They kicked off their shoes and moved further onto the bedspread, taking turns holding each other's glass while they got comfortable against the many oversize pillows. "What's that?" She pointed to a cloudy sticker that hung precariously from the ceiling.

"Hard to say since it's daytime, but it looks like Saturn."

Now Catherine saw the half-circle shape with a slightly darker ring in the middle. "Why, yes it does. But here's a better question: Why is Saturn slipping from your ceiling?"

"Tommy. And I suppose Danielle had some say in it. A few years ago — he was probably five or six — they visited and he refused to sleep upstairs. He wanted to sleep here between us." Fred motioned to the middle of the bed and Catherine momentarily imagined Tommy could be her grandson too. "Just like grandpa, he's not much of a sleeper. So I had this great idea to put up a few glow-in-the-dark stars, you know, just to have something to talk about late at night. But Danielle said if you are going to do that, you might as well *teach* him something, which is how we ended up with the

318

entire solar system on our ceiling." He turned to her, perhaps to gauge if she were following him, perhaps to see if he were boring her with details. "I think there are few things in life as wonderful as the stars."

With that, Catherine looked more carefully and saw other pale stickers above them — red-tinged Mars and blue-flecked Neptune. "But what's that?" She pointed to a yellowish square sticker in the corner.

"That, my dear, is SpongeBob."

Fred wondered how he could have missed the Old Course photograph during his cleanup. Like a real estate agent who removes personal objects so potential buyers can picture themselves in a house, he had placed Lissa's things in a plastic container and moved it to the attic. He'd cleared the novels from her dresser, her shoes from underneath the mattress, and the second toothbrush in the bathroom. He'd hoped to transform his bedroom into a neutral landscape where Catherine might feel comfortable enough to relax. To stay. To nap.

To nap? You're killing me. Are you kindergartners? Lissa said.

Do you think you're helping?

I'm encouraging you.

What? To get on with it?

319

You don't have all the time in the world, sweet cheeks.

Fred appreciated Lissa's support, if that's what it was, but he needed to focus on Catherine.

He was glad she liked the wine. He imagined being with her on a passenger train in Europe, offering her a drink from whatever region they were passing through — ouzo or prosecco or Chianti — with complementary cheese. On a picnic, he could feed her grapes pulled directly from an arbor. He wanted to take care of her; maybe he could give her what Ralph didn't or couldn't. Maybe he could find a way. After a moment of comfortable silence he said, "I don't know if I've told you, but you are absolutely beautiful." He had told her, of course. As they sat in his car the night before, as they walked toward the playground swings earlier that day. A smile spread across her face. *Like sunrise on an ocean,* he thought.

"I am?"

"Your eyes. Your kindness." Then he added, "And I'm not telling you that just to seduce you." Though once he said it he knew he was lying, not about her being kind but about the endgame. Of course he'd like to sleep with her. Lissa was right — Lissa was always right. Their make out sessions had awakened a dormant desire, a door that had been sealed shut but was slowly swinging open.

Without planning his next step he took her glass. He'd thought about refilling it but found that he placed it next to his own on the bedside table. He turned back to her and propped himself up on his right elbow, his head resting on his palm. He reached with his left hand to tuck another piece of hair behind her ear. Then he moved his fingers slowly to her cheek, her chin, her neck, her collarbone.

He could hear her breathe faster, and she closed her eyes.

"May I?" he asked.

Her voice answered yes before she'd even considered the question. She could feel him undoing the first button on her shirt. Then the second. She felt a tingling to her nipples and a wetness between her legs though he barely touched her. With her eyes closed, she imagined the scene from above. The two of them splayed comfortably across his bedspread, pillows jumbled beneath them, acting like two hormonal teenagers. But teenagers wouldn't proceed this slowly, wouldn't understand the excruciatingly divine interval between moments.

His fingers approached the third button on her shirt. "Yes?"

She nodded.

When he undid the final button, her blouse opened. She was glad she'd worn a lace bra. Glad she'd taken extra time to dress and wash her hair and shave her legs. Glad she'd moisturized and exfoliated. Lying on her back, she saw that her stomach looked almost flat, but she wanted to show him the fullness of her breasts and so leaned over onto her side to face him.

He didn't rip open her shirt as she'd seen in movies, only slipped his hand beneath the cotton. She felt his warm fingers on her waist. "Are you okay?" he asked.

She'd never met anyone so concerned, so hyperaware of her feelings. "I am more than okay."

He brought his hand to the top edge of the lacy cup, where he hooked his index finger. While he pulled down the bra her nipples ached for him. Finally, after what seemed like hours, her right breast fell free. He did the same to her left and she arched unexpectedly, moving her naked breasts into his hand, feeling as if she could have done a backbend had she been asked.

He brought his mouth to her collarbone, kissed the flesh above her heart, then moved downward and sucked at her dark areola, taking each hard nipple into his mouth. He spent long minutes kissing both breasts, as if he couldn't decide between them. "Catherine, Catherine, Catherine," she heard him whisper.

She grabbed his head in her hands and held it tightly while he explored her torso with his mouth. Then he started to move lower, from her ribs to her stomach and belly button, slowly making his way to the top of her skirt. She clutched his head to her body. Then she reached down and grabbed for his belt and before she knew it, his pants were off, his erection pushing up through his cotton boxers.

They both stopped for a moment and caught their breath as if breaking through the surface after a deep-sea dive.

As he moved back up toward her he felt fully alive. He couldn't believe that she wanted or needed him. *It's just too perfect,* he thought.

And then it was.

"You know I'm married," she whispered.

He knew it had to come. It had been right there in Fred's subconscious all along, but he'd been afraid to access it lest he wake from a dream. "Yes, Cath-er-ine." He pronounced each syllable of her name, its sound echoing the staccato triplets of his heart.

"It's complicated, you know?"

He wasn't sure if she was looking for support or advice or sympathy. Did she want to be convinced that this — whatever *this* was, whatever the consequences were — was worth it? He didn't want to rush her, but felt an urgent need. To push her into the mattress and make love to her. He was drawn back to her perfect, full breasts, and so instead of speaking he kissed the tips of them.

She continued, "I mean, because my husband and I are so different."

He could feel her pulling away from him, as obvious as if she were pulling out of a parking place.

"We didn't always use to be. When we first started dating, a hundred years ago, we were happy. But retirement changes things, doesn't it? People become irrelevant."

He tried to will her to come back, to stop wherever she was going, to do a U-turn. But she was gone, barreling down the highway. And so he sat up and handed her the glass. "Look," he said, "we don't have to do anything more. I'm willing to wait until you get your feelings sorted out."

■ ■ ■ ■

As soon as Catherine said she needed to use the bathroom, Fred scrambled to her side of the bed to assist her. She held on to his arm and stood, felt light-headed again, and wondered if it was just the wine. Rather shyly, she lifted her bra cups to cover her breasts and closed the front of her shirt in mock embarrassment. Then she smoothed her skirt. Although she wasn't prudish about her body, the phrase *cue the body double* drifted through her head, and she imagined calling in a gate pass for Michelle Pfeiffer or Jane Fonda.

Once in the bathroom, she closed the door and stood before the mirror. Even her flushed face with starbursts of pink brightening her cheeks couldn't hide her crow's-feet and the parentheses around her mouth. She was sorry that she didn't have the toned thighs and tight buttocks Fred might be hoping for or used to. Sorry she'd stopped playing tennis when she'd moved to Seven Oaks and hadn't spent afternoons at the gym with Amity. She remembered when she was thirty, then thirty-five, then forty. But suddenly she was sixty-five. How had this happened?

She was surprised to see that much of her hair had fallen out of her ponytail, as if she were in the middle of a tight three-set match, so she reached into the top drawer of the bathroom vanity between the two sinks. Fred's razor and shaving cream and toothpaste sat next to one sink, while the other was empty except for a ceramic tumbler. It was impossible not to think of Fred's wife and to imagine the woman she was. Catherine found a brush and saw grayish-red hair in its bristles and wondered how her life might have been different if she'd been with a man like Fred. If Fred and she had met and married forty years ago, maybe she would have had photos of a daughter and grandson on her piano instead of Ralph holding a putter. Instead of a man who smiled only when asked.

She took the elastic out of her ponytail and pulled the brush through her hair, letting the white strands fall onto her shoulders. Then she splashed water on her face and dried her hands and face with a towel. She leaned close to the mirror and pinched both cheeks, suggesting a dab of rouge. She pursed her lips tightly together, over and over, until they reddened. She looked at herself, at her red face and excitable eyes.

After stepping out of her skirt and removing her bra and panties, she spied Fred's bathrobe on the door hook. It was green flannel, the color of a starting flag in a car race. *It's a sign,* she thought. *It's time.* She put it on, tied it loosely in front, then moved back into the bedroom.

Fred had fluffed some pillows and placed others on the floor. He'd also refilled her wineglass.

"Very nice," he said, eyes wide. "It looks much better on you."

Before thinking of repercussions and why she was there and what she was doing she went directly over and stood before him. He looked up at her and took hold of the belt. Though the previous half hour had been dangerously slow, now he pulled it urgently.

Without a word they fell together onto the bed, arms and legs and bodies pushing against each other. The movement was so natural they might have done this a hundred times before. Every step perfectly choreographed. If she'd ever fantasized about this sort of thing — a sexual encounter with a virtual stranger — she might have imagined wriggling limbs, bungling embraces, awkward silences. But their movements were as smooth as a river flowing over timeworn rocks. She fell forward and onto him, straddling his body.

He entered her almost immediately. She gasped at her completeness. There was no searching for Viagra or grappling with personal lubricant or waiting for an erection. Just a brightness of energy and motion while he said her name again and again. *Catherine. Catherine. Catherine.* As if every dark corner of her world had been illuminated.

CHAPTER 32

The next morning Catherine stood at the stove absentmindedly flipping pancakes. All she could think of was Fred and their afternoon together. How the two of them had found each other and had fallen, hand in hand it seemed, down a rabbit hole of desire. *Would you like a blanket? Can I get you anything?* She'd been touched by his attention after their lovemaking and had fallen into a profound sleep. When she woke, she heard Karma snoring sweetly on the bed between them, and felt positively euphoric it hadn't been just a dream.

With spatula in hand, Catherine hoped Ralph would get up so they could talk, confident the buttery smells would lift him out of bed and into the kitchen. But it was after nine o'clock and he was still asleep. They'd missed each other the day before: Ralph returning from golf, then at a doctor's appointment; she home after her interlude with Fred, then off alone at dusk on the nature trail, looking for Sequoia, thinking things through; Ralph out to dinner with his poker group; she fast asleep when he got home, happily exhausted from her escape.

So as she waited, the pancakes bubbled and browned. To pass the time she put away dishes from the dishwasher, wiped the counters, refilled the hand soap dispenser. As she considered nonstick pans and all the crazy inventions in the world — robotic vacuums and ten-speed juicers — she wished someone would create an iPhone app that would assist in making personal decisions. As if it were as easy as plugging in her dentist's address and having Siri tell her which way to go: "Take DeRenne Avenue and head west. In a half mile turn on Paulsen." And then when she was where she was supposed to be: "You have arrived at your destination."

But that was the problem. She didn't know what the destination was or even what direction she should be heading in. She knew her marriage was falling apart. *I'm supposed to feel guilty,* she thought, *but I don't.* Really, she and Ralph were just cordial roommates, intimately familiar with each other's bathroom and sleeping habits. Even a marathon has a finish line. After twenty-six miles, a thin yellow tape signifies the end, while exhausted participants collapse to the pavement and mutter, "Thank god *that's* over." But where was the yellow tape in a decades-long marriage?

As nine thirty approached, she prepared more batter and cooked more pancakes. She set the table with maple syrup for her and peanut butter for Ralph, and placed the *Savannah Morning News* by his place mat. Then she defrosted and cooked a package of sweet sausage. Then one of bacon. Even Karma rose from his doggie bed to come in and stare at her, his beady eyes asking, *Are you okay?*

Finally Catherine heard Ralph's slippers shuffling along the living room floor. He entered the kitchen, head bent low and clearing his throat, then brushed past her toward the coffee.

And good morning to you too, she thought.

He poured coffee into the mug she'd left out. He didn't like to speak before his caffeine fix. In fact, when they first got married she'd given him a mud-colored T-shirt with jagged lettering: NO COFFEE, NO TALKIE. Before taking a sip, he brought it up to his nose. "Hazelnut? Really? Are you trying to poison me?" He was probably kidding, but the words stuck: *Poison him. I can poison him.* She took a moment to let the scene play out. An EMT standing over his body. A solemn memorial. Then an endless string of afternoons in Fred's bedroom.

"Just a little to give it some zip." She usually made the coffee with hazelnut or mocha or gingerbread flavoring, but he never seemed to notice. What he didn't know wouldn't hurt him.

She had a lot to say, questions to ask and things to discuss, but wasn't sure where to begin. With asking about Audrey? With telling him about the dog park or even referencing Fred? With asking what they were doing and where their marriage was going?

He sat at the table and Catherine scooped a pile of overcooked pancakes onto a plate and placed them in front of him.

"Are we having a party?" he asked.

A party? That's the feeling she had that she couldn't identify. Being with Fred felt like a soiree with colored streamers and sweet sponge cake. Yesterday afternoon was a celebration of life, the flannel bathrobe tie a fanciful ribbon on a gift. A party for two.

Ralph jerked the paper open, then folded it.

She might have said something about the weather, about how it would promise to be a fine day for golf. Maybe he could even get in thirty-six holes. After the big storm the other night, crews would have finished clearing fairways of fallen branches. Since the forecast called for cloudless skies, it would be prudent to bring extra sunscreen. But suddenly she felt reluctant to talk, as if some words held more weight than others, some canaries and others cannonballs. As if she wouldn't be able to control blurting out what she had done.

"So what's going on? What were you doing yesterday?" Ralph asked.

It was the last thing she'd expected. It hardly occurred to her he'd notice or care she was gone. "At the dog park. I helped a new friend look for his Great Dane."

"Did you find him?"

"Who?" Momentarily she thought he meant Fred. *Did you find Fred? Did you get what you were looking for?*

"The dog."

"Sequoia," she said firmly. Somehow saying the Great Dane's name made the afternoon real. "No. She's still missing."

"Cute."

"What?"

"Sequoia. For a big dog. I like that."

Catherine was sorry she'd mentioned the detail.

"And the park. How was that?"

She considered describing the tall picket fence and the back woods. The comfortable bench where two people might spend an afternoon.

"Catherine?" Ralph asked. "Hell-ooo. You there?"

"It was lovely. The people were friendly."

Ralph retied the string to his flannel pajama bottoms and his belly hung over the edge as if he were five months pregnant. He unscrewed the top of the peanut butter jar and looked inside. "You're running out," he said.

"Pardon?"

"You are running out," he repeated, louder.

"*I* am?"

"Okay, Catherine. I get it. *We*. *We* are running out of peanut butter. Is that better?" He scraped the flat edge of a knife along the jar's inside. "But do me a favor, do *us* a favor, and get smooth. You got crunchy last time."

She watched him spread a dollop on his pancakes. Thick brown crumbs fell onto his plate like crusted scabs from an incision.

Maybe he mistook her silence for confusion. Maybe he thought she hadn't heard him. "You know these little nuts stick in my teeth. It takes forever to work them out."

"Smooth," she said.

"Right here." He opened his mouth and pointed to a small gap between a canine and molar. It was a dark, empty space she never imagined he had and had been right there inside him all the time.

"Yes." She nodded, but now she was standing on a street corner holding a virtual suitcase that held her hopes, dreams, and all the things her future self might need. She imagined Fred somewhere nearby, ready to meet her and whistle for a taxi to the airport.

"I mean, I can floss it out. But smooth's better." Ralph's tone softened. "Okay?"

A dog was lost, Ralph. Our dog was lost, she thought. Suddenly she wanted to tell him everything, as if she were at confession. She wanted to explain that things happen without reason. That life can do an about-face when you least expect it. That fate brings people together in strange ways. "Karma was gone too."

"What?"

"We were looking for Karma, too. Not just the Great Dane."

"Oh, I see."

But he didn't see. He didn't understand and it didn't matter that there had been a storm and a kiss. Things had changed.

After taking another bite of pancake he smoothed the business section with one hand. "I'm thinking we should consider changing our investment strategy. Maybe go into real estate."

Catherine made a plate of pancakes for herself, sat down, and grabbed Mrs. Butterworth's waist and tilted her sideways, watching the amber liquid stream from her head as if she'd had a brain injury.

"There are some terrific opportunities out there," he said.

Opportunities? Life is filled with opportunities. We don't always know to embrace them but we can. Life is filled with choices and chances and changes. Dogs get lost. People fall out of love.

Then he added, "Downtown has some cool old buildings that need attention. And just think of all that foot traffic by Ellis Square."

I need attention, she thought. "Do you really know anything about this market?" Catherine remembered Charleston and how for two years before he retired they talked about getting a little historic house with an outdoor plaque — BUILT 1858 — and a brass door knocker. How they imagined they could buy close enough to the wharf to watch the boats come in with the tides. But their tech stocks had taken a big hit and all they could afford was an unremarkable neighborhood in Mount Pleasant. "Isn't it a little soon?" She was going to say *idiotic. Isn't it a little idiotic?* But she didn't, because she suddenly thought of Fred and realized that sometimes the world works in mysterious ways. Miracles happen. If they hadn't moved to Savannah, she wouldn't have met *him.*

"I'm just kicking the idea around at this point."

"Oh."

"Audrey has shown me some properties downtown that are interesting. That may make sense in the long term."

"Audrey?" Catherine felt a stiffness in her back.

"Look. The investments are my department. *This* is your department." He motioned his upturned hands to the kitchen. To the refrigerator and stove and microwave. To the empty jar of peanut butter. "Did you see she won salesperson of the month again?" He took his thumb and jabbed it into his mouth, trying to work out a nut, then poured more creamer into his coffee. "And I think that's it for the cream," he added. "You're out of cream."

And that was it. Without another thought

or a fight or even a word she let herself go. She gave herself permission to set off into the universe. She even left Karma, just for the morning. "I'll get some."

She stood, grabbed her purse and car keys from the counter, and let his voice fall flat in the empty well of the back stairs. Maybe he added some items to her grocery list. Butter or beer or bacon. Maybe called after her to pick up a book of stamps or a stick of antiperspirant. But she was already in the car, checking the mirrors, double-checking that the car was in reverse. With breath measured and mind focused, she backed out, being sure not to rush, not to let her heart control the gas pedal.

Then she put the car in drive and pulled out of the driveway and forward to the stop sign. She thought of the iridescent, delicate wings of a monarch butterfly, a butterfly that changes from egg to chrysalis to adult in a matter of weeks. A butterfly that uses the sun and an internal compass to find its way in the world. And so she followed her own instinctual feeling. Instead of taking a right to the wide aisles of Piggly Wiggly, she turned left toward Fred's house.

CHAPTER 33

Ida Blue couldn't believe her good luck, as if she'd cracked open a fortune cookie to find a scrap of paper that read *YOU WON!*

Fred had arrived late on the previous afternoon to pick up his dog. When she opened the door she noticed his grin, as big as a Triple Whopper. He thanked her for working Sequoia into her busy schedule — like she had anything else to do — and handed her a hundred-dollar bill.

Ida Blue flipped it over, expecting it could pay for Marvin Gardens or Baltic Avenue, anticipating *Not Legal Tender* or Rich Uncle Pennybags on the back. "Seriously?" she asked.

"I've never been more serious in my life," he answered. "And if you're willing, I'll need you mornings and hopefully some afternoons too."

"I'll try to fit you in."

Sequoia had wandered to Fred's side to

enjoy an ear rub, but when Ida Blue pocketed the money, the dog turned and approached, nuzzling Ida Blue's hip. She knew it was just the Slim Jim in her pocket but felt appreciated nonetheless.

"She's always been friendly," Fred said, "but I've never seen her like this. She just adores you."

"And the feeling is mutual."

"Look, I'm anticipating some longer trips, too. Maybe to Europe or the Caribbean."

"I'm here as much as you need me." Ida Blue fondled the beef jerky, then brought her hand out so the dog's wide tongue could smack at her fingers. "We seem to have a real connection."

At eight o'clock the following morning, Fred brought Sequoia back to Ida Blue's house. The dog practically raced through her front door, and Fred carried in her bed, some chew toys, a retractable leash, and a tub of food. He gave Ida Blue complete instructions for his dog's care, as if Sequoia were being dropped off at summer camp. He apologized for his vagueness but said he didn't really know when he'd return. He had an important appointment. Ida Blue couldn't be more pleased. She had no pressing engagements besides her talk shows and realized that missing yesterday's programs hadn't been nearly as difficult as she'd expected. She'd thought she'd crave Kathie Lee and Hoda the way a chain-smoker misses a cigarette, but she seemed to have quit cold turkey without any signs of withdrawal.

After feeding Sequoia a light breakfast and sitting out back to watch her root around in the yard, she decided to take the dog for a walk. The first thing Ida Blue needed was a workout outfit, but the closest thing she could find were polyester shorts with a wide elastic waistband and a Hawaiian shortsleeved top. She didn't have running shoes, so she settled for canvas slip-ons and found a bright pink sweatband to complete the ensemble.

As Ida Blue stood in her small closet, Sequoia seemed genuinely interested in her, her eyes following her every movement, her tail hitting the floor. Maybe it wasn't all about her Slim Jim. "Girls rule and boys drool," she whispered, then quickly apologized as she saw drool forming on Sequoia's lower lip. Next, Ida Blue headed to her garage to get the backpack filled with her flyers and removed them. The papers had been in there for weeks, corners wilting from the humidity. *Dog-eared!* she thought. With her new dogsitting empire supported by the patronage of Fred, maybe her days of marketing in hot parking lots were over.

Sally Ride didn't prepare for space just by watching *Star Trek,* so Ida Blue decided it was time to get serious. Inside the empty backpack she placed a half-dozen plastic bags, a thermos of water, three granola bars, a survival whistle, a travel umbrella, and bandages — in case either she or the dog developed blisters. She mapped out a mile loop from a pullout plan in the Seven Oaks phone book. Ambitious, but she was ready for a challenge. She could almost hear Oprah speaking directly to her: *Every journey starts with a step.*

She hooked the leash to Sequoia's collar and set off. After they passed her mailbox she had to stop to readjust her shoe, and Sequoia waited patiently. A few minutes later they reached the sidewalk and she stopped to sip water. If she was going to keep up this pace, she needed to stay hydrated. To keep her legs moving, her arms swinging, and her mind occupied, she started humming the tune of "Erie Canal": *I've got an old dog and she's a Great Dane / Fifteen miles on Oak Bluff Lane.*

After a bit, she stopped for a granola bar, feeling like Lance Armstrong in the Tour de France. Sweat dripped from her armpits and trickled down her sides. A mile was going to be a challenge but worth the pain. *Where there is no struggle, there is no strength.* Her thighs rubbed together and she was sorry she hadn't brought a tub of Vaseline. Surprisingly, the dog seemed fine, a worthy training partner. Sequoia would walk a few feet ahead of Ida Blue, pushing her to be the best she could be, then wait as Ida Blue caught her breath. As people passed in golf carts or on bicycles they tipped their hats or waved encouragingly, as if they were all living in the Olympic Village.

Then a dark-blue car passed. She noticed it because it was going fast, above the twenty-eight-miles-per-hour speed limit, but it suddenly slowed and pulled over. After a minute, it backed up until it reached her.

Ida Blue would have to get used to this, people wanting to chat about her fitness regimen, to enquire if she and her dog were training for the Rock 'n' Roll Marathon. She'd have to factor public relations into her schedule.

The car pulled alongside her and a white-haired woman rolled down the passenger-side window and leaned over to talk to her. "Is that dog yours?"

Ida Blue had seen shows about how often

dogs look like their owners, how people subconsciously choose pets that mirror themselves, so it was natural for this woman to make that assumption. Ida Blue had the same oversize head and strong body. The same gentle disposition too, though she knew the woman couldn't see that. "We're not exactly related by birth."

"No, I mean, isn't that Sequoia?"

The dog sniffed the air and wagged her tail. "Yes, baby." Ida Blue ran her hand along the dog's neck and held the leash tight. "Yes."

"What about Fred? Does Fred know you have her?"

"Of course."

"Of course?"

"He's my neighbor. We sort of share her."

"Wait." The woman shook her head as if trying to shoo away a bee. "You *share* Sequoia?"

"I'm his dog walker, but I prefer to think of it as *joint custody.*" Ida Blue liked the way that sounded. *Joint custody.* It was a phrase tossed around on daytime TV and *Divorce Court* when people wrangled over children or estates in the Hamptons. "He's asked me to be on call for a few days. He has *business* to attend to." *Business* might have been an overstatement, because she assumed he was retired, but it made her feel like they were all part of something big.

"Did he tell you that?"

Ida Blue wasn't sure what the woman was getting at. "Why sure. Mornings. Afternoons. It all depends. He's a pretty busy fellow."

The woman ran her hands through her hair, then looked into the rearview mirror though no one was behind her. "The other night. The storm. Wasn't Sequoia lost?"

"Lost?" That was the night Sequoia had come into Ida Blue's garage. The night her luck had changed. "Not so much lost as found. They were in my garage."

"They?"

"She was with another dog. A Boston terrier."

"Oh," the woman said quietly.

"Sort of brown and white. *Brindle* is the term for it." It was nice to be able to share some of her canine knowledge with the public. Maybe one day she could cohost a game show with Cesar Milan. Have Drew Carey on standby with *The Pooch Is Right.*

"I see."

"Are you all right?" Ida Blue asked. The woman's face had flushed crimson as if her car's air-conditioning had just gone on the fritz.

"You say you're a dogsitter?"

"Sitter. Trainer. Handler. I do it all."

"I'm sorry, what's your name?"

"Ida Blue."

"Ida Blue the pet psychic?"

"Yes, I mean I *was* a pet psychic, but truth be told, getting a good connection is sort of like finding love on *The Bachelor*."

"I called you a few months ago about Ralph."

It must have been one of her free ten-minute consultations. It was so draining dealing with people who believed in clairvoyance. Thank goodness those days were over. "Well, take what I said with a grain of salt. I was transitioning between careers."

"Ralph isn't my dog. He's my husband."

"You called me about your husband?"

"Sorry, but I don't have issues with my dog."

Was this one of the hundred fake calls she'd gotten over the years? People who made prank phone calls just to get her goat. *May I speak with Mr. and Mrs. Wall? No Walls there? Then what's holding up your house?*

Well, Sequoia isn't really mine, either, Ida Blue thought, *so we'll all just play along with each other.* "Here's a newsflash, lady. I'm not a real pet psychic, so pardon me if I take my dog." She tugged Sequoia back to

346

the sidewalk to make the final push toward home while the blue car pulled out into the road. Clearly, the driver had forgotten where she was rushing, as she made a sharp U-turn and returned in the direction she'd come.

CHAPTER 34

Fred felt like a teenager. He kept running back and forth to his dining room window to see if Catherine's car had pulled in. They had made a plan that she would swing by around nine, and although she was almost an hour late it didn't matter. All that mattered was seeing her again. He hoped they would fetch Sequoia and he could explain his dogsitting arrangement to her. The plan wasn't to deceive Catherine; the plan was to get to know her. He wanted to tell her about the pain of losing Lissa and his struggle to connect with Danielle. He might brag about Tommy. He could ask about her marriage or even about Ralph, while remarking how lucky a man he must be to have spent a lifetime in her company. He would have her tell him stories of Karma as a puppy and her own childhood, of summer camp or New Jersey winters or exotic trips she'd taken. He wondered if she preferred the beach or the mountains. Maybe one day he could bring her to Lewiston for the holidays, then rent a cabin near Sunday River or Sugarloaf. He hadn't skied in years but couldn't remember why he'd stopped.

Finally he spied her blue car parked outside, and he opened the door before she even knocked. She stood before him wearing a bright skirt and a short-sleeved shirt that flattered her figure. "Why hello there," he said breathlessly, as if he'd just been on a training run to get to this moment, the starting line of his last and best race. Fred had hoped that Catherine would jump into his arms as in a scene straight out of a Cary Grant movie. Instead she just stood on the stairs.

"I found Sequoia," she told him.

Momentarily, he'd forgotten that she hadn't been in on the details. Her quiet voice told him that the world had shifted. "You did?"

He needed to be the one to explain to her how their dogs had stayed together during the storm and had somehow found refuge in Ida Blue's garage. How Sequoia and Karma had navigated Seven Oaks' trails and worked as a team. He hoped the serendipity of the storm and their own united quest to find the dogs would make a romantic anecdote in years to come.

"I think she's in good hands with the 'pet psychic.' " Catherine put air quotes around the words, saying them weakly, as if they weren't worth the effort.

Fred couldn't imagine Catherine just running into Ida Blue, couldn't picture the oversize dogsitter venturing to the park or the nature trail. But it didn't matter. All that mattered was that he was losing Catherine. "I'm sorry," he said. "I was going to straighten things out this morning."

"Were you?" She held a macramé key chain in her hands and fingered the frayed edges.

"Yes, of course I was." He was going to tell her that his attraction to her was immediate and pure. How the last thing he imagined at his age was falling in love, but it seemed he'd caught a game-winning ball in the bottom of the ninth. He would tell her that if it didn't storm that afternoon, they could take the dogs for a walk along the harbor. Karma and Sequoia might enjoy a ride in the golf cart and the heady smells of salt and sand. He imagined Karma chasing crabs down the long docks, Sequoia relaxing with him and Catherine at a picnic table. He'd pack a cooler of cheese and fruit, and sweet tea — maybe even new chew toys for the dogs. He could find out what Catherine liked to eat. What her favorite movie was. Who she was. He wanted to know every inch of her, as if exploring a beautiful beach for the first time.

Then she took off her sunglasses and Fred could see she'd been crying. Her eyes were puffy and red, her eyelashes moist.

"Is it Ralph?" he asked. "Did he hurt you?" Had her husband learned of their encounter? Perhaps she'd felt compelled to tell him. "What's going on?" He stepped forward to reach for her, hoping to pull her toward him, to comfort her as best he could, but she twisted away.

"Listen, Fred, I'm sorry. I'm married. I was so taken with you — but it was a lie. I was wrong. I don't know what I was thinking."

"We weren't thinking. That's just it. We didn't *have* to think." The words came from a groundswell deep in his chest. "You see, we just followed our hearts. We let the afternoon carry us. Don't you understand —"

She held up her hand, palm wide and fingers extended. Her wedding ring glinted in the sun. "I can't and I won't. And I'm sorry too." Then she spun around, walked down the stairs, and started for her car.

Fred felt a push from behind and heard Lissa's voice: *Get her, you damn fool.*

Without wasting a moment, he took the stairs two at a time, forgetting even to hold the rail or watch his bad hip. Once on the walkway he jogged to her car and put himself between her and the driver's door. "I am *so* sorry." He grabbed her forearm. "I don't know about Ida Blue being psychic, but I do know she's my neighbor and a wonderful petsitter. Sequoia adores her. And our dogs found their way to her, after all."

Catherine shifted her gaze from the ground to his face. Her forehead creased, and he sensed she might cry.

Keep going, pal. You are losing her!

"I felt a connection between you and me. An understanding. Something beyond us both. I just want to know everything about you. About your childhood and dreams. I even want to get to know your sister."

Catherine smiled briefly before shaking her head. And then the tears came, large clear pearls rolling down her cheek.

Fred thought about their drive together in the rain and how they kissed. For the first time in twenty years, he didn't have to grasp for a word for his emotions but could have instead recited the dictionary: *Affection.*

Exhilaration. Expectation. Hope. Longing. Reverie.

What, do you get paid by the hour around here?

He reached for Catherine and pulled her close so that her cheek rested against his button-down shirt. She didn't resist, and her tears became hiccuping gulps. Though they were standing in his driveway, plain as day to any neighbor who might drive by, it didn't matter. He didn't care who saw. She was meant to be pressed against him, her forehead resting on his chest. They were meant to be together. And if there were time, he would tell her other things. That life is too short. That love is precious and dangerous and important. That things happen outside their control.

She broke away, and pushed his arms down. "I just wasn't thinking," she said, her soft hands now balled into fists as she thumped his chest several times. "And neither were you."

And Fred thought of his own marriage. How Lissa had somehow veered off course a few years after their own wedding. But how, if love is strong enough, two people can work things out.

We can and we did and I'm sorry. I'll always be sorry. You know that.

And then, as if Catherine couldn't hear him or the universal forces that wanted to pull them together, she spun around and departed, leaving an empty space inside him.

CHAPTER 35

Catherine had thought she'd feel safe at Seven Oaks. She'd equated living in a gated community with being sheltered, protected from Colombian cartels, grifters, and door-to-door vacuum salesmen. But she'd been bamboozled by Fred, an attractive man who had simply shown her a bit of attention. Catherine knew about online dating scandals and identity theft. She was a sensible woman who didn't use her social security number as a password, though her wedding anniversary as a garage security code seemed low-risk enough. So she felt foolish for believing Prince Charming would miraculously come into her life and fill her heart like a helium balloon at a fair. Every time she'd seen Fred she'd felt lighter, floating toward something real.

Though it seemed unlikely, part of her wondered if she'd been just one of several women seduced by Fred's charm. She felt like a fool, a willing spectator at a magic show who is called up to the stage after shouting "Me! Me! Me!" only to have both legs sawed off. She considered reporting the matter to security but realized that was ridiculous. What would she do? Fill out an incident report and admit that she'd been duped by Fred's kind smile, a friendly dog, and a few glasses of French wine?

She knew Fred had tried to call her several times. She answered the phone once and heard his hopeful voice. "Hello? Catherine? Is that you?" She clicked the phone off before he could say anything else. When Ralph answered the home phone calls he'd say, "Hello? Hello? If you can hear me, take us off your goddamned telemarketing list!"

Then there was the matter of her marriage vows. Of course she felt guilty. How could she not? But she didn't feel the need to confess anything to Ralph. What she needed was advice. Experience. Someone who knew her. She decided to phone Amity. When her voice mail clicked on, Catherine suggested meeting amid the art students at one of the organic beaneries downtown.

There was only one other person whom she could trust and who knew a thing or two about the vagaries of romance. Her sister.

"I met someone special."

"Wait, what?"

"I met a man."

"You didn't."

"I did." Catherine heard Martha's sudden intake of breath, as if she'd been hit by a toaster oven. "And why shouldn't I?"

"It's just, I thought you were happily married."

"Really?"

"I'm kidding!" Her sister snorted. "Don't be ridiculous."

Catherine heard voices in the background. "Where are you?"

"Waiting to play bocce. League semifinals. Team Boccelism versus Barack O'Bocce. So what happened?"

"I thought I was in love," Catherine said.

"No way. Who is he?"

"I don't know."

And she didn't. Was Fred a charlatan after her money? His house was as big as her own, so that hardly made sense. But she didn't understand the intricacies of penny stock frauds or Ponzi schemes, and the closest she'd come to money laundering was collecting Ralph's pocket change from the washing machine.

"So how did you meet him?"

"Our dogs ran off together during a

storm. One thing led to another."

"You mean he *seduced* you?"

"Hook, line, and sucker."

"Is he hot?"

Hotter than a solar flare, she thought. "Let's just say if he lived at the Villages there'd be an entire club devoted to him."

"And younger I trust."

"Older."

"On average, women live five years longer than men, Catherine. Do the math."

There were other things Catherine might have told Martha, if they hadn't sounded so pathetic. That her afternoon with Fred was the highlight not just of her week, but of her last thirty years. That in the few days she'd spent with Fred, she could imagine a lifetime with him.

"I can't say I'm surprised. I mean, what do you and Ralph really have in *common?*" Martha asked.

It's something Catherine had asked herself a hundred times in the last week. *We have only each other in common,* she thought. A shared past of dinners eaten and addresses lived. A lifetime of sitting side by side on a couch watching the same TV shows.

Then Martha added gently: "You know, just because it's old doesn't always mean it's worth saving. A rusted car in the backyard doesn't necessarily become a classic. Sometimes it's just a motel for stray cats."

"Maybe Ralph and I just ran out of gas."

"Could be. You wouldn't be the first."

Catherine sensed an unfamiliar wistfulness in her sister's voice, something akin to regret, but it was gone as soon as she'd identified it.

"So what's next? Do I hear *divorce*?"

"I don't know. I haven't gotten that far."

"Trust me. If you do divorce, you'll get the shaft. Been there. Done that."

Catherine hadn't considered not reaching an amicable financial settlement. Ralph would be generous, wouldn't he?

"You could work," Martha said.

"The last job I had was in a library with card catalogs and hand-crank pencil sharpeners."

"Teach?"

"Learn CPR? Get vaccinated for HPV?" Just saying *HPV* made Catherine think of the Villages' hot tubs.

"Does Ralph know?"

"No, but he suspects I'm unhappy. In the last week he's been trying a little harder."

"How so?"

"I came home yesterday afternoon and found all the spices arranged alphabetically: allspice, basil, cinnamon, dill." She might have mentioned the other things too. The folded bath towels and reorganized dog toys. All the pencils in the kitchen sharpened, points facing up. He'd even taken out the garbage without being asked, but she felt her sister slipping away. "I mean, it's not the most romantic gesture ever, but maybe it's a start."

"Listen," Martha said before she hung up to get back to the bocce party. "Enjoy yourself, make sure this dude isn't married, and find out if he has a kid brother for me."

CHAPTER 36

As Fred waited outside and watched the cars circle the Portland terminal, he felt like a suitcase abandoned in baggage claim. Finally he saw Danielle's gray minivan. She pulled up to the curb, got out, and came around to him.

"Sorry. Traffic." They hugged awkwardly as his shoulder bag fell between them. "Welcome to Maine," she said. Fred wheeled his suitcase to the rear door but his daughter took it from him. "Don't hurt yourself." Then using just one hand she flung it into the backseat.

"Where's Tommy?" he asked.

"Soccer practice. Tuesdays, Thursdays, and Saturdays."

"Oh." Fred opened the front passenger door and moved a pair of sneakers and a Superman figure from the seat.

"I thought I told you."

After settling in, Fred leaned forward and

grabbed a plastic candy wrapper stuck to his loafer. He was going to raise it up and ask, *You won't be needing this, will you?* Or *Melts on your feet, not in your hands.* But he didn't.

Before he could congratulate himself on his discretion, she breathed deeply, as if lifting a heavy weight. "Please don't start," she said.

Traffic was light as they headed north on I-95 and toward Yarmouth. Fred tried to think of something neutral. A common thread that would pull them together, a pleasant conversation they might enjoy if they were polite strangers on a bus. But she spoke first. "So, how was your flight?"

"Long, of course." As soon as he said it he had a vague recollection of an argument years ago, maybe when she'd first followed her boyfriend to Maine. About how far away Lewiston was and why she couldn't just settle in Atlanta.

"Security is the worst." Danielle imitated the deep voice of a TSA officer: "Take off your shoes. Take off your belt."

And then without conscious effort to stop it, he imagined Catherine whispering: *Take off your pants.* During the flight he'd tried to distract himself from Catherine with the airline magazine — a half-completed crossword puzzle and an article about cruising alone — but his thoughts kept coming back to her. He felt devastated not only that he'd deeply hurt her, but also, selfishly, that he might have lost his last chance for love.

They drove mostly in silence. Occasionally Danielle mentioned something about a recital or a meeting at Tommy's school, but they didn't discuss Lissa or how empty the car felt without her. Fred promised himself he wouldn't take the role of lawyer by asking whether she was receiving her child support promptly. So he tried to focus on things outside his heart and was struck by the many signs indicating recreational areas and the heady abundance of pine trees, several shades darker than Catherine's eyes.

As they turned off the expressway Fred heard a thud in the backseat. "What's that?"

"A soccer ball. Sometimes we stop and practice."

"I see," he said, though he didn't really. Weren't they taking this a bit too seriously? Had he missed the announcement that his grandson had been recruited for the 2028 Olympic team? It was one thing to enjoy a hobby. It was quite another to focus obsessively on a sport that involved head butting. What happened to giving Tommy tennis or golf lessons? Learning to swing a racket or a driver was more fun than running laps and wearing knee socks.

Don't meddle in their lives, he heard Lissa say.

Fred and Danielle arrived at her house a little after six. She took the suitcase from the back and he grabbed the shoulder bag. They entered through the back door into a narrow hallway. Lightweight jackets, shin guards, and backpacks cluttered the built-in shelves, while sneakers and cleats lay scattered across the floor.

Fred wondered whom she'd gotten it from. Both he and Lissa were reasonable, prudent people who understood the importance of a clean home. They made beds and swept floors and wiped counters. They tried to teach their daughter that a clean house translated into a clean mind. This looked like the handiwork of a madwoman.

"You don't have to say anything," Danielle said when she saw he had stopped. "This is my version of organized."

Entering the kitchen, Fred smelled garlic and sausage. *Aglio e olio.* Right away he recognized it as Lissa's recipe. For years she would serve the dish on Sunday nights when the three of them sat down together as a family. No friends. No boyfriends. No neighbors. They'd review the upcoming week and sometimes take a drive to the Tybee Island lighthouse or just get hot fudge sundaes at Leopold's. He wished Lissa were here now, holding up a yellow penalty card when the play became rough.

And what makes you think I'm not? He heard her as plainly as if she were right beside him. *You are doing fine. Just don't be a nudge.*

A nudge?

You know, don't push her. She's angry. She's grieving. Just like you.

I'm not angry.

Okay, you're not angry. You've gotten over it.

It was a long, long time ago.

He remembered the living room from their last visit, sitting with Lissa on the L-shaped couch and listening to Tommy muddle through "Twinkle, Twinkle, Little Star" on the upright piano. Back then Danielle had a photo of the four of them on the narrow wooden top. Now it was a virtual shrine to his wife. With flowers and votive candles and photos. Lissa as a schoolgirl in pigtails and pinafore. Lissa as a college graduate. Lissa holding Danielle while they sat on a haystack at a county fair.

Then a small voice interrupted him. "Hi, Grandpa."

Fred turned and saw Tommy standing shyly, wearing athletic shorts that appeared to be three sizes too big for him. His red curls were pressed against his forehead and dirt stippled his white shirt. "Why if it isn't Pelé!" Fred shouted a little too loudly.

"Who's Pelé?"

"Never mind." He went over and bent down to give the boy a hug. Fred felt his knees creak and wondered if he could get back up again. "My, my, you've grown."

And then he heard Danielle's stage whisper from the kitchen: "If you ever logged onto Facebook you might know what he looks like."

After dropping Tommy at school the next day Fred and Danielle passed the Lewiston town library and pulled into a shopping center that Fred recognized from their last visit. They'd taken Tommy for ice cream just south of here. His grandson had wanted praline marshmallow swirl but Danielle had steered him toward vanilla.

"See that?" Danielle pointed to a new building in the distance. Several hulking bulldozers leveled the gray earth, and a line of traffic cones indicated future sidewalks. "This is going to be Maine's newest retirement community."

White stickers on the windows reminded Fred of remaindered books in a library sale. "Bingo and everything?" he asked.

"No, really. It's going to be amazing. It'll have an indoor pool and cottages for independent living."

"Chair fitness? Balloon volleyball?"

"No, watercolor classes and world history lectures."

He could hear the hardness in her voice. When Lissa got angry, she'd do the same thing. Of course, Danielle's concern was related to her mother's death. When Fred and Lissa had each other, his daughter hardly worried. But now that he was alone, Danielle probably imagined him padding barefoot around Seven Oaks. As if now that he was seventy-five at any moment he might head straight out the front door, down the steps, and into the ground.

"Look, I know this is hard for you, Dad. It's hard for all of us. But I need you to stop thinking of yourself just for a minute. Stop being so selfish."

Selfish? He considered himself independent, self-sufficient, low maintenance. He might have told her about his few remaining friends who expected, even demanded, that their children call every Sunday. To send photographs and copies of report cards. To keep them updated on what their grandchildren ate for breakfast. He did nothing of the sort.

She tried again, a little softer: "If anything happens to you, we're sunk. I'd have to give up everything to take care of you. As you may recall, I don't have brothers or sisters to rely on."

"What are you saying?"

"I'm saying it's me. Me, me, me." She thumped the steering wheel with both hands. "I'm saying it's time to give up that house and that gated community. It's time to move here. Maybe we need you."

CHAPTER 37

It had stormed almost every afternoon that week. The rain fell in thick sheets so powerful that Catherine wondered if perhaps a nice community on a flat, dry golf course in Phoenix might have been a better retirement decision.

Although Ralph's schedule wasn't put off by the weather — canceled golf games morphed into lunch and an afternoon of liar's poker at the clubhouse — Catherine felt out of sorts. Her mind became a matinee that spooled endlessly, replaying the moments she'd spent with Fred. To distract herself, she took Karma for long walks in the mornings, to the Seven Oaks playground to watch the swings sway in the wind or past the dog park, to see if she could find Fred's car. She didn't. Toward the end of the week she ran into Ernie at the Piggly Wiggly, and he told her that Fred had flown to Maine to visit family. She couldn't believe he was gone, a shooting star that had flashed momentarily through her world. She threw herself into household projects — scrubbing the vegetable drawer, sorting the recycling, sweeping the attic — and then found herself on the couch at midday, paragraphs into a novel, then somewhere far away. A rocket ship to nowhere.

She met Amity once downtown to go walking. After lunch, they headed to Colonial Park Cemetery, to wander among the mossy headstones of early Savannahians and heroes of the American Revolution. General Lachlan McIntosh and Archibald Bulloch and Button Gwinnett. Real people who had fought for something they believed in. Catherine even suggested breaking into another house, hoping the rush of adrenaline would surpass the feeling she'd had with Fred, but Amity told her she was trying to cut back. Trying to kick the creeping habit.

The only thing that brought Catherine temporary relief was strapping Karma into his doggie seat and taking afternoon drives with no particular destination in mind. She cruised along the whimsical cottages of Isle of Hope and the antebellum-style mansions of Victory Drive. After crossing the Talmadge Bridge one dreary afternoon with the hypnotic *thwap-thwap-thwap* of windshield wipers, she lost herself in her science CD. Before she knew it, she found herself window-shopping on Calhoun Street in Bluffton, South Carolina. As warm mist rose from the pavement around her, she pictured renting a one-bedroom bungalow in the community, deciding what antiques to keep in her living room and which planets to stick to her ceiling.

Six days into his visit, Fred approached Danielle in the kitchen. "A nine-year-old shouldn't have math club."

She stopped unloading the dishwasher. "Pardon?"

"A nine-year-old should be out exploring trails or catching frogs. Not have every minute of his day accounted for."

"He's in the sixtieth percentile. If his grades don't get better, he won't get into a good college."

He's in third grade, Fred thought.

"Look, I know you're trying to help, and you *do,* but if he doesn't get word problems then he won't understand algebra. Next thing you know he'll be behind in trigonometry which means he's out of AP Math. He can kiss a college scholarship good-bye."

"Hello. Good-bye," Tommy said as he

walked into the room, a gargantuan book bag hanging from his narrow shoulders.

Fred looked at the boy and saw a bit of himself in his tired posture. "Can Grandpa help with your homework?"

Tommy nodded, so Fred followed him to the living room and settled next to him on the couch. Danielle came into the room carrying a plate of apple slices and set it on the coffee table. "Grandpa will be *happy* to help you with word problems, won't he?" She looked toward Fred.

"Happy, happy, happy," he answered.

Fred took a deep breath and looked around the room at the collection of board games and puzzles on the bookshelf. Even Legos weren't Legos anymore but ridiculous collections of spaceships and cowboy hats and faces. When Danielle was a child they were just red, yellow, blue, and white plastic rectangles and squares. Fred would sit with her and they would snap together a building with a pencil bridge. Now every box had a theme. Tommy could build the Empire State Building or the Brandenburg Gate or the Sydney Opera House without leaving the room.

Tommy grabbed an apple slice and wiggled it playfully in front of Fred. "Wanna bite, Grandpa?"

Fred took the bait and leaned forward, growling like a lion. He snatched the apple between his teeth, then devoured it with sloppy, exaggerated chews. As Tommy belly-laughed, Fred noticed his long eyelashes, just like Lissa's, fluttering. Even though the world had changed, some things stayed the same, generation after generation. Old math worked just as well as new math. He could teach his grandson that he didn't need a step-by-step colored diagram to have or do or become anything.

Tommy dug into his bag, then handed Fred a canary-yellow work sheet. After Fred found his glasses in his front shirt pocket, he read the first question. "Okay, a man has ten dollars to spend at a fair. Every ride costs three dollars. How many rides can he go on?"

"I need a dividend," Tommy said.

Fred placed the paper on the coffee table, then his gaze rested on the photo of Lissa and Danielle at the fair. Taken on the same day as the one Catherine had asked him about, with Danielle as an astronaut. "You're making it complicated. It's not."

"I need a dividend, quotient, and divisor. My teacher said."

"It's ten dollars and rides cost three dollars apiece." He thought of Catherine and imagined they might have taken Tommy to the Coastal Empire Fair if things had worked out differently.

"What rides are there?"

"A Ferris wheel," Fred started. "A giant Ferris wheel with wide comfortable seats and spokes lit up like a birthday cake." Fred could hear Catherine's nervous laugh as they rose higher into a starry night. Tommy wrote down a three. "And then a merry-go-round. A merry-go-round so wonderful the horses are real."

"And we could ride them?"

"Of course we can." Fred motioned to the paper and Tommy crossed off the three and wrote down a six. "Finally, there's a tunnel of love."

"What's that?"

"I don't know if they have them anymore. It's a small boat you row through a dark building." Tommy replaced the six with a nine. "And remember he had ten dollars to start with."

"So the dividend is ten and the quotient is three."

"So the remainder? What's left over when everything else is accounted for?"

"They went on three rides and the remainder is one."

And Fred thought of Catherine again and

reminded himself there wouldn't be a Ferris wheel or merry-go-round or tunnel of love. *The remainder is me,* he thought.

CHAPTER 38

Fred and Danielle sat side by side on folding camping chairs as they watched a scrimmage. Red versus blue. His grandson was somewhere in the middle of the pack, but Fred kept losing sight of him.

"I just think you might be micromanaging him, what with math club and travel soccer and everything. He'll have fifty years of showing up. Showing up for work and showing up for marriage."

"Is that what marriage was for you? Something you just showed up for?" Danielle chewed her upper lip, then pulled out a phone to take a photo of the boys.

"No, I didn't just show up for marriage. I loved your mother. We had a wonderful marriage. I'm sorry she got sick and I'm sorry you lost your mom."

"Thank you." He couldn't see her eyes behind her dark glasses, but he didn't need to be psychic to hear her anger.

"I'm sorry you think I could have done more. Is that what this is about?"

"Or less."

"Pardon?"

"You could have done less. She told me."

"Told you what?"

"About your relationship. About what happened. She told me everything."

"What did she say?"

"She said you and she separated because there'd been *others.*"

She was the flirt, he wanted to shout. *She* was the one. *She* had others. Then a soccer ball rolled off the field and past them. Several boys started to follow it but stopped when Danielle stood. She jogged to where it lay and threw it back onto the field. On her way back she stopped to talk to other parents.

It was so very long ago, and they were all just doing the best they could. His wife was just a person. She didn't have X-ray vision, sonic speed, or even superhuman strength to resist opportunity. Marriages are like Legos, he wanted to tell Danielle. They can snap apart and either remain detached single blocks or be rebuilt even stronger. They can take on different, unique shapes and stand the test of time when two people work together.

Then he heard Lissa: *I started to tell her, Freddie.*

It's ancient history.

I was going to tell her why we split up. She was just a little girl.

It was a long, long time ago.

But she was always so angry after that. I should have told her it was me, not you. I intended to, you know.

You and I got past it.

But she never did. That's the thing. I was going to make it right between you two. Before I left. And I started to do that last week — I really did — I told her how marriage is a journey that sometimes takes routes you don't expect. Of course, she understood that part. I was going to tell her how I was wrong to leave you but I saw her face and then put it off.

So you didn't.

She said she didn't want to get into it. Didn't want that conversation to be what she remembered of our last weeks together. I thought there'd be more time.

But there wasn't.

No, there never is. But I'm trying to make it up to you. I'm trying to give you another chance.

Fred and Tommy moved forward in the movie line. After the game, Danielle had dropped them at the theater. The boy was tired, leaning, his curls resting against Fred's chest. A gray-haired woman and her granddaughter stood ahead of them at the concession counter. The woman wore a sky-blue jacket embroidered with yellow flowers. It was something he imagined Catherine would wear for a spring day. Something that might cheer up other people. He was sorry that Catherine wasn't standing in line with them. That she would never get to know his grandson.

The children glanced awkwardly at each other. The girl waved, but Tommy stood still as a toy soldier.

"Do you know her?" Fred whispered.

"No. Not really," he said and turned away.

"Grandpa?"

"Yes?"

"Can we get popcorn?"

"You know your mom said no popcorn," he said, winking dramatically. Once at the front of the line he ordered a buttered jumbo bucket as big as a soccer ball.

As they headed into the dimly lit corridor he imagined how a senior center would feel. Carpeted, safe, predictable. There would be no sharp objects or inherent dangers besides the most obvious one — getting older one day at a time. There would be no opportunity to break a hip while slow dancing in the living room. And as he looked at the glowing red exit signs he wondered if it was in fact time to leave Seven Oaks. After all, who was waiting for him when he got back? Ernie and Lulu?

They found two seats toward the front of the theater. During the opening credits the lights dimmed and Tommy rested his head against his shoulder, so Fred lifted his arm and wrapped it around his grandson. He was an old fool to believe that Catherine would have ever really fallen for him. Would have left her marriage to run off with him in the — what? — ten good years he might have left. And he doubted if she would even forgive him for his deception.

The smell of suntan lotion revived Fred, and he wondered what he could teach the boy. Not about quotients or dividends or divisors but about love. One day he could teach him how to lead a woman on a dance floor and how to build a strong fire that would last through the night. He would teach him that love may come only a few times in a lifetime, but whether it lasted for thirty years or three days, it was worth the pain. And finally, he could teach the boy that a lie, no matter how small and insignificant, can take down an empire.

CHAPTER 39

"Wait, I thought you said Fred *returned* Karma to you." Amity was having trouble following Catherine and the drama.

"Yes, but you see he told me he didn't know where the Great Dane was. He made me believe something that wasn't true."

Amity was thankful that Catherine had called to suggest coffee, but her friend was jumping around as if she'd already drunk too much espresso.

"And besides," Catherine continued, "how do I know Fred and Ida Blue didn't lure Karma away from the dog park on *purpose*?"

"So what does Ralph have to do with this?"

"Maybe they're all connected."

Amity knew about people keeping secrets, both large and small, but she also knew that Catherine was acting crazy. It wasn't Fred that Catherine needed protection from, it was Ralph, who kept a gun in his file cabinet. People keep guns for protection, of course, but not hidden from their wives beneath piles of paperwork.

"Don't you see?" Catherine's voice had a tinge of exasperation. "I don't even know if Sequoia is Fred's dog at all."

Amity sipped her cappuccino and nodded politely. For the first time she felt thankful that she'd gotten out of her doomed marriage early and hadn't let the charade run for thirty or forty years, hadn't become a wife on the edge of insanity. "So you think it's a *conspiracy*?"

"Could be." Catherine shrugged and then looked down into her muffin as if she might find the answer there. "I mean, Fred and I had all these wonderful moments over just a few days, but maybe they weren't real at all."

"Listen, there are lots of things that aren't real but serve a purpose." Amity thought of Buddy, her invisible dog, whose leash allowed her to go anywhere in search of him. "Plastic Christmas trees. Artificial sweetener" — a waitress walked by with a dessert tray — "mock apple pie. Even our creeping. It's not a real thing, just a temporary fix that makes us feel better momentarily. People don't just lie in wait at the dog park hoping to encounter dupes. From what you've said, Fred sounds like a sweet guy."

"Fred *is* a sweet guy."

Every time Catherine said his name, she seemed anxious, looking around as if expecting him to be sitting in the next booth or entering when the front doorbell chimed. Although Catherine hadn't mentioned any physical contact, Amity knew a love connection when she saw it.

"But what I can't figure out is, why would he have gone through all the *trouble* to hide Sequoia?" Catherine asked.

"I think maybe he likes you that much."

"You do?" Catherine leaned forward across the table. "Really?"

From creeping in Catherine's house, Amity felt like she understood her friend a little better. She was glad she could help her on occasion, as sort of a domestic secret Santa, refilling the soap dispenser, folding laundry, whatever needed to be done. But she kept coming back to Ralph's gun, which didn't quite fit into their tidy house. Maybe he suspected his wife had a boyfriend. Maybe Catherine was in trouble. She'd like to warn her, but couldn't let her know she'd been a regular interloper in her house. "And do you think this psychic sitter had something to do with the dognapping?"

"Maybe Fred and Ida Blue are secretly *sleeping* together." Catherine sounded jealous. "Maybe they've had me in their crosshairs for months and Ralph is even in on the action. Maybe Fred was meant to lure me to a truck stop in Pooler so they could chop me into little pieces and Ralph could move on."

"Their crosshairs? Have you ever tried skeet or trap shooting? Does Ralph have an interest in sporting clays?"

"Pardon?"

Amity had to rein herself in. As when she taught English, she couldn't jump into diagramming on the first day: *Ralph (noun) keeps (transitive verb) a hidden (adjective) gun (direct object).* She sipped her cappuccino and came back to Catherine. "You're getting a tad ahead of yourself." Amity hadn't realized Catherine had such a vivid imagination. She wondered if taking her creeping had shown her a darker way of living and opened up a dangerous skylight in her mind. Truth be told, after her own near overdose, Amity decided creeping wasn't an effective coping mechanism, though a climactic farewell before starting therapy might be in order. She was even starting to think like Catherine, as she imagined jimmying the lock on the golf maintenance building and taking a fairway mower for a joyride. "Okay, Catherine, so now what are you going to *do*? You can't just sit on it."

"Do you know Audrey Cunningham?" Catherine asked.

"I know who she is." Amity recalled a glossy ad for Seven Oaks in *Savannah* magazine with a photo of a Realtor in a revealing button-down blouse and the tagline: "Let Audrey Cunningham Take You Home!" "I mean, who can forget that kind of brazen marketing? But I've never met her. My ex and I only worked with an agent downtown. We didn't think to consider the *safety* behind the gates." Amity was surprised by her own facetious laugh.

"I need your expertise."

"How so?"

"You found out about your husband, even though it wasn't what you wanted or expected."

"I did."

"But you didn't stop there. You *left* him. It's the bravest thing in the world."

Amity hadn't considered it bravery, only simple survival, but she still wasn't following. "So?"

"So I need you to help me figure out what Ralph and Audrey are up to. I need to know if they're having an affair."

Amity might have said, *Careful what you ask for,* but for someone as needy as Catherine, she wanted to be a little more concrete without mentioning the gun. "Husbands keep secrets. Trust me on this. I'm sure yours does too."

"Which is why you are the woman for the job. You understand why this is so important to me."

"What can I do?"

"Get me into Audrey's office."

Chapter 40

Audrey strode through the welcome center and closed her office door. Everything was annoying her — the other salespeople, the rain, Leona. Since it had stormed all week, clients wanted to talk only about the weather and global warming. No one wanted to look at a house or sign a contract. No one wanted to see how granite counters, marble floors, or a media room could enhance their pathetic lives.

Resting her high-heeled shoes on her desk, Audrey leaned back in the leather chair and looked out the office to the dark lagoon. Its crusted top resembled congealed chicken soup boiled too hard for too long. That's how she felt too, as if she'd been on slow simmer for years. She was getting tired of hustling, trying to sell people things they didn't need or appreciate or even understand.

Even Leona, dear sweet Leona, was making a general nuisance of herself. It wasn't necessarily the dog's fault. Leona had barely been outside for three rainy days, and the lightning and electrical surges were making the shih tzu crazy. An hour earlier Audrey had found her peeing on the rug under the conference table, and Audrey was damn well not going to get down on her hands and knees to sponge it up.

And to top it all off, Ralph was becoming a nervous wreck. A regular Larry Liability. What was he waiting for? A red carpet and an embossed invitation to join the deal? All he had to do was write her a check. It's not as if a hundred thousand dollars would sink him, for god's sake. He could take out a second mortgage, sell the Porsche, redeem some stocks. If he kept growing out his hair maybe he could sell it to some wig company. Maybe a balding twelve-year-old with alopecia was in the market for a gray ponytail. All it took was a little creative budgeting. If the world moved as slowly as he acted, they'd all live under a busted red light.

She knew Ralph was interested in her, of course. He'd made that perfectly clear. So she needed to continue to reel him in carefully, pushing the advantages of her investments without addressing any fringe benefits. She was not ready to tell him that it was his wallet, not his wee willie wonka, she was interested in.

The only one who had seemed at peace during the last few days was Mr. Peabody. The alligator lay for hours in the rain, in his little nest of leaves and sticks on the lagoon's overgrown island. Sometimes he moved a few feet or disappeared into the dark water, his laser-white front teeth always ready for a photo shoot, the end of his long mouth curled into a smile. If Audrey were in charge, she'd get rid of the alligator and truss it up in exchange for a nice pair of pumps or a briefcase. She'd install a fountain with some photogenic mallards, practical wildlife the club chefs could use for *duck à l'orange* in a pinch.

The ringing phone startled her. "Hello, Audrey Cunningham."

"Hello Miss Cunningham, this is Fred Wolfe. I've seen you once or twice at the dog park over the years and you dropped me a note recently." She couldn't quite picture him, so thankfully he added, "I have the Great Dane."

"Yes, yes, of course." How could she forget that dog? Each bowel movement must be like a souvenir from a bricklayer's convention. A loudspeaker drowned whatever else Fred said. "Pardon?"

"I'm sorry, I'm calling from the airport."

Though she couldn't exactly picture him, she remembered he had marshfront property, so she opened her file cabinet where she kept notes on every wealthy homeowner over sixty. These older prospects would all die at some point, and she would be ready when they did. She flipped open a manila file to find the obituary she'd cut from the paper. There was his deceased wife — Lissa Amelia Wolfe — in a boxy headshot sporting a wide grin and a string of pearls, dolled up as if on her way to a White House dinner. When it was Audrey's time, she would take out a full-page ad in the *Savannah Morning News* with the headline "See You Later, Alligators!" A scribbled note on the obituary confirmed she'd sent Fred a condolence letter and brochure about the Terraces, the local assisted-living facility.

If his Great Dane conveniently died before a closing in the next month, she could sell him the priciest model at the Terraces, which didn't allow pets. She might even spring for a silver urn in the shape of a paw print. Or, if this was her lucky day, Fred might have a chronic cough or a low white blood cell count, and she could get a nice commission for sending him directly to twenty-four-hour residential care.

"How's Sycamore?"

"It's Sequoia. Yes, she's hanging in there." *That dog should have died when the broad died. They usually did.* "So how can I help you?"

"I'd like to sell my house."

It was refreshing to see a clown who knew when it was time to pack up the tent. Nothing worse than the two-hundred-year-old geezers who rattled around the island in oversize Cadillacs, their cataracts as big as sunglasses. "You're on Jolly Badger, right?" Checking his address, she could picture exactly where he was, one of the original houses on a double lot. They could bulldoze the place in a day or two and build a sleek, modern residence closer to the marsh with an infinity pool. A few years ago, Audrey had had a brief affair with the building inspector, who helped her tweak the zoning ordinance. A single phone call to him and his wife at dinnertime would do the trick.

"Yes, that's right. We were original owners. Going on thirty-five years."

Good lord, she thought. She'd have to meet Fred for a walk-through to ooh and aah over a nightmare of wood paneling, shag carpeting, and a million fading photographs of his dead wife. If Audrey didn't think it'd offend him, she'd prefer to tour the interior in crime scene protective gear — a white jumpsuit and a respirator. She could probably have the place condemned within a week. "When would you like to meet?"

"My plane arrives at five ten. I can be at your office by six."

"Six tonight?" She liked a motivated seller, but really, what was the rush?

As if sensing her hesitation he added, "At seventy-five, you never put off to tomorrow what you can do today."

CHAPTER 41

The drive from the Savannah airport took longer than expected. Flooding on De-Renne Avenue forced Fred to take Veterans Parkway to Route 204, so he was half an hour late to his appointment with Audrey Cunningham. Yet he didn't think she'd mind. She struck him as a woman who might wait for another ice age if it meant a possible commission.

He used to wish he could remain in his house until the end of his days, but a week in Maine had forced his decision. Even if he couldn't write a happy ending to his own life, at least he might make a difference in Tommy's. As the boy grew, he could fill the empty space of a father figure, which his grandson needed. And maybe, just maybe, he could make peace with Danielle. His only regret in leaving Seven Oaks was not handling things differently with Catherine. Though he understood she had her own path to follow, he should have fought harder for her. Should have had the courage to tell her all that he felt. Should have grabbed her and held her as if his life depended on it.

He pulled into the real estate center and realized he hadn't been there in years. He had forgotten or maybe had never known that there were spaces for golf carts and bicycles and now there was even room and a charger for an electric car, as if next time there'd be one for an electric blender or blanket. Parked in front of a sign that read SALESPERSON OF THE MONTH sat another car, a black Mercedes sedan. Inside he saw Audrey Cunningham in the driver's seat, speaking emphatically into her cell phone. She gave him a quick salute, finished her call, then stepped out to greet him.

"Sorry I'm late. I hadn't anticipated the flooding," he explained as they shook hands.

"No problem at all. You've missed a rough week weather-wise." Audrey held Leona, the shih tzu. Fred didn't remember the agent well from the dog park, but he recognized her from her advertising campaign. He sensed a distinct neediness in her, with her low-cut blouses and tight skirts. He understood this was about marketing, about attracting attention, but he much preferred the refined way Catherine dressed, without the need to broadcast her body. Then in an instant he imagined Catherine in slacks and a shirt, an exquisite Christmas present that he'd like to unwrap but would never have the pleasure to again.

Audrey and Fred exchanged pleasantries as they approached the locked front door. "We closed at five," Audrey explained, "so we'll have the place to ourselves."

An empty reception desk stood before them, and to the right was a waiting area decorated with a tall grandfather's clock and shelves filled with novels and knickknacks. If he hadn't known better, he might have thought he'd wandered into someone's living room.

"Come this way." Audrey extended her hand to the welcome center ahead, and Fred was impressed by several flat-screen TVs and tall racks of glossy brochures. Wide four-color posters on the wall depicted the active lifestyle of Seven Oaks — a couple chipping onto a carpeted green, a family of five enjoying an oyster roast at sunset, a woman walking a brindle-colored dog on a wide sidewalk. Fred knew it wasn't Catherine and Karma — the model was a young woman in her forties — but he still did a double take.

"Wow, this is new." Fred stood before a

three-dimensional glass-cased diorama. Miniature figurines posed with frozen smiles on plastic faces. He vaguely recalled a rough Styrofoam display when he and Lissa had first visited Seven Oaks. Fred quickly followed Seven Oaks Way South, bordered by plexiglass lagoons and forest-green foam hedges, and found his house. All he could picture was being alone on his back deck, flipping a single hamburger on the grill.

Audrey laughed. "New? It's almost fifteen years old and heading to recycling next month to make room for an interactive touch table." She motioned to what looked like a full wet bar and pantry. "Would you like a cappuccino?"

"No, I'm fine," he said.

"Come." She took his elbow, as if she thought he might slip on the carpeting, and escorted him to her glass-walled office, where they both sat. "So we can talk about selling, but let's also figure out where you're going to *live* once you move." She said *live* emphatically, as if it involved salsa dancing.

"Frankly, I'm not interested in buying. I'll be moving out of state."

"The Terraces have some wonderful units. I think I can get you a discount if you make a deposit by the end of the month."

He thought of Lissa and Catherine. How

life skirts by quickly. How investments made don't always pay off. "Miss Cunningham, have you ever known love?"

Audrey shuffled papers on her desk. "Excuse me?"

"Love."

"I've never been married, if that's your roundabout way of asking me." She brushed her bleached blond hair back from her face with both hands.

Fred sensed she was flirting with him, but he ignored her. "No, not marriage. Marriage may have complications. People can make mistakes, can hurt each other without meaning to. I'm talking love with a capital *L.* I'm talking desire and intensity. *Losing* yourself."

"I love selling real estate." She looked around her office and motioned to the trophies behind her. They all wore tiny sailor caps made of what looked like diapers. Audrey stood, picked off the hats, and dropped them into the garbage. "And of course I love the safety and convenience of Seven Oaks."

"I'm talking about passion. Distinct and pure joy."

"I'm passionate about the new fitness center and our social clubs."

"No. Love. Pure and simple. For a *per-*

son." Perhaps he was overstepping his bounds, but it didn't matter. She could chalk up his animated comments to senility, to an old man who doesn't know any better. "About being so passionate about someone you don't even know what *hits* you." It felt good to speak his truth. If nothing else, he could spend the last years of his life teaching people about the power of love, and he would start with Tommy and Danielle and Audrey Cunningham.

"Love." Audrey said the word slowly. "I love Leona."

"Your dog, yes. But nothing else?"

"Speaking of love, where is that damn shit-zoo? Leona!" Audrey yelled. "Get your shiny behind in here!"

Fred heard tiny legs thundering down the hallway toward them, but the dog ran straight past the open doorway. He would pick up Sequoia from Ida Blue after his business here and, if it had stopped sprinkling, take her for an evening walk. "You see, it's all about love. There *is* nothing else." *Audrey is still young,* Fred thought. *She can stand to take advice from someone who's been around the proverbial block.* "When you are old, like me, you will not remember the contracts or the checks or the accolades."

"Leona, come!" The dog flew inside the office and skidded to a stop in front of Audrey. She sniffed wildly at the door and the rug and the desk, then put her tiny paws on the file cabinet and even sniffed there.

"You see, I've known true love twice in my life, which is two times more than many men. One woman I was married to for almost fifty years, and the other I met recently and just knew for a day or two."

"Uh-huh." Audrey nodded, but he knew she wasn't following. She was watching her dog, who was taking deep breaths of the rug by the closet. Sequoia did that when she was onto a squirrel.

"Although the circumstances were different, the feelings were the same. They were equally strong and equally powerful. I've been a lucky man and don't deserve the blessings I've had. It just feels right to quit while I'm ahead."

"But what if I get you a nice two-bedroom unit with a view?" The dog started to paw at the closet door, her tiny nails scraping the wood. "Cool it, Leona!"

He was so very tired. He would have liked to have said it was the plane ride, the tight connection in Atlanta, or even the emotional toll of deciding to move. But it was more than that. It was because he'd lost Catherine. "There is no life here for me without love," he said simply.

And then they both heard a movement in the closet, a shuffling of a jacket, and the rattle of the door as it slid open.

Catherine popped her head out. "You're leaving?" she asked, incredulous.

CHAPTER 42

Both Audrey and Fred turned suddenly to look at her. Audrey's eyes opened wide and she screamed, "What the —"

"Catherine?" Fred interrupted.

Catherine pushed her way past Audrey's blazers, golf umbrellas, and SOLD! signs and stepped out of the closet, into the room. "Did you mean what you said?" Catherine asked Fred.

Audrey jumped up to grab the phone but Fred picked up the handset first. He held it tightly to his chest. "Take it easy," he told Audrey. Then to Catherine: "Are you all right? What are you doing?"

What *was* she doing? Sneaking around the Seven Oaks real estate office like a common criminal. Browsing Audrey Cunningham's filing cabinet to see if she could find evidence of an affair with Ralph. Swan-diving into Audrey's closet when she heard voices approaching. "I'm falling apart," she answered. "I fell apart after I lost you."

"After you lost *him*?" Audrey asked.

Then they all heard the front bell and the anxious rattle of a locked door. Leona barked wildly, a child throwing a tantrum.

"Well if this just ain't Grand Central Terminal," Audrey muttered, leaving the room.

"You did?" Fred asked. "You fell apart?"

"I lost my compass," Catherine said, flatly. She sat down in a corner chair. "My north star." Even in the confusion of the moment she wanted to go to Fred and have him wrap her in his arms. Perhaps she'd over-reacted about his "lost" dog. Certainly she'd underestimated her need for him. But before she could explain anything to him she heard a familiar voice in the welcome center.

"Don't call security, Audrey, I've already alerted them." Ralph stepped into the office to face Fred. "Is this the guy?"

"I beg your pardon?" Fred asked.

"You've been pretty busy with practical jokes, eh?"

"Look, I'm not sure —"

"Audrey told me about you. The authorities are on their way." Ralph took off his windbreaker, hooked it around a chair, then took a step closer to Fred. "Conveniently

402

delayed till after office hours, huh?" They stood almost chest to chest. "And you keep yourself busy breaking into vacant houses, do you? You enjoy making prank phone calls to agents *impersonating* a seller when all you really want is to frighten someone with a dead raccoon? That's just sick."

Catherine waved to Ralph from her seated position in the corner. "Not him. That would be me."

Ralph turned to her and stepped back. "What are *you* doing here?"

Leona raced back into the room and, unclear whom to address, barked wildly, moving from Ralph to Fred to Catherine.

"Can't you keep this thing quiet for a change?" Ralph asked Audrey.

"Don't you dare tell me what to do," she responded.

Ralph opened the glass door and Leona scooted out to the wet lawn. They all were momentarily mesmerized as they watched her run back and forth along the unseen edge of the underground fence. The drizzle had stopped but the sky remained slate gray. Mist rose from the dark lagoon.

"Let me get this straight." Audrey took a deep breath and glared at Catherine. "It was *you* who called about the house on Fletcher Lane?"

Catherine nodded, feeling a strange satisfaction. Amity had taught her it was good to get out of her comfort zone.

They heard a low rumble, as if someone were moving furniture upstairs, and the overhead lights flickered and went out.

"Oh great," Audrey said, looking up to the ceiling, then clicking her computer's dead keyboard. "Just terrific." It wouldn't get dark for another hour, so there was still plenty of light to illuminate the confounded faces.

"So what brings *you* here, Ralph?" Catherine asked.

It was Fred's turn. "*This* is Ralph?"

Audrey interjected and pointed a finger at Catherine: "*You* are hiding in my office. *You* are making prank phone calls. *I'm* the one who should be asking the questions."

Catherine didn't hesitate. "And *you* are using my husband as a bodyguard? Do you always ask him to check up on you after hours? Do you share everything?"

Ralph countered, "Technically she didn't ask me. I just thought there might be trouble. I mean this guy" — Ralph pointed a thumb at Fred — "only called this morning. Who's in that much of a rush to sell a house? And besides, he had to meet after the office closed? It seemed a little suspi-

404

cious, if you ask me."

"So you're now in the security business?" Catherine asked her husband.

"No, but maybe it *is* my business."

Audrey arched her eyebrows. She had taken a seat at her desk, forearms resting on the surface as if ready for negotiation. "Oh, so *now* you're ready?"

Ralph ignored her and stayed facing Catherine. "Yes, so it *is* my business." He took a moment to clear his throat. "After all, we'll be investing together."

"Oh?" Catherine felt her stomach plummet.

"Riverwalk on Bay Street, a development of one- and two-bedroom condos, retail, and restaurants. Just west of City Hall, near Ellis Square." As Ralph spoke he gained momentum, gesticulating wildly as if conducting a tone-deaf orchestra. "There'll even be thirty thousand square feet of office space and a stand-alone parking structure." He pulled a hand through his long hair. "Don't look so hurt. Like you're suddenly going to start taking an interest in what I do? I mean, what do *you* do all day?"

"I take care of you."

"Like I need taking care of?"

"I keep a clean house and I cook you dinner. I get god-knows-what stains out of your golf shorts *and* your underwear." Catherine had never spoken to Ralph this way. "I even keep you swimming in smooth peanut butter. Smooth. Not chunky. Gets in your teeth. Gives you gingivitis. Imagine that."

"Well, I'm not your child or your baby."

"I've been taking care of you for thirty-eight years."

"Don't kid yourself. If that's your job, it's time to retire."

Catherine wondered if he meant it or was just showing off for Audrey. "I take care of the house and the dog and —"

"No, what do you *do*?"

Then she thought not of cleaning or grocery shopping or laundering but of the last five months at Seven Oaks. Of creeping with Amity and being pushed on a swing by Fred and taking drives with Karma to antique stores in Bluffton. She'd done more since they'd moved than she had in her lifetime. Her days here had been filled with excitement and emotion. And, since she'd met Fred, hope and — dare she think it — love.

"Your life is as empty as a black hole."

Catherine steeled herself before speaking. "Black holes aren't empty."

"What?"

"Black holes are infinitely dense."

"And you are so obsessed with that dog you can barely look out the window."

"That dog?" Catherine asked. "You mean our dog?"

And then Audrey shouted: "Leona!"

They all turned to see that the shih tzu had wandered to the lagoon's embankment. The dog was on the muddy edge, peering down to the water. "The Invisible Fence is out!" Audrey rose from her seat, fled past Ralph and Fred, and out the door. She kicked off her high heels and, arms pumping, raced across the lawn. Ralph followed.

"Did you mean what you said?" Catherine asked Fred. "You know, about passion? About love?"

"Every word," he answered.

Catherine thought of the afternoon she'd made love to Fred and remembered his gentleness and kindness. She'd laughed that day and felt hope. She'd been happy.

Before either could continue they heard Audrey scream and both turned. As if in slow motion, the earth gave way beneath the real estate agent and her small dog. Several feet of the bank disappeared into the water. Catherine lost sight of them as they fell.

Catherine and Fred made it outside just as Ralph reached the edge. As he called to

Audrey, the crusty earth below him collapsed too and he dropped into the lagoon. The surprise of the fall caused him to tumble forward onto his hands and knees.

Catherine felt Fred's hand grab her elbow.

"Don't get too close," he said. "The rains must have eroded the bank."

Audrey was near hysterics, yelling to her dog. "Come! Leona, come!" With her blond bob now wet and plastered to her scalp, the real estate agent struggled forward, taking one step at a time. Leona, several feet in front of her, dog-paddled for dear life.

Fred grabbed a fallen oak branch and moved as close as he could to the edge without risking another collapse. He called to Ralph, who scrambled forward to grab it, but it was too short. Then Catherine heard a golf cart's quiet whirr and turned to see Amity pull up to the building. She'd forgotten that her friend was waiting for her to emerge from the office.

Amity was the one who screamed and pointed: "Look out!"

All heads turned to the island to see Mr. Peabody waddle forward. He slipped from the bank, into the water. His long tail twitched eagerly as he swam slowly toward them.

With arms cartwheeling, Audrey somehow

caught Leona. She held the small dog above her head as she waded back toward shore. The murky water was only one or two feet deep, but with every third step she sank to her thighs.

Ralph turned to see Mr. Peabody, now forty yards away, then shouted to the group, "My jacket! Get the gun!"

Amity, closest to the office, rushed to the building and the open door.

"It's hooked on the chair!" Catherine called, and in what seemed like only a few moments later, Amity was back out on the grass beside her.

Mr. Peabody's eyes, visible just above the water, locked on Leona and Audrey. He barely made a ripple as he skimmed past lily pads and through green moss. Ralph turned and yelled something at the gator, but Mr. Peabody didn't stop. He neither slowed nor sped, just kept coming with wide eyes and spiked tire-tread back.

A panicked sound came out of Amity, so Catherine turned to her and watched as Amity did the only thing any of them could do. She tightened her index finger around the gun's trigger, straightened her arms, raised the weapon, and took the shot.

CHAPTER 43

Catherine slammed her hands over her ears as the bullet screamed straight up into the air and the gun whipped behind Amity's head. Meanwhile, Ralph dove toward the muddy shore where he crouched in the duck-and-cover position. Instantaneously, the alligator splashed beneath the water and disappeared.

"Holy fuck." Amity looked at the gun in her hands, to Catherine, then back to the lagoon. "Holy, holy fuck."

Everyone remained still, as if the shot had signaled a pause in a disastrous game of freeze tag. Audrey, cradling Leona, stood perfectly still exactly where she'd been, brown water up to her knees.

"Oh my god! What *happened*?!" Amity asked Catherine. "I get you into the real estate center and the whole world shows up and decides to go for a swim?"

But Catherine was too lost in anxious

thought to reply, replaying the image of Mr. Peabody streaming toward the shore, imagining this was how it all would end.

Ralph stood slowly and limped toward the left side of the lagoon. He found an exposed root to stand on and, using a clump of spartina grass, pulled himself up to the lawn. "Oh shit," Catherine heard him mumble as he hobbled toward them, grabbing his calf.

"You better get out of there!" Amity shouted to Audrey, then moved to assist Ralph.

Ralph turned to Catherine. "What's wrong with you? I said I've been *hit*!"

"Don't be ridiculous." Catherine was sure she'd seen Amity point the gun skyward at the last second, but perhaps the bullet had ricocheted off an overhead branch, hit the thick wood of an oak tree, and executed an abrupt U-turn, somehow nicking Ralph along the way. She might have felt sympathy or fear for her husband, but she felt nothing. Meanwhile, Amity pulled a dog leash out of her fanny pack. With Ralph now sitting on the wet grass, she tied the leash as a tourniquet around his slacks above where he held his leg.

Then Fred scrambled crab-style down the embankment.

"It's slippery!" Catherine shouted. "Be

411

careful!"

The coffee-colored water reached Fred's shins, and he high-stepped toward Audrey. Because Leona was so uncharacteristically quiet in Audrey's arms, Catherine wondered if the renegade shot had somehow hit the shih tzu, a single bullet shard through her peanut heart.

Catherine felt something close to jealousy when Fred reached Audrey and placed one hand on her elbow, his other around her waist. She heard the outline of his voice calming her as he might a skittish animal. "It's okay. C'mon. That's right."

And then next to her, Amity gasped. "Jesus," she said, breathless. "He's back!"

He's back. Catherine recognized the line as straight from a bad horror movie, from a final scene where the monster — stake through heart and spike through head — roars back to life. A scene where the audience understands anyone still alive is a goner. Fifty yards away, Mr. Peabody wasn't taking no for an answer. He floated lower in the water, only black eyes and wide snout visible.

Fred grabbed Audrey and half-carried, half-dragged her toward shore.

Catherine was going to tell Amity to fire another warning shot, to scare the alligator and be sure to keep Fred safe, but before she could find her voice she heard the click of an empty cartridge. She turned to see Amity holding the gun skyward like a referee starting a hundred-yard dash, in a wide-legged stance, prepared for the gun's recoil. Amity pulled the trigger over and over. Empty clicks on a quiet soundstage.

"Hurry!" Catherine shouted, though clearly there was nothing more her friend could do.

For a moment Catherine imagined that Fred and Audrey were partners at a picnic, in a three-legged race for their lives. Mr. Peabody continued forward steadily. He did not lurch or flail as in a *National Geographic* special, but swam intently, a premeditated killer focused on his prey.

As the gator advanced to thirty yards, Catherine felt her whole future evaporating. She heard herself screaming wildly, shouting who knows what into the world, and praying suddenly to a god she'd never called on. When Fred and Audrey reached the mucky shoreline, Mr. Peabody was only twenty yards away. Catherine searched the manicured lawn for something to throw, a rock or a branch or even a pinecone, but found nothing.

Then she heard a siren from the direction

of the clubhouse and caught a glimpse of a flashing blue light as a Prius raced toward them. She lost sight of the car after it tore straight across the golf course, through a bunker, then dipped into the fairway. As it approached, Catherine recognized the red-haired security officer at the wheel and beside him what looked like a large blow-up doll, like drivers used in high-occupancy lanes of the New Jersey Turnpike. After skirting a clump of pampas grass, the Prius slammed to a stop beside her and Amity and Ralph. Both occupants jumped out and Catherine recognized the passenger as Fred's dog walker, Ida Blue.

The uniformed security guard pulled out his holstered gun as the alligator closed within ten yards. He fiddled with the safety until the large woman elbowed him aside and grabbed his weapon. She clicked open the lever, knelt, and fired.

The bullet splashed within a foot of the alligator's snout. Mr. Peabody bucked backward and his long tail whipped high into the air and down, making a splash as big as Catherine had ever seen. Within seconds, the dark shadow retreated to the far end of the lagoon. Catherine lost sight of the gator as he fled behind the island.

The guard returned to the Prius, where

he pulled out a nylon rope and first aid kit. He tied the rope into a lasso and threw it to Fred. "Get her out of there."

Fred grabbed the rope and looped it gently over Audrey's head and shoulders as he took Leona from her. "It's over," he told Audrey. "Just hold on tight."

Her eyes wide and blinking, Audrey did as she was told. Fred pushed her, one hand on her buttocks, up the incline while the guard grabbed her outstretched arms. Once safe, the security guard threw the rope to Fred, who was able to scramble up the hill. They all gathered in a ragged circle on the grass as Ralph clutched his leg.

"She shot me!" Ralph cried to the security officer, pointing to Amity. An inch-long rip and what looked like drops of ketchup stained his khakis.

"Okay. Relax. Take a deep breath." Catherine saw the guard's name tag — RUSTY — as he bent down, untied the dog leash, and pulled up the hem of Ralph's pants.

"I can't bear to watch," Ralph said, looking away.

"Looks like you were bitten."

"The gator *bit* me?"

"Nope." The guard snapped his gum. "Mighta been a rusty nine iron."

"Huh?"

415

"You got stuck by a broken golf club shaft. I didn't invent the game, in fact I don't even know why people play if it's so damn frustrating. Can you imagine if this club had *teeth*?" He laughed until he saw no one thought it was funny. "But for sure you're gonna need a tetanus shot."

Ida Blue pulled a pouch from the first aid kit. As she unfolded it, it became a metallic poncho that she wrapped around Audrey, still silent and pale. Catherine imagined an aluminum-foil turkey about to be baked.

"Well, your timing was perfect, but how'd you know to come?" Fred asked.

"A golf club?" Ralph interrupted. "Are you *sure*?"

Rusty nodded to Ralph, then answered Fred: "Got a call from a Mr. Ralph. Said there was suspicious activity. An after-hours arrival to the real estate center. And this little lady" — he turned to Ida Blue — "confirmed it. You see, she's *psychic,*" he explained.

"A *psy*-chic *side*-kick," she added, smiling.

"We need all the help we can get 'round here. Prank phone calls. Half-dozen reports of home entry. Nothing taken, just evidence of intruders. Can't have those shenanigans at Seven Oaks." Catherine and Amity made eye contact. "That's the problem here. People figuring gates keep nut jobs out. I reckon that's what keeps 'em *in.* Islands make people go crazy."

"Just look at *Bachelor in Paradise,*" Ida Blue said, helpfully.

Fred put his hand on Ida Blue's shoulder. "I know you're a damn good dogsitter, but how'd you learn to *shoot* like that?" he asked.

"My uncle made us shoot apples off Princess Diana's tiara," she explained, though nobody understood the reference. Then, in the distance, they heard a muffled, barely discernible rumble of thunder. There would be no more rain that evening.

Catherine looked to Ralph, who was staring into his cut, a wound barely bigger than he'd get shaving. He looked up to her and smiled sheepishly before picking out slimy marsh grass from his shoes and pathetically trying to sweep soupy moss from his khakis.

"Catherine, honey?" Ralph asked her. "Would you mind getting me a towel?"

She stood exactly where she was, next to Fred. Then, for the first time in her life, she felt sorry for her husband. "A gun, Ralph? Really?"

"We moved to Georgia," he replied. "You *know* it's south of the Mason-Dixon Line."

Then Catherine looked back to Ralph's pants. *Audrey's going to have a helluva time getting those stains out,* she thought.

CHAPTER 44

Six weeks later

"Yee-haw!" Ida Blue shouted when she saw the golden retriever veer off the sidewalk and toward a fire hydrant. She yanked the dog's leash while the other dogs kept their forward momentum. Within moments all five were back on track, a peloton in the Tour de France, heading home from their third walk of the day.

As they turned down her street, a minivan passed and beeped. Ida Blue waved wildly, yet she could barely keep track of her clients anymore. After her recent *Good Morning Savannah* appearance she was now the hometown hero, too busy to watch daytime TV, to hang on Dr. Phil's every word. Instead of telling obsessive housewives that their parakeets needed more exercise or their dogs didn't like hats, she had commitments to dogsit and to lecture skeet-and-trap clubs about gun safety.

"Whoa!" she shouted as the pack neared her mailbox. As they careened to a stop, she transferred the leashes to one hand, then reached inside to find grocery coupons and a handwritten envelope with *MISS IDA BLUE* written in big oily letters. Without opening it, she recognized Rusty's scrawl. Each week he dropped off a hand-drawn card or placed a colorful bouquet at her door. On two occasions, he'd even regifted presents from his housesitting clients — a book on trout fishing and a ten-dollar gift certificate to the Waffle House.

With mail in hand, she led the pack to her side gate. Her new enclosure might have been outside her budget if she had the wherewithal to keep one. All she knew was that the money was coming in faster than she could buy rope toys, grooming brushes, and do-it-yourself plastic fencing. She unhooked the leashes and the dogs rushed forward to cool off in the kiddie pool, a plastic tub decorated with goldfish floating in clouds. It reminded her to check her YouTube channel. In her latest three-minute clip, while she sat in a swimsuit and matching tasseled swim cap, she discussed the importance of keeping pets hydrated in the heat. As she did, tailed torpedoes splashed around her. Forget dancing cats, she had photogenic dogs, and within the first two weeks the video had received more than a hundred thumbs-up.

Once inside the house, she called in the dogs for dinner and toweled them off, one by one. During mealtime Ida Blue felt like Alice in *The Brady Bunch*. In charge of a family that wasn't even her own, but was just where she belonged.

After feeding the dogs, she hustled to her closet. She'd forgotten she'd already chosen her evening outfit, so her polyester slacks and floral tunic hung from the door as she entered, as if some part of her were already dressed for the magic show, ready for the next chapter of her life. Though she felt more complete than she ever had, there was still a small part of her that neither a chewy-chip granola bar nor a like on Facebook could fill.

Much to her delight, she found a single vacant parking spot by the community center's front door. Another cosmic give-away from her fairy godmother. Although she hadn't seen the ghostly older woman since the night of the big storm, since she'd received the unexpected gift of Sequoia and Karma, she felt her presence whenever she noticed a happy coincidence. Like when she encountered a string of green traffic lights, strung like a Christmas tree, or some nice pink pork chops on sale — ONE DAY ONLY! — just when she was in the mood.

She pushed open the wide doors, passed the crowded bingo hall, and followed the MCSWEENEY HOUDINI TONIGHT signs to a smaller room off the lobby. She'd sat for a few minutes in the front row when a woman approached. "Just so you know, the show doesn't start until eight."

"Yes, yes," Ida Blue replied. "I wanted to make sure I get a good seat."

"Oh, I see." The woman looked around the empty room and laughed, then added, "Say, aren't you that woman from the lagoon?"

Ida Blue nodded. "Why yes."

"I just want to say, and I can speak for our whole community, everyone at Seven Oaks owes you a debt of gratitude. Saving all those people's lives, sparing that poor alligator . . ." Her voice trailed off.

"Thank you," Ida Blue answered, finally understanding how Oprah must feel when approached by a fan in a grocery store.

At precisely eight o'clock, an emcee wandered onto the stage, welcomed the sparse audience, then reminded them of upcoming events — a ventriloquist in July, a puppeteer in late September. Then the *Hawaii Five-O* theme song roared to life from a geriatric speaker. With no curtain, McSweeney emerged from a side door, which might have been a broom closet. While waving to the audience, he stumbled forward but caught himself before landing face-first. No one laughed except for Ida Blue and a set of pig-tailed girls sitting behind her.

Although McSweeney looked older, she recognized him immediately and felt an excitement rise in her chest. As a teenager he'd been tall and gangly, but now he was so slender she wondered if he'd eaten a real meal in twenty years. He wore black slacks and a long-sleeved shirt under a glittery vest. Horn-rimmed glasses sat on his crooked nose, and his thinning hair swooped sideways across his head. When McSweeney looked out to the audience, she tried to get his attention, mouthing "Hello" to him and giving a little fist pump by her hip, but he didn't seem to notice her.

To start the show, McSweeney pulled a silk handkerchief out of his breast pocket. With a dramatic flourish, he shook it and it became a silver wand. Then he dazzled the crowd, or at least Ida Blue, with balloon art, which led to a balloon rabbit that became an actual rabbit that scampered across the stage leaving decidedly real pellets. Next he performed a routine that climaxed with him juggling a toaster, a hairbrush, and a woman's sandal. After McSweeney changed a disgruntled gentleman's twenty-dollar bill into an issue of *TV Guide,* the rear speaker roared to life again with a thumping drumroll.

"And now I need a volunteer," McSweeney announced. While other spectators checked their watches and turned to identify exit signs, Ida Blue waved her hand. "You! The pretty lady in the front row." The magician pointed to her, and Ida Blue flew up the four steps to the stage. All of her walking had paid off. "Welcome," he said.

Ida Blue waited for him to recognize her. It had been twenty years, but surely he must. "Hello McSweeney," she whispered.

He wheeled a metal table forward, then opened a briefcase in front of her. Inside, Ida Blue spied some oversize playing cards and a dog-eared copy of *Playboy* as well as a printed sign that read ANSWER "NO" TO ALL QUESTIONS.

"Now tell me, miss, do you believe in magic?"

"Yes!" Ida Blue thundered.

"Let's try again." With the briefcase blocking the audience's view, he pointed to the sign, moving his index finger as if tapping out Morse code. "Do you think I can create something out of nothing with just a wave of this magic wand?"

"I think you can do anything you put your mind to. You're McSweeney Houdini!" The audience laughed.

"It's true we've never met, correct?" He looked at her as if he had something stuck in his eyeball.

"But we have!" she shouted.

McSweeney pursed his lips in irritation. He cocked his head and pushed his glasses farther onto his nose.

"Don't you remember? We used to go parking at Flo's Drive-In." The audience roared, and Ida Blue wondered if a busload of people had arrived since she'd been selected for the spotlight. She might have seen a flicker of recognition, but it was not the reunion she expected. "I'm Ida Blue Childs," she said, weakly. Perhaps he didn't recognize her now that she'd shrunk to a size twenty-four, thinner than she'd been since seventh grade.

"Ida Blue?" he asked, confused. She felt suddenly tired and hoped there'd be a way to drift inconspicuously offstage, but she heard: "Is it really *you*?" She felt his hand, hard on her elbow, and he spun her around.

While doing so, he reached behind her and pushed something solid into her elastic waistband. "Yes, we *do* know each other." He twirled back to the front of the stage. "And yes, we *did* use to park at the submarine shop." He gave an exaggerated wink and a murmur rose.

Then the music started again, the beat thumping as if someone was stuck in a car trunk. Within minutes, in a final routine of unimaginable precision, he broke apart solid linked hoops, then swallowed a steel sword. With steady applause he bowed dramatically before her, one hand on his torso, one behind his back. "Thank you, milady." Then he reached into her elastic waistband and presented her with a flapping, if somewhat dazed, white dove.

She waited in front of the men's locker room door for several minutes. Although she'd imagined she'd be sharing the lobby with autograph-seeking fans, she stood alone, the distant hum of a vacuum in the background. Although part of her wanted to go back to her dogs, another part of her needed to see him.

But then, as if someone were right next to her, she heard: *Stand up straight. Don't be afraid. Let your smile be your umbrella.*

426

With head up and shoulders back she brushed any lingering dog hair from her outfit and knocked lightly. No answer. After a minute, she knocked again. "Just a sec!" Ida Blue heard anger in his voice and wondered if she'd interrupted a TV interview.

The door opened and McSweeney Houdini popped his head out. Slowly, he opened the door and stood before her, sweat staining his undershirt. He held a half-empty bottle of bourbon. Their eyes locked and his mouth melted into a smile. "Ida Blue Childs," McSweeney said sweetly and softly this time, like he meant it.

She stood frozen but felt a firm push from an invisible hand.

Let the magic begin.

CHAPTER 45

After a full day of teaching summer school, Amity drove straight to the natural food store south of Forsyth Park. As she pushed her half-full grocery cart outside, she noted the rising moon behind the wide live oak trees and thought of Catherine. Before her friend had left on vacation, Catherine had told her a story about the Sea of Tranquillity and how the ancients looked for signs in the stars.

Okay, okay, she thought. *So show me a sign already.*

As she maneuvered down the flare in the sidewalk, that's when she saw PUPPY'S FOR SALE — $10. On another evening she might not have been bothered by the grammatical error. PUPPY'S. Or she may have noticed, but not made it her business to care, but Amity *had* asked for a sign. She wheeled her groceries to a grizzled older man sitting on a plastic chair with a small fold-out table beside him from which the scotch-taped sign hung. She would stop just for a moment. The low-fat ice cream and vegetarian pizza and frozen organic peas were going to melt.

"Your sign," Amity said, motioning to the cardboard message.

"Want a puppy?"

"No. Your sign. It should be plural, not possessive."

The man looked at her, his head tilted slightly to the right as if he'd lost feeling in his neck.

At once she realized her mistake. She should just mind her own business. But he was marketing puppies to an upscale crowd. She started again, "I'm a teacher. I can't help myself sometimes."

"*I* before *e* 'cept after *c*, right?" He smiled when he spoke, his teeth lurching forward.

"Yes. Of course." She might have offered other mnemonics, but she was determined to stick to the problem at hand.

"Wanna puppy?" he asked again.

"Pardon?"

"A puppy." He pointed to the box.

She hadn't even looked in, they'd been so quiet. So she took a step forward and peered down. She was surprised by the still heads, closed eyes, and limbs splayed in every direction. *Oh my god, they're dead,* she thought.

"Got four left and Mama ain't doing so hot."

"I don't know." After getting to know Catherine and spending time walking with Karma she had certainly thought a dog might be nice one day. But this wasn't the right time.

"If so, yer in luck," the man continued.

It sounded like *Your in luck* or even worse, *urine luck.*

She could have turned to go, bid him goodnight, wished him well, or just handed him ten dollars to get a good shave, but just then a puppy awakened. He scrambled onto his hind legs and peered at her over the top of the corrugated carton.

"Cute, huh?" The man lifted an eyebrow solicitously.

But *cute* wasn't what Amity was thinking. *Desperate. Sad. Heartbreaking.* To begin life in a cardboard box on a hard sidewalk on a warm June evening. "What kind are they?" *Not that I care,* she thought.

"They're what you might call high-birds."

"Pardon?"

"Mutts."

She had groceries to bring home, dinner to make, soy milk and cottage cheese to get

430

to the fridge. She even had a load of gym clothes to wash before morning. "How old are they?" *As if it makes a difference.*

"Four weeks. Need their shots is all." A second puppy popped his head over the edge of the box. "Two boys and two girls all that's left."

Boys and girls, like they're little people. Like they are babies.

Then the third one popped up.

"The one back there." The man pointed to the final puppy. "He's the one always sleeps."

And then Amity heard high-pitched childish chatter behind her. She turned to see a young girl of three or four sitting with a red lollipop in the seat of a grocery cart pushed by her mother.

"Puppies!" the little girl shouted.

The mother laughed. "Yes, puppies," as if her daughter had just identified a new species of vertebrate.

The man shifted his focus. "Puppies!" he sang out. "Ain't they cute?" He had directed his question to the girl, but winked at her mother. "Only ten bucks."

You snooze, you lose, Amity thought and managed to smile at the two. The mother wheeled her cart and child closer. The three puppies clambered together as one squirm-

431

ing three-headed monster while the fourth remained still, a lifeless lump in the back.

"Look at the sleepy one!" the girl shouted.

And that's when Amity really stopped herself. She peered into the box again as if looking into the Grand Canyon for the first time. She was overwhelmed by the possibility it contained, amazed the tiny creature could experience sleep or perhaps serenity in the darkening parking lot.

"Yes, he's dreamy dreaming," said the mother, fluent in the nonsensical talk of all parents. "Just like you get."

"I like that one, Mommy. He's so pretty."

"I'll take him." Amity spoke loudly and suddenly. They all turned to her with surprise. Even the young girl stopped licking her lollipop, her mouth open, cherry tongue hanging halfway out. Before the man said anything, before the child started to cry, before the woman could meet her ten dollars and raise her twenty, Amity opened her purse, pulled out her wallet, and grabbed a fistful of bills. She counted out a five and five singles, thumbing them quickly into the outstretched hand of the man.

Puppy's for $10. Your in luck. A high-bird. Boys and girls. It would make a nice story for her students.

Just as the man placed the warm and

432

sleepy puppy into Amity's arms and she pulled him to her breast, she looked down at her sneakers. On the pavement by her feet was a large puddle. Her frozen ice cream and pizza and peas had started to melt, as if her water had just broken and her womb was crying with joy.

CHAPTER 46

"On the court today," Fred said, taking a sip of wine from his plastic cup, "you were good."

"I was *rusty.*" Catherine leaned back in her beach chair and looked up into the dark Maine night. She had one arm hooked around Karma, who lay heavy in her lap, exhausted from their first day of vacation. Sequoia snored on a large beach towel at their feet.

"We are all rusty. Anyone over fifty has a little oxidation. But give yourself a break. You haven't played in forever." Fred stood and stoked the fire with a thick branch. They both watched the flames dance, then he sat back down. "Our goal this week is to blow out those cobwebs from your chassis."

"Blow out my chassis? Really?" Catherine wasn't sure if he was flirting with her or she with him, but it hardly mattered. They both laughed.

She'd so wanted to impress him with her tennis, but she'd never found her racket's sweet spot. Her timing had been off as she'd swung too early on volleys, too late on ground strokes. Despite her own disappointment, she'd been pleasantly surprised by *his* game. In the four months they'd known each other, Fred had never told her he was good, never made a deal out of it the way Ralph would have. Ralph would have bragged about playing tennis in college or having box seats at the US Open.

"By the end of the week you'll be good as new," Fred promised. "And no more excuses about not playing when we get home."

But Catherine knew there hadn't been excuses so much as other commitments. After the shoot-out at the Seven Oaks corral, Audrey had threatened to prosecute her for breaking and entering into the real estate center and the house on Fletcher Lane, but in both cases it was just Audrey's word against her own. No fingerprints. No forced entry. Amity had taught her well. Besides, Catherine made it clear that if charges were filed, she would tell everyone at the dog park that Audrey stole her husband. It wasn't true, as Catherine learned, but rumors have a way of rebounding and imploding within the protective boundaries of a gated community.

In a single meeting with a mediator, Ralph and Catherine agreed to separate. They worked out the preliminaries of a financial arrangement involving the house and retirement assets. Without further drama, Ralph moved his golf clubs and Civil War memorabilia downtown, to a two-bedroom rental Audrey found for him on Whitaker Street. Thoughtfully, Fred kept Catherine busy, organizing picnics with the dogs and museum and lecture outings for just the two of them. He even took her on a haunted walking tour, though their tour guide, dressed in top hat and tails, looked more like a judge at Westminster than a ghost hunter.

"My forehand wasn't working." Catherine buried her toes into the sand, still warm from the afternoon. "That's usually the best part of my game."

"Could be, but distracting me with your legs was a wonderful strategy."

Catherine still couldn't get used to his compliments, whether it was about her dinner rolls or her dancing. And although she was still self-conscious in the bedroom, Fred was infinitely patient during their lovemaking, paying careful attention to her needs. *Are you all right? Would you like me to touch you here? Does this feel good?*

Fred cleared his throat. "There's a regular Sunday round-robin I think we should join when we return. I've already inquired and they'd be happy to have us."

"So we're a team?"

"If you'll have me as a partner, it's official."

Catherine felt excitement rise in her throat. She might have even shouted for joy had it not been for the sleeping dogs. "This is cause for celebration," Catherine said, sitting forward.

Karma stirred briefly, sleepy eyes half-open, as Catherine transferred him to Fred. Their dogs were exhausted from their morning walk in West Quoddy Head, with the silver-gray fog creeping in from the sea and the distant moan of a foghorn. After they had returned to the cabin, they played in the lake for hours as the sky cleared, Fred and Catherine throwing tennis balls to Karma, while Sequoia stood knee deep, slapping the water with her forepaws, trying to grab fish.

"I'll be right back," Catherine said.

She followed the gravel path to the two-bedroom log cabin. It wasn't fancy, but with an unobstructed view of the lake and plenty of privacy, the rental suited them perfectly. A collection of antique leather-and-wood snowshoes hung from the walls; Mason jars filled with dark smooth rocks populated the heavy bookshelves. Much to her relief, the moose head over the stone fireplace was hand sewn and looked as if it had been pieced together from flannel pajamas. The master suite held a comfortable king-size bed with a colorful quilt and extra wool blankets should the weather turn. Catherine was secretly excited by the prospect of rain in the forecast during their week at the lake.

Once in the kitchen, she retrieved the half-filled bottle of white wine from the refrigerator. They were going to have only one glass before bedtime, but the evening had been so pleasant they'd lost track of time. As she moved back toward the screen door, her ringing cell phone surprised her. Catherine hadn't realized it was on and had barely considered whether she'd get a signal so far from town.

"Hello?"

"Well if it ain't Amelia Earhart, off on a great adventure," Martha said.

"It's late, isn't it?"

"Only ten o'clock. I figure you spent your first full day in the sack anyway. You've got to get up and eat sometime. Got to keep your energy up, among other things."

"Yes, I suppose we do." Catherine looked

out the window and saw the orange glow from the fire.

"Have you met his daughter yet?"

"No. We're stopping in Lewiston on the drive home. Just for two nights, but I'm looking forward to it."

"Speaking of swinging by, I've been thinking, why wait for Thanksgiving? Maybe I'll visit in September for your birthday."

"My birthday? What's the catch?"

"No catch. I just want to meet Fred."

"Oh?"

"But since you mentioned it, I *did* do a little regional search on Match.com. I figured if I were coming your way this fall anyway, I might see what's out there, and voilà, I've struck up a lovely correspondence with someone."

"What?" Catherine couldn't imagine Martha looking outside the excitement of the Villages.

"I'm done with bocce players. They can keep their balls." Martha laughed. "This guy I've been talking to, his original post said: 'Loyal companion likes late-night cuddling, playing fetch, getting his belly rubbed, and treats.' Under 'hobbies,' he wrote, 'Looking for tennis balls.' Clever, isn't it?"

"Sure. What's his name?"

"Lou. Lives right there in Seven Oaks. He

even has a dog."

"Does he go to the dog park?" *Maybe Fred knows him.*

"Didn't think to ask but, FYI, you have no idea how many people on your little island are looking for love. There are, like, hundreds of posts. Like you're on freaking Bora-Bora. I guess, same as here, you can have the security of gates but no one can protect you from loneliness."

Catherine thought of Ralph and their marriage. "So how old is he?"

"Says he's ten in dog years. What's that, seventy? But I'm not worried about the math."

"And his photo?"

"His profile shows an adorable mutt with a mop of white fur. He says, like most people, he looks like his dog but since she's cuter, she's the poster child."

"A mop of hair and a white beard? Like Santa Claus?"

"He got the dog for his grandkids who, by the way, call him Lou Lou."

Lulu. Ernie. "You've talked on the phone?"

"A few times. I don't know if it's his deadpan humor or what but he's straight-forward. I've decided it shouldn't matter. I've spent too much time basing everything I do on whether a guy can bench-press my

Medicare statements. My new policy is substance over style. Engine over chrome."

After hanging up, Catherine grabbed the wine and flashlight and followed the pale beam back to the fire. Fred had swaddled Karma in a towel and was holding him in the crook of his arm. She refilled their glasses and sat back on her beach chair.

Catherine reached over and stroked Karma's head. "I'd say my little baby is tired and happy."

"And may I say the same thing about you?"

Catherine leaned into Fred's shoulder. "If only you knew."

They remained silent for several minutes, watching the fire curl upward. Then the heady call of a loon pierced the night. From across the lake they heard a distant response. Catherine imagined it might just be the dying fire, but the stars seemed brighter since she'd returned outside. She'd meant to bring her science CDs to share with Fred on the long drive north, but she'd forgotten them in the excitement of packing tennis outfits and new lingerie.

"Martha called," Catherine said, breaking the silence. "She's got a new romantic interest."

"Excellent," Fred said. " 'Tis the season."

441

Catherine thought about mentioning Ernie. Fred would admire his friend's tenacity and maybe be surprised that he was lonely enough to post a personal ad. But it was better for that relationship to take its course, at least for now. Catherine wouldn't have chosen Ernie for her sister, but love is unpredictable. She knew it could show up in the unlikeliest places, appear out of nowhere, like a renegade thunderstorm on a clear spring day.

While Catherine looked skyward, Fred found himself watching her. He admired the smooth slope of her neck and the outer edges of her lips curling into a smile whenever she thought she'd identified a constellation.

"Okay, there's the Little Dipper, but is that Orion?" Catherine motioned to several bright stars in the southern sky.

"No, that's Cassiopeia." He was thrilled she was interested.

And then he heard Lissa, who'd been silent for weeks. *I was interested.*

I know. You were a class act.

Thank you. She's a class act too, but you've got to give me a little credit.

Oh?

It's not as if these things just happen.

442

Well then, thank you. Thank you very much. And Danielle will like her, trust me.

We're visiting them next weekend.

I know, I know.

Tommy asked me to teach him to build something. Maybe even a doghouse. It's a start.

It is indeed.

Fred considered stoking the fire again, but something held him where he was. He wasn't finished.

It's all worked out, hasn't it?

What?

This. What you have.

I miss you, but I'm happy. Yes.

And you forgive me?

I forgave you years and years ago. You know that.

I needed to be sure.

I forgive you. I forgive you. I forgive you.

Fred heard the crackle of fire before him and felt Catherine's arm against his own as she stroked her dog. He waited patiently, then heard Lissa one last time.

Thank you. I can't just hang around here forever, you know.

I know.

I've got things to do.

You always had things to do.

And now I'm late to meet Jack Klugman for drinks.

"Fred?" Catherine asked.

He didn't know where he'd been but came to. "Sorry. Just on a little nostalgic walk-about."

"Is everything okay?"

"Everything is wonderful." He liked the feeling of her head hard against his shoulder.

"So is that Venus?"

Instead of looking up to follow her arm, he adjusted Karma in his lap, then leaned across Catherine so his right hand rested on the outer edge of her thigh. His knees ached from playing tennis, but he'd been happy to get back on the court. Catherine shifted, so he placed his open hand on her lower back and pulled her whole body toward him. Every bit of him felt alive when their lips touched. He considered dropping back — they had the entire week to kiss — but he felt the urgency of passing time, of seconds clicking by then lost forever, so he pulled her even tighter.

Suddenly Sequoia shook her massive head, her collar and ID tags jangling. They both pulled back and looked at her. Her nose twitched wildly.

"Looks like Sleeping Beauty smells something," Catherine said.

To their surprise, Sequoia stood stiffly, then ambled in front of them, past the fire, and to the shore.

"What is it, girl?" Fred asked.

His Great Dane took a few steps into the lake and leaned forward into the night.

As Fred watched her, his attention moved back to the fire, to a snap of wood sap and a bright spark that lifted skyward. As if it had been transformed into a firefly, it rose higher and higher, a flicker of light. It became a larger beacon as it floated away but remained visible, a Chinese lantern made of rice paper, a child's illuminated kite, a hot air balloon.

"Do you *see* that?" Catherine asked, breathless.

But Fred remained still and silent, focused on what was now a distant rocket ship, the reverse of a falling star. Just as it reached the edge of the visible universe, he saw a bright flare like a Fourth of July sparkler and then, though he couldn't be sure, he thought he heard the whisper of laughter.

ACKNOWLEDGMENTS

While writing is a solitary endeavor, publishing is a team sport. Fortunately, I have a wonderful team.

First, thanks to my Savannah Scribes writing group: Nancy Brandon, Amy Paige Condon, Judy Fogarty, Lyn Gregory, and K. W. Oxnard, all talented writers, thoughtful editors, and invaluable friends. I feel blessed to have had your encouragement when I had only a few chapters about a well-intentioned pet psychic who needed to meet her neighbors.

I appreciate comments from dear friends who read an early draft of this novel: Lydia Angle, Denise Farrell, Emily Sorokin Kessler, and Janine Steel Zane. I'm indebted to all other friends and family, near and far, who encouraged me with phone calls, distracted me with games of tennis, or took Gussie (our spirited Boston terrier) and me for walks. In particular, Marilyn Brady provided inimitable style and social media advice, Monica Hughes calmed me with her generous spirit, Jim Guerard tendered his ample photography skills, and Charlotte Sequeira always offered me a clear space at her magical desk. I am indebted to my parents, wherever their spirits are soaring, for their encouragement of creativity and humor.

I treasure The Landings community on Skidaway Island in Savannah, Georgia that provided the inspiration for this fictional book but not the central casting. Thank you to Eileen Galves for her real estate savvy and to The Landings security staff, for a fun and informative afternoon of tooling around with them in a Prius in the name of research.

I am indebted to Dan and Pat Lynch who passed along my story to their good friend Leah Wasielewski, and I am in awe of the editorial, sales, publicity, and marketing talent at HarperCollins. Heartfelt thanks to my talented and razor-sharp editor, Emily Griffin, who believed in this book when it showed up, unbidden, on her desk and then used her formidable skills to shape it. I so appreciate the support of Allison Hunter, my impossibly wise agent at Janklow and Nesbit. (And here's a big shout-out to the fine folks at Stuart Krichevsky Literary Agency.)

Finally, thanks to my husband, Bill, for his unflagging support, unwavering enthusiasm, and unswerving good humor. The best karma of all is that we found each other in this great big world.

P.S.
INSIGHTS,
INTERVIEWS & MORE . . .

■ ■ ■ ■

ABOUT THE BOOK

■ ■ ■ ■

A NOTE FROM THE AUTHOR

Good Karma is not only the title of my novel, it's also the essence of how this book came to be.

My personal definition of karma doesn't involve big-picture, earth-shattering collisions of coincidence, but unexpected gifts the universe delivers when someone is good and ready. My version involves an unlikely string of green traffic lights or a tennis ball that hovers at the top of a net and becomes the match point winner in a tiebreaker. When *Good Karma* is published I'll be fifty-four, well into my metaphorical second set, but exactly how old I needed to be to find my voice as a novelist.

I wasn't a voracious reader growing up, but I had a singular fascination with words. While peers devoured classics, I delighted in anagrams, palindromes, and rebus puzzles. I was a word mechanic, my head in the engine of language, who didn't care much about driving. Then I attended Vassar College and majored in English literature because, frankly, they didn't offer a degree in puns.

My first job out of school was as assistant to the national sales manager at Random House. I had a romantic idea that after a distinguished six months of typing memos and photocopying reports, I'd be promoted to trade rep and start my illustrious career presenting spools of bound words to charming booksellers. After a year, I was politely informed that sales might not suit my rather whimsical personality, so I resigned to prove them wrong and peddled advertising space for a regional magazine. (Alas, the scouting reports were spot-on.) But karma interceded and I took an unlikely turn into editorial, just where I belonged. In 1992 I ended up at the Iowa Writers' Workshop in a small class of brooding novelists. And so I became one myself, tamping down my humor and playful bon mots in order to write "serious" fiction. At graduation I ended up with an MFA and a rather depressing novel (which, as luck would have it, the world didn't want or need).

Fast-forward, I put my fiction aside to travel and enjoy eclectic positions as charter yacht cook, dogsitter, tennis professional, and crossword puzzle constructor. Pushing forty, I met and married my husband (nineteen years my senior), settled in Westchester, New York, and became a stepmother to two and doting but spry step*grandmother* to six. I wrote articles for periodicals, but I didn't see how I could use my quirky fictional voice to say something important about love and life.

But then my husband retired in 2010 and everything changed.

After an exhaustive search, we relocated to a lively island community in Savannah, Georgia. Contrary to what I expected, retirement (at least for us) wasn't relaxing into an armchair of late middle age — it was a tornado of social adventures, new opportunities, and temptations. It is an intersection, both physical and psychological, where the body starts to fail just when most people have the time and occasion to use it. I discovered an entire generation of women who experienced difficult transitions with long-independent husbands suddenly wanting to know what was for lunch. Likewise, many floundered in relationships with grown children, distant grandchildren, and, in some cases, aged parents. A nation of baby boomers was breaking up and hooking up.

With my newfound inspiration and ample time, I began writing again. *Good Karma* started out with one character — a slightly off-kilter pet psychic who wanted to meet her neighbors. After a few pages, a kind-hearted widower arrived on the scene, followed by a troubled younger woman who breaks into houses just to lead other people's lives. I didn't set out to have a dog in the book, but our high-energy Boston terrier forever thumps me with her tennis ball when I write, so Karma, the dog, came to life. Finally, Catherine entered the story. Shy and self-conscious at first, she began to speak the loudest to me. She was a woman at the crossroads of her marriage and her life. Catherine was thoughtful and funny and patient and she taught me that as long as you speak the truth, a little quirk can be good.

So I hope you enjoy *Good Karma,* my non-brooding first published novel in which both Catherine and I found our voices.

■ ■ ■ ■

READ ON

■ ■ ■ ■

READING GROUP GUIDE:
DISCUSSION QUESTIONS FOR
GOOD KARMA

1. What are your first impressions of Catherine and Ralph, and what do their reactions to each other reveal about their marriage? What do you think each of them wants or fears? Did your impressions prove to be correct?

2. Security is paramount to Catherine: in her sense of self, in her marriage, and in her home. Do you think she's overly focused on it? Is she more secure or less so by the novel's end?

3. What do you think of gated communities like Seven Oaks? Is Christina Kelly's depiction of such a community accurate, or is it satirical? When you retire, would you consider moving to such a place? If you have a partner, have you discussed your expectations of retirement?

4. Throughout the novel, Fred hears the voice of his late wife in his head. Do you read Lissa's voice as literal or something Fred imagines? Have you ever felt that you could hear the voice of a deceased loved one? If not, would you want to?

5. How does Fred and Danielle's relationship change after Lissa's death? What are the sources of Danielle's anger or impatience? Are they justified?

6. Do we all have an impulse to "lead other people's lives," as Amity does? If so, have you ever acted on this feeling? Does Amity's rationale for creeping and taking advantage of others' lapses in security reveal something about her character?

7. Why does Ida Blue pretend to be a pet psychic? Is what she does wrong? Does it matter, if her heart is in the right place?

8. The point of view alternates among several characters throughout the novel. Did you relate to one point of view or voice more than the others?

9. The author juxtaposes humor and pathos. Did you find them balanced? Are some

individuals more prone to see one than the other in a given situation?

10. Several characters in the novel are "stuck" (as Fred tells his therapist), needing to take action but being unable to do so. What events compel each character to act? Are most people you know content in their marriages, careers, and lives? For those who aren't, what holds them back from taking steps toward change?

11. Dogs play a big role in *Good Karma.* How do Sequoia and Karma act as vehicles for character development? How do Karma, Sequoia, Leona, and Lulu mirror their owners' personalities? If the other characters were to get dogs, what breeds would they choose?

12. What is your definition of karma? In what ways do the characters experience good karma? When have you encountered good karma in your own life?

ABOUT THE AUTHOR

Christina Kelly is a graduate of the Iowa Writers' Workshop and an occasional contributor to the *New York Times* crossword section. A native of Westchester, New York, she now lives with her husband in Savannah, Georgia. *Good Karma* is her first novel.